FROM GARDEN TO GRAVE

THE LEAFY HOLLOW MYSTERIES, BOOK 1

RICKIE BLAIR

BARKLEY
BOOKS

FROM GARDEN TO GRAVE
Copyright © 2017 by Rickie Blair.
Published in Canada in 2017 by Barkley Books.

This book is a work of fiction. Names, characters, places and incidents are
products of the author's imagination or are used fictitiously. Any resemblance
to actual events or locales or persons, living or dead, is coincidental.

ISBN-13: 978-0-9950981-4-5

To receive information about new releases and occasional special offers,
please sign up at www.rickieblair.com.

Cover art by: http://www.coverkicks.com

For Grace-ann, with gratitude

FROM GARDEN TO GRAVE

CHAPTER 1

I ALMOST DIDN'T ANSWER the call that changed my life. *Telemarketer*, I thought, burying my head in the pillow with a groan. But in my family, a phone ringing in the middle of the night always signaled disaster. So I was genetically wired to jab that loudspeaker icon and croak, "Hello?"

"There's been an accident. Your aunt is missing."

"Who?"

"Your aunt," said a man's voice.

"Are you sure you have the right number?" I reached for my robe and slipped in an arm. After flailing about, I realized I'd grabbed a pair of jeans. Forget the robe. It wasn't as if anybody was in my bedroom to ogle. I dropped the jeans back on the floor.

"Are you Verity Hawkes, Adeline Hawkes' niece?"

I groaned again, inwardly this time. I hadn't spoken to my estranged—and slightly deranged—aunt in years.

"That's me." I sat on the edge of the bed, rubbing my

eyes, as the caller droned on. Given Aunt Adeline's talent for getting into, and out of, sticky situations, I decided not to panic for now.

"Who are you?" I asked.

"Wilfred Mullins, Adeline's lawyer. I'm sorry I didn't get in touch earlier, but—"

"What's she done now?" I asked, cutting him off as I padded along the hall to the kitchen.

Mullins said the police had dragged her empty car from the river a week ago. There was still no sign of my aunt, who was "presumed dead."

"I'm sorry for your loss," he added.

I refused to believe it. Not Aunt Adeline. Just because her car was in the river didn't mean she was in it when it pitched over the railing. Besides, my aunt could survive a plunge over Niagara Falls. Possibly without a barrel.

"She's not dead," I said.

"The police think—"

"They're wrong."

I slipped a pod into the coffeemaker and turned it on. Then I walked into the living room to open the blinds. The morning's first rays of sunlight spilled into the room, illuminating stacks of self-help books, a ragged sofa the color of mud, and dust bunnies big enough to form their own union. I did my daily count of construction booms in the blocks around my apartment. Seven. One more than a month ago, but no new ones. For now, my view of a sliver of Vancouver's Burrard Inlet was intact.

"I realize it's difficult for you to accept," the lawyer said, his voice echoing from the phone on the kitchen counter. "It's a shock for all of us. But somebody in your family has to come to Leafy Hollow and deal with this, and you're the closest."

I walked back to the kitchen, eased my filled mug from the coffeemaker, slopped in a dash of cream, and took a long swallow before replying.

"I'm two thousand miles away," I countered.

"Still the closest," the lawyer insisted.

I assumed that was a reference to my dad. He probably refused to drag his latest new bride from Australia to a tiny village in southern Ontario because a former sister-in-law had disappeared. Particularly since the sister-in-law considered him a useless dolt and was never reluctant to say so.

That left only me. Verity Hawkes, a twenty-eight-year-old unemployed bookkeeper with no idea how to find a missing sixty-five-year-old woman. And even less idea of what to do if she couldn't be found.

Or didn't want to be found.

While the lawyer carried on about powers of attorney and something called holographic wills, I thought back to the whispered late-night phone calls I'd overheard as a child. Back then, Aunt Adeline ran an office-services company and risked, at most, paper cuts. But my mother's panicked expressions had suggested something more dangerous than mail merges.

In fact, what my only aunt did to earn a living was one of the great mysteries of my childhood, eclipsed only by sex—and why the Backstreet Boys didn't come to my birthday party when I was nine.

I took the phone into the living room, pushed aside my copy of *Ten Paths to Clarity through Tidying Up*, and collapsed onto the sofa with my bare feet on the coffee table. I explained to Mullins that I hadn't left my apartment building in two years. Normally, I didn't mention this to strangers, but it was unavoidable given the circumstances.

It wasn't technically true, either, since I had visited the bookstore across the street a day earlier. I liked to take a self-help book with me to the basement laundromat, and then smile and nod above its cover at the neighbors who insisted I come to dinner now that I was alone. I found that *Help for the Overly Hirsute* best deflected unwanted conversations, and the bookstore had called to tell me of a new illustrated edition.

The lawyer ignored my objections, preferring to prattle on about flight times and unaffordable limo services. My gaze fell on the dracaena plant I purchased after reading *Achieving Peace through Nature*. I must have skipped the chapter on maintenance because the dracaena's formerly lush green leaves were the same color as the sofa.

"If you took the red-eye, you could be here by this time tomorrow," Mullins intoned.

He wasn't listening.

With a flash of irritation, I picked up the dead dracaena and tossed it through the opening in the wall between the kitchen and living room. The potted plant plopped into the garbage container that sat open on the kitchen floor, rocking the bin. I pumped my fist. A three-pointer.

"Miss Hawkes? Are you listening?"

"I'm thinking."

To be honest, I regretted my ongoing feud with Aunt Adeline. But her current predicament was a problem that required the grown-up Verity. I wasn't sure I wanted that Verity back.

I stretched my arms overhead, mulling it over. Although it had been years since I'd been in Leafy Hollow, the village lived on in my memory as a perpetually green and blissful refuge. A place where no one was too rushed to offer a friendly wave, well-mannered children in pastel overalls traded Pokémon cards, and rain never dampened the world's most adorable homes.

With a twinge of guilt, I shifted my gaze to the framed photo over the television. Matthew wouldn't have wanted me to be sad. And how could I be sad at Rose Cottage, surrounded by the intoxicating scents and colors of Adeline Hawkes' magnificent garden? The woman might be eccentric, but her dahlias were legendary. She never would have killed a dracaena.

"Okay," I said. "I'll come. Give me a day or two."

I barely had time to change into yoga pants and a hoodie and call up flight prices on my phone before I heard a *tap-tap-tap* at my door. I held my breath. If I was quiet, my neighbor Patty might think I was asleep. Maybe even in a coma.

"Ver-i-ty," came a singsong voice from the hall. "I know you're in there, hon."

Rats. She must have been watching through her peephole, waiting for me to emerge from across the hall, and got tired of waiting. I was one of Patty's projects, like the caps she knitted for newborns, but I hadn't talked to her in days. If I didn't open the door, a contingent of firefighters might knock it down within minutes.

I hesitated because, well, firefighters. Then I pulled back the door.

Patty Ferris swept in, ponytail bouncing. She held a Tupperware container in one hand. "Hi there, hon. Guess what?" she asked, hoisting the container aloft. "I made triple-fudge three-alarm chipotle brownies yesterday, and I said to Clark, 'Who do we know that loves brownies?' He said, 'Verity!' So, I had to bring them over. It's my newest recipe. I added a touch of turmeric this time."

I doubted Patty's husband Clark had looked up from ESPN long enough to hear the question, never mind answer it, but I kept that to myself as I closed the door and smiled at her.

"That's sweet of—"

"There are no nuts in these brownies," Patty continued without drawing breath. "Not a morsel. I didn't forget your allergy." She thrust the container at me while launching into an update on our new neighbors down the hall. Patty suspected them of running a marijuana grow-op in their bathroom. "That light is on day and night," she said in a stage whisper. "*Day and night.* You can see it from the street."

My hand sagged under the weight of the brownies. I wasn't allergic to nuts. But since Patty's baked goods were inedible, I always trashed them. Until the day she came back for a forgotten oven glove and spotted her caramel-Worcester-shire nut tart at the top of my garbage. The only explanation I came up with on short notice was an allergy to nuts I had neglected to mention.

I cautiously patted the container as I placed it on the counter, hoping it wouldn't burn through the plastic before I could dump the contents. "Thanks. I'll enjoy these."

"Why don't we eat one now with a cup of tea?" Patty asked, bustling over to the stove to fill the kettle.

"Oh," I said hastily. "I can't." I took the kettle from her and replaced it on the stove. "Sorry, but I'm... packing."

"Packing? You're going somewhere?" She gripped my arm and shrieked as my words sank in. "Oooooh, you're going somewhere. Finally. Where to, hon?"

"Back East. Family stuff."

"You're not worried, are you? You look tense."

"I'm fine."

And I would be, as soon as my heart rate slowed to a more normal one-hundred-sixty or so. And the vein in my neck stopped throbbing.

"I'm a little anxious," I admitted, "but once I get on the plane, I'll be okay."

At my mention of a plane, Patty sprang back with a look of horror. "You'll need something to eat during the flight. They don't serve meals anymore."

I tried to head her off. "I don't need any food, honestly."

"How about a nice egg salad with candied capers and—"

"No need," I blurted, hustling over to the door and opening it. "I've got the brownies, remember?"

"Wait," she said on her way out, slapping a hand against the door before I closed it. "Won't you need me to water your plants?"

I glanced at the garbage container in the kitchen, where a crispy dracaena leaf curled over the rim like a poker player clutching for a cocktail after fifteen hours of bad beats. I shook my head.

"Thanks, but that won't be necessary." I gently closed the door behind her.

Patty's concern agitated the butterflies in my stomach I was doing my best to ignore. The early-morning call from Aunt Adeline's lawyer had dredged up disturbing memories of my aunt's behavior over the years.

Like the summer I turned twelve—all arms and legs and boy crazy. Mom sent me to Leafy Hollow to help Aunt Adeline recover from the dislocated shoulder, broken jaw, and bruises she suffered in a car accident. But when I arrived, my aunt said she didn't need my help. She suggested I spend my school break learning Krav Maga at the community center instead.

I didn't see how that would help me attract boys. And I said so.

"Boysh?" my aunt asked, as anyone would with a wired jaw, but I believe she was genuinely puzzled about the purpose of my objective. Since I didn't understand it either, I agreed to learn about martial-arts kicks and strikes instead of the opposite sex. Our class included grappling and ground fighting—skills applicable to both pursuits, I realized later.

Meanwhile, the Volvo station wagon in Aunt Adeline's garage that summer didn't have a scratch on it. My aunt rebuffed my attempts to pry loose the details of her accident. So I went home at the end of the summer none the wiser— but able to inflict a mean head butt.

Years later, my ongoing curiosity about Adeline's true calling was squelched for good when she skipped Mom's funeral. To my mind, showing up at her sister's interment disguised in gravedigger's overalls, huge sunglasses, and a curly red wig didn't count as proper attendance.

She yanked me aside moments after I threw the final clod of earth onto Mom's casket. Not realizing who she was at first, I drew back my hand for an inside chop until she hissed in my ear.

"Sssshhh. It's me. Don't say a word, Verity."

I gawked at her. "Aunt Adeline? Where have you been?"

She cast furtive looks around the cemetery. "I can't tell you that."

I took a step back to consider this, pressing my lips together so hard they almost split. This was a normal day for my crackpot aunt. Except it wasn't a normal day. It was *my mother's funeral*. The hurt and anger I'd held in for weeks erupted in a vicious, two-handed shove that flung my aunt off her feet. Aunt Adeline landed on her rear amid two toppled tiers of flower arrangements. I fervently hoped the roses had thorns.

"Stay away," I shouted. "I never want to see you again."

My aunt brushed wilted chrysanthemums from her face and spit out a spray of baby's breath. "Verity, wait. You don't understand—"

I whirled on one foot and stalked off. "Not listening," I called over my shoulder.

That was five years ago, and we hadn't talked since. Whenever her name popped up on my call display, I clicked on "Decline." Eventually, she stopped calling, and I started a new life.

I didn't want to think about how that had turned out.

With a sigh that echoed deep in my core, I pulled my dusty suitcase from the closet.

CHAPTER 2

I HELD my anxiety at bay during my red-eye flight by reading *Organize Your Way to a Better Life* and trying not to imagine what awaited me in Leafy Hollow. As we flew east over the Rockies, I muttered the book's advice like a mantra: "Empty your cupboards, keep what's important, toss the rest."

Far from helping, it only emphasized the eerie similarities between my life and a home-improvement project. Still muttering, I fell asleep. The book slid off the seat and under my feet.

During our three-hour stopover in Calgary, I riffled through the now-battered pages of *Organize*, intending to skip ahead to the promised happy ending. Instead, I nodded off in the waiting room.

The nighttime runway lights were shutting off as our second plane touched down in Toronto. Armed with two super-sized lattes, I staggered aboard a Greyhound bus headed west for the next leg of my journey. Two hours later, the bus pulled into Strathcona's busy downtown station. I wheeled my suitcase across the street and settled into the backseat of a taxi, feeling like a contestant on *The Amazing Race*. Strathcona was the nearest big city to Leafy Hollow, but my journey wasn't over yet.

The cab headed for the highway. Over an hour later, we left the freeway to veer onto the one-lane country road that led to the village, nestled into a valley at the foot of the Niagara Escarpment.

The taxi swept through the tranquil hills I had loved as a child. Black ash and sugar maples, spruce and cedar, sassafras and tulip trees billowed in green clouds across the landscape. Lacy white caps of wildflowers along the road nodded in the breeze as we passed. When I lowered my window to take a deep gulp of cedar-infused air, a red-tailed hawk soared past, its wings slicing through the deep azure sky. My misgivings fell away, replaced by eagerness to see the charming stone facade of Rose Cottage once more.

"We're here," the driver said as he pulled up outside my aunt's home.

I straightened up to look. Then I opened the door and stumbled out, my mouth hanging open.

My aunt's house looked as if it had been plucked from a horror movie. The mortar in its fieldstone walls was cracked and crumbling, the roof's cedar shingles showed gaps, and killer vines twined through the rotted front steps. Dead blooms hung from the climbing roses on the front walls. Drawn curtains strengthened my impression of the two front windows as glaring, crazy eyes.

Faded gold letters on a crooked sign by the stairs read:

R SE C TT G E

Watch Your Step was scrawled in felt marker underneath.

The driver hauled my suitcase out of the trunk and placed it on the walk as I counted out the fare and handed it over. He leaned back on his heels to inspect the cottage.

"What happened here? Death in the family?"

"Certainly not," I blurted. "Why would you say that?"

The cabbie gave me a pitying glance and craned his neck to assess the shabby roof. I followed his gaze. Two red squirrels chased each other across the splintered cedar shingles, breaking off bits of moss that tumbled into the packed gutters. The squirrels leaped into the branches of the giant elm overhead and disappeared, probably disgusted with the available lodgings.

I knew how they felt.

"We passed a nice bed-and-breakfast in the village," the cabbie said. "I could take you there."

"Tempting," I said with a sigh, "but no."

I bent to collect my suitcase, then halted, struck by the sensation of being watched. I twisted my head to one side. A stranger stood fifty feet away, behind the wire fence that separated my aunt's property from the one next door. He was in his mid-sixties—judging by the gray samurai topknot that matched his mustache and goatee—and wore blue-tinted octagonal glasses.

A feeling of unease crept over me under his focused gaze. But as I straightened up and stepped closer, he pivoted on one foot and ducked behind a hedge. I tried to peer through the foliage, unable to shake the feeling that I had seen him before.

Behind me, the taxi driver shut his door and drove past with a brief wave, dust rising from the unpaved shoulder in his wake. I returned his wave before resuming my scrutiny of the hedge.

The stranger was gone.

Great—a nosy neighbor. I should feel right at home.

I hauled my suitcase up the ramshackle stairs, pausing to yank a strand of murderous vine off a step. I regretted bringing along my entire self-help library. *Top Ten Tips for Success: The Workbook Edition* alone weighed five pounds. Still, that was only half a pound per tip.

I retrieved the key from under a flowerpot and twisted it into the lock. It took a shove from my shoulder before the door burst open. I toggled the light switch, but the bulb over the foyer did not flicker. The cottage smelled musty, as if it hadn't been aired out for days.

Leaving the door ajar, I pulled back the heavy curtains over the front window. A dim light filtered through the elm branches, enough to show the cluttered interior. The windows and floors looked clean, but when I ran a finger across the coffee table, it came away coated with dust. Knick-knacks cluttered the mantel of the stone fireplace on the far side of the room. An aluminum pail sat under a damp spot in the ceiling.

With a grimace, I remembered the cabbie saying the forecast called for rain.

Clicks and whirs sounded above my head. I halted, my heart in my throat, and looked up. Was someone in the attic?

The clock on the mantel ticked loudly while I stood there, listening.

Silence.

My over-caffeinated imagination was on hyperdrive.

Shaking my head, I wheeled my suitcase across the pine floors and into the front bedroom. Rose Cottage was built in the late nineteenth century in the simple style known as a worker's cottage. It had four small rooms, plus a lean-to kitchen at the back that was added decades later. I knew from my aunt's lectures over the years that the fieldstone in the walls was collected, piece by piece, from nearby fields and streams. Then it was split and laid in mortar by the Scottish stonemasons who settled here.

Judging from the state of the exterior walls, one of those Victorian-era masons would be a welcome visitor today.

I flung the suitcase onto my aunt's four-poster bed and zipped open the lid. Folded T-shirts, yoga pants, underwear, and hoodies nestled alongside each other like cabbage rolls at a fall fair. *Packing for the Infrequent Traveler* provided no suggestions for framed photos, however. I sat on the bed beside the suitcase and dug out Matthew's picture, intending to place it on the bedside table.

Every atom of that photo was engraved on my heart, from the white-capped mountains in the background to the grin on Matthew's tanned face—even the scuffed hiking boots on his feet. I ran my fingers along the frame, recalling our trip to the Yukon, feeling the familiar twinge in my chest.

Then I tossed the photo back into the suitcase, slammed the lid, and shoved the case under the bed. This trip was hard enough—why make it worse? I was here to find my aunt and go home, not redecorate.

I marched back into the living room, where a silvery glint on the cluttered roll-top desk caught my eye. Under a sheaf of papers, I found a state-of-the-art laptop, incongruous on the desk's antique surface.

"Anyone home?" a voice called from the front door.

I gave a start and twisted to face the entrance, dropping the papers onto the floor. They fluttered in every direction.

A woman stood in the open doorway, her penciled black brows, jet-black hair, and blood-red lipstick in vivid contrast to her chalky white skin. I estimated her age at the wrong side of fifty, but suspected she wouldn't admit to more than thirty-five. Her red fingernails matched the lipstick, and her tummy pooched under a skintight black leather skirt.

She stepped in and swiveled her gaze around the room, letting it rest for a moment on the aluminum pail. Then she placed her hands on her hips. "This is a mess, isn't it?"

I assumed she meant my aunt's cottage, and I prepared a sarcastic reply. Before I could open my mouth, she spoke again.

"My grass should have been cut three days ago." She tapped a stiletto heel on my aunt's pine floor and raised her penciled brows.

I rubbed my chin, trying to work out if this was a joke or an escaped psychiatric patient. Finally, I clued in. This was one of Aunt Adeline's landscaping clients.

"I'm sorry about your lawn, but my aunt—"

"Is not here. You're the niece; I know that." She cocked her head. "Why do you use her last name, by the way?"

I swallowed hard before replying. "Long story." *And none of your business,* I mentally added.

Her brisk wave indicated a complete lack of interest in the details. "Whatever. Your aunt must have a backup plan. Who's going to cut my lawn?"

"I don't think anyone is. Not from here, anyway."

"Need I remind you that I paid in advance? For the whole season?"

I stared at her in astonishment. I didn't know if my aunt's bank account was healthy enough to refund a season's worth of lawn-care payments, but mine wasn't. I hadn't had a full-time job in over two years, and my savings were almost gone.

I decided to play the sympathy card.

"My aunt is probably dead."

The visitor brushed a hand over her bouffant hairdo. "They haven't found a body, have they?"

"No, but—"

"Meanwhile, my lawn is very much alive. And with the book club arriving this afternoon, it has to be cut. I insist."

"I'm sorry, but—"

She didn't even stop talking. "And what about the pruning? Adeline," she added, pointing a finger at me, "promised to prune my wisteria."

"I'm sorry my aunt couldn't cut your lawn, but under the circumstances..."

My visitor held out a hand to admire her nails, and then flicked an invisible speck from the sleeve of her blouse. "Typical," she said.

"Excuse me?"

"I meant that your aunt was a... what do they call it? Free spirit? And the pups never stray far from the bitch."

"Meaning?" I asked through clenched teeth, choking back the urge to throttle her.

"Oh, don't be offended," she said with an airy wave of her hand. "It's only a saying. But if your aunt has abandoned her responsibilities, is it too much to expect that her relatives should pick up the slack?"

"She didn't abandon—"

"I've heard about you. You're the lazy one, right?"

"What?" I reminded myself that Krav Maga was intended for defense, not offense. Even so, I yearned to flip her over that aluminum pail and smack her onto the floor. My therapist would have attributed that urge to "unresolved anger." *Count to ten, Verity.*

"Sorry, am I wrong?" she continued. "I heard that you're the niece who gave up working and became a recluse when your husband died. Or was that someone else? I guess it must be, because that woman never leaves her apartment, right?"

For a full second, I couldn't move. My heart gave a thump so sharp that I looked down, half-expecting to see a weapon sticking out of my chest.

"No," I whispered, "that was me." My throat closed, choking off any other response. I ground my fingernails into my palms to ward off tears because no way would I give her the satisfaction. "Are you done?" I asked, a bitter note in my voice. "Because you need to leave. Now."

I knelt to round up the scattered documents. As I reached for the farthest ones, a hand thrust a stack of papers under my nose. I looked over and found my visitor crouched on the floor beside me, gathering up the rest of the papers.

"I'm a widow myself," she said. "You can't let the bastards win."

She shoved more papers at me. I took them, speechless.

"You came all this way," she said, "so you must have a plan. Or did you intend to stay in this room?"

"That's none of your business."

"Perhaps. But whatever your goal, you'll need money. Forget about my advance payments. Cut my lawn this afternoon and I'll pay you double your aunt's usual rate—in cash."

Rising to her feet, she flexed her surgically taut cheeks into the semblance of a smile. "It's just business," she said. "You don't need to like me. You only need to cut my lawn. Deal?"

I tapped the edges of the papers on the floor to straighten them before standing up. I was a bookkeeper, so I understood billing and receivables. Nobody offers to pay you twice, never mind at double the rate. So I was tempted by her offer, even though part of me still wanted to slam her face into the floor.

"I'll think about it," I said.

She pivoted on her high heels to strut across the porch and down the steps.

I hoped the rotted stairs would choose now as the ideal time to collapse. No such luck.

"I'll expect you within the hour," she said over her shoulder. "Twelve Peppermint Lane. Yvonne Skalding. Don't forget to prune the wisteria."

Following her onto the porch, I opened my mouth to say I had no idea how to prune a wisteria, whatever that was. I gave up as the driver's door of her pale blue Volvo thudded shut, and she drove off.

I scuffed the toe of my running shoe across the porch floor. A strip of dried blue paint lifted off the worn boards and crumbled into fragments over my shoe. "I should go home before things get worse," I muttered to myself while shaking the paint chips off my foot.

The words caught in my throat. The police had given up on my aunt, and now I wanted to do the same. I'd come two thousand miles because I didn't believe she was dead. I couldn't turn my back on her now.

I reached out my hand to run a finger along the cracked mortar in the stone walls. If I gave up on Rose Cottage, what would happen to it? A bulldozer and a monster home, most likely. My aunt loved this house. So had my mother. I owed it to both of them not to abandon it.

But if the police thought my aunt was dead, who was I to disagree?

I rubbed my hand along the wall, bumping over the rough stones, and then straightened up to my full five-foot-ten. Maybe I couldn't dispute the official version of my aunt's accident—not yet—but I could look for evidence on my own. Meanwhile, I could fix up Rose Cottage and sell it to someone who would love this old house as much as my aunt did.

And then—I let out a deep sigh—I could pack up my photos and my books and go home.

I studied the boards at my feet, kicking the paint chips to one side. It would take money to rebuild this porch and fix the roof, though. Which meant I had to cut Yvonne Skalding's lawn.

Unfortunately, I had no idea how.

I headed for the garage, hoping to find a mower. With instructions.

CHAPTER 3

I STOPPED at the threshold of Aunt Adeline's garage, surprised by its resemblance to a giant jigsaw puzzle. Dozens of hand tools hung on the back wall, each one outlined with black marker on pegboard to show where it belonged. Unlike my aunt's cluttered desk, her garage was tidy and peaceful.

Then I looked up.

Another illusion shattered.

Circles of iron with vicious-toothed edges hung on rusted chains from the rafters. I hoped those traps were meant to be decorative antiques, like the rusting plows you see at the end of farm driveways. Otherwise, one of those could take a leg off, no problem.

I returned my attention to the pegboard tools. Along a side wall, rows of hooks neatly corralled the long, wooden handles of much bigger implements. I recognized the hoes and shovels, but the other tools were a mystery. Still, how much equipment did you need to trim a few shrubs?

My forced tranquility soon evaporated. The pegboard

outlines weren't labeled, so they didn't help me figure out which gadgets I needed. And my aunt's lawnmower was the size of a sofa. It took me an hour to wrestle it up the loading ramp and onto the truck bed. I couldn't find any operating instructions, either, so I Googled it on my phone and scribbled them onto a sheet of paper. By the time I'd added a rake and some sharp, pointy things—including heavy-duty blades that I hoped were pruning shears—and jammed a baseball cap on my head, it was two in the afternoon.

It took me another hour to find Yvonne Skalding's house.

The problem with driving in the country is that there's no one to ask for directions when you're lost. My chest grew tight and my breathing ragged as I drove past miles of nothing but corn fields, pastured horses, and farmhouses set so far back from the road they could have been mirages. I pulled over at the top of a sun-baked hill and turned off the engine. With a hand pressed to my stomach, I straightened up to start the breathing exercises recommended by my therapist.

In, out. Try as I might, I couldn't calm my thoughts. Why hadn't I stayed in Vancouver? I'd be settling in to watch *Jeopardy* right about now.

In, out. And I was halfway through a 1,500-piece jigsaw of Vita Sackville-West's Sissinghurst Castle that I really wanted to finish.

In, out. A crow landed on the truck's hood and hopped up to the windshield. I watched out of the corner of my eye while it stared at the peace medallion hanging from the rearview mirror. The bird took a hop in my direction and tilted a flinty eye at me.

We locked glances for a moment.

Then it gave a harsh caw, lifting into the air with a sweep of its wings and a splat of droppings across the windshield.

Shit.

No, really, shit. I gaped as the stuff ran down the windshield.

"Oh, come on," I muttered. Most of the time, my face didn't scare crows. In fact, my five-foot-ten frame, brown eyes, and thick brunette hair had been favorably compared to a supermodel's. Yes, it had been a friend of my mother's who made the comparison. And yes, the "supermodel" had been a clerk at the local mall who did TV commercials on the side. But still.

I flicked on the wipers. *Snick-snick.* That only spread the stuff around. I had forgotten to check the truck's washer fluid reservoir before leaving the garage. It was empty, of course. I giggled. My giggles soon turned into full belly laughs. *Welcome to Leafy Hollow, Verity Hawkes. Don't get too comfortable.*

Still chuckling, I reached for the rags tucked under the seat and stepped out of the cab. After several minutes of swiping and swearing, the glass was still streaked. But at least it was clear enough to see through.

I tossed the dirty rags into the bed of the truck and turned to lean back against the truck's sun-warmed panels. Brown wrens skittered through the weeds at the edge of the road, darting after insects and seeds, while cicadas droned in the background.

The corners of my mouth lifted. *Jeopardy? Jigsaws?* When did I turn into such an old woman?

I gazed down the hill with a hand shading my eyes. From

this elevated vantage point, the twisted roads of Leafy Hollow actually looked like the map I'd reviewed on my phone before setting out. Peppermint Lane was easy to spot. It was no more than ten minutes away.

Back in the truck, I did a U-turn and roared up the road.

A siren wailed.

I looked in the rearview mirror. A black-and-white Ontario Provincial Police car was gaining on me. I slapped a hand on the steering wheel with a muttered curse. Where was this cop when I was lost?

After pulling over on the shoulder, I watched in the side mirror as the OPP officer emerged from his cruiser behind me and walked up to my window. He was tall and lean, with straight black hair, dark eyes, and cheekbones you could cut yourself on. The name tag on his uniform read, J. KATSURO. As he lowered his head to the window, I thought I detected a faint whiff of Old Spice.

I pasted on a smile. "Hello, Officer. How can I help you?"

"That was a stop sign back there."

"I know. I stopped at it."

"No, you did not. You performed a rolling stop, not a complete halt. Your license, please."

I pulled it from my wallet and handed it over, my stomach sinking. I couldn't afford a fine. Or a jail sentence. Or whatever the penalty was for a rolling stop.

He nodded at my license and handed it back.

"Verity Hawkes. Adeline's niece, right?" He didn't wait for my answer. "People who live in big cities think it's safe to speed along country roads—"

"I would never—"

"—but it's not. That intersection, with the stop sign you ignored—"

"To be fair, I didn't exactly ignore—"

"That you ignored," he repeated. "That same intersection was the scene of a hit and run that killed two people."

"I'm sorry. I won't do it again."

He stepped back from the window, his face impassive. "Take it easy in future."

I watched as he returned to his cruiser and drove past me with a brief wave, but I wasn't thinking about the stop sign anymore. I was wondering how so many people in Leafy Hollow knew that I was Adeline Hawkes' niece and whether that was nice—or creepy.

<hr>

When I pulled up outside her sprawling, red-brick ranch house, Yvonne Skalding was standing on the porch with an amber drink in her hand. I suspected it wasn't ginger ale. She gave her watch a pointed glance.

"Sorry I'm late," I called while scrambling out of the truck, "but you didn't give me directions."

Yvonne rolled her eyes. "It's a five-minute drive." She disappeared inside after yelling, "Not too short."

I puzzled over that, since I towered over most women, until I realized she meant the grass. Not a problem. Surely, the mower would take care of that.

After hauling it off the truck, I re-read my scribbled instructions and tucked them into the pocket of my jeans. It took a dozen tries to start the engine. Once it roared into life, I pulled back the levers on the handle. The mower shot out from under me and bolted over the grass, leaving me to hang on and run after it—not realizing I had my hand clamped over the lever that kept the engine turned on.

After several harrowing moments, I realized my error and brought the machine to a halt.

Then I looked over my shoulder. My mowed lane jerked across the lawn like an alien crop circle. Not quite *Downton Abbey*, but a start. Perhaps the edges needed tidying, though.

I was cutting another strip when a blur of brown-and-white feathers topped with a red cockscomb darted across the lawn in front of me. With a shriek, I released the levers. The mower's engine coughed and stalled—as did the rooster, which then tilted its head to study the lawn. A caterpillar had caught its attention. The black Death Eater lawnmower inches from its bony legs, however, it ignored.

A woman wearing a huge, striped sunhat ran across the grass and scooped up the bird.

The rooster jerked its head in that bobble-headed way peculiar to chickens everywhere, annoyed to have missed out on the caterpillar.

"I'm sorry," the woman said. "Damn bird is always running off." Her broad-brimmed hat cast a mysterious shadow over her features. At least, it would have been mysterious if the thick lenses of her glasses didn't give her such a goggle-eyed expression.

"I didn't know Mrs. Skalding kept chickens," I said.

"Just the one. Yvonne got it so she could claim she keeps livestock." The woman gave the rooster a baleful look while tucking it under her arm. "She probably imagined this useless bird would lay eggs." She held out her hand. "I'm Imogen West, the housekeeper."

I could tell from her accent that Imogen was from the north of England, possibly Yorkshire. I'd heard Patty's husband, Chuck, yelling at his beloved Leeds United on television often enough.

"Verity Hawkes." I shook her hand, keeping a wary eye on the rooster's pointy beak.

"Adeline's niece?"

"That's right." I wiped the back of my neck. My hand came away damp with sweat. "Any chance of a glass of water?"

"Yvonne won't let you into the house in your work clothes, I'm afraid. But there's a hose on the patio. By the deck chairs. I'll show you."

"What did you mean by livestock?" I asked as we walked to the patio. I was still curious about the rooster. "Isn't it a pet?"

"Yvonne doesn't keep pets. They might damage something," she said, with a curl to her upper lip on the word *damage*. "She bought it because farmers who own livestock can shoot predators on their property. Yvonne thinks that having a rooster means she can call the police to shoot stray moggies that get into her geraniums."

I halted in surprise. "And do they? Shoot stray cats for her, I mean?"

Imogen snorted. "Certainly not. They have better things to do than harass small animals." After pointing out the hose, she turned to go.

"Wait," I said. "Do I mow that big field behind the house?"

Imogen adjusted the struggling rooster to a more secure position. "No, that's not Yvonne's. It belongs to developers who want to build a subdivision, but Yvonne won't sell the land they need for an access road." Imogen stared into the distance, gazing at the field as if I wasn't there. "She doesn't need the money," she muttered, "and she enjoys being disagreeable."

Imogen disappeared behind the house, clutching the bird. I had flashbacks to Thanksgiving dinner.

I picked up the hose and twisted the crosshatched brass nozzle as far as it would go. Water whooshed out in a wide stream, spraying the wall and the patio, and splashing back on me. I tried to turn it off, but only succeeded in soaking the cushions on the deck chairs. I frantically twisted the nozzle in the other direction. The spray slowed to a fine mist and stopped.

My T-shirt and jeans were sopping, and water dripped from my hair. When I took a step, my feet squelched in my running shoes. As I wrung out the edge of my shirt, I eyed the patio furniture. Hopefully, Yvonne wasn't planning to sit out here anytime soon.

I sloshed my way back to the grass and restarted the mower. This part of the lawn was tougher going, with little hills and valleys. A few times, the mower bogged down. Eventually, it sputtered and stopped. After several tries at restarting it, I bent down and looked at the wheels. They were coated in mud and grass clippings. When I checked the strip I'd mowed, I found bare spots and muddy patches. That was odd—where did the grass go?

Turning back to the mower, I yanked on the cord and recoiled as gasoline fumes filled the air. I yanked a few more times. Then I gave the mower a kick and slumped onto the ground with my cap in my hand, wiping the sweat from my face with my other hand.

I couldn't salvage my aunt's landscaping business. I couldn't even operate a lawnmower.

A shadow fell over me. I looked up, squinting against the sun. A man stood over me.

"Need any help?" he asked.

I got to my feet, settling the baseball cap on my head to shade my eyes from the sunlight. A gold logo on his green T-shirt read, *Fields' Landscaping*. That tight shirt spanned impressive pecs. "I'm fine," I said, trying not to stare.

A smile played over his lips. One of those slow, sexy smiles. I realized that my wet T-shirt clung to my chest—what there was of it. My chest, I mean. I moved behind the lawn-mower, but the handle didn't offer much cover.

"You don't look fine," he said.

"Thanks."

His smile became a wince. "I didn't mean—"

"Forget it." I gripped the lawnmower handle as my face flushed. I wanted to move away, but I had no idea what was wrong with the mower. Or how to fix it.

"Let me take a look," he said, reaching a tanned, muscular arm past me and gently taking the mower's handle.

I stepped back, watching as he removed a tiny metal

cylinder—the spark plug, he said—from the mower and cleaned it on his shirt.

"Let me guess," he said as he replaced the spark plug. "You're Adeline Hawkes' niece."

"Verity, that's right. Thanks for fixing my lawnmower, um..."

He smiled again, revealing blindingly white teeth. "Ryker Fields. And it's no problem. Your mower should be fine for now, but you'll need a tune-up. You should also wear ear protection and safety glasses when you operate heavy machinery." He glanced over his shoulder at the strip I'd cut. "And raise the wheels. You're scalping the lawn."

Well, excuse me, Mr. Know-It-All. He probably also thought his deep blue eyes and two-day stubble made him irresistible. He was probably right. But not to me, of course. I was not in the market for tall, blond, and irresistible. Not anymore.

"Thank you," I said, brushing past him and grabbing the mower handle. "I can take it from here."

"Uh-huh," he said, nodding. "Listen, I'm on my way to Tim Hortons. If you'd like—"

I yanked the cord on the mower. The engine roared, and I pretended I couldn't hear him. Before I could push off, I felt a hand on my arm. He held out a business card and shouted in my ear, "Call me if you need any help."

I stuck the card under my hat and resumed my mowing. As he drove away, I peeked at the black four-door pickup with "Fields' Landscaping" painted on the side in green and gold. It looked brand new.

When I finished the lawn, I put the mower back in the

truck's bed, picked up the pruning shears and my aunt's aluminum ladder, and headed to the backyard in search of Mrs. Skalding's wisteria. According to the Internet, it was a robust climbing vine that blooms in early spring.

I rounded the corner, and there it was, smothering a wooden arbor and reaching out to mount the trees on either side. "Robust" was an understatement. This plant could have starred in *Little Shop of Horrors*.

I studied the massive vine, wondering which bits needed pruning. Leafy tendrils trailed over the edges of the arbor and rustled in the breeze. The effect was charming. It seemed a shame to nip them off, but that's what I'd been hired to do.

After placing the ladder against the arbor, I climbed to the top and cut off the branches that curled over the edges. When I finished, the bare twigs left behind didn't line up along the arbor's edge, so I trimmed a little more. I climbed down from the ladder to assess my efforts.

It didn't look right. I climbed back up and trimmed the branches a bit more. They still weren't straight, so I started over, reminded of my ill-fated high school experiment with bangs. I had to sneak into class with a kerchief to cover the tufts sticking up from my forehead. This wisteria might look the same if I didn't stop soon.

My hands were stinging. When I turned them over, I found blisters on my palms. Too late, I remembered that my aunt always wore gardening gloves.

After one last snip, I decided to call it quits.

As I climbed down from the ladder, the back door opened. Mrs. Skalding came out onto the patio. Her face was beet red, and she was gasping for air.

I reached for my cell phone, thinking I might need to call nine-one-one.

"What did you do to my lawn?" Yvonne shrieked, pointing to the front of the house. "It's all..." She paused, looking over my shoulder, and clapped one hand to her mouth.

I followed her gaze. *Yes, the wisteria looked good*, I thought. Not bad for a first attempt.

Mrs. Skalding was dumbstruck. It couldn't last.

It didn't.

"You stupid, stupid girl. What have you done?" she wailed. "That looks terrible."

I was wet, muddy, and exhausted. My nose was sunburned, my damp jeans chafed my thighs, and my palms were blistered raw. So I think it's understandable that I wasn't as conciliatory as I could have been.

"What have I done? What have I done?" I waved the shears in frustration. "I pruned the bloody thing. Isn't that what you wanted?"

"Not like that. Don't you know anything?"

I pointed the shears at the arbor. "What exactly is wrong with it? It's shorter, isn't it?"

Yvonne muttered at the wisteria, rubbing her hands together so furiously that I expected her acrylic nails to pop off.

"You're supposed to cut off the spurs, not the whole branch. Why didn't you tell me you didn't know how to prune wisteria?"

I was swaying from exhaustion. If I didn't sit down soon, I'd fall over. Why was this woman yelling at me? I didn't volunteer to prune her damn vine. She showed up on my doorstep and practically forced me. And what the heck were spurs?

"You insisted that I come over here to cut your lawn—"

I had no chance to finish before she was running off at the mouth again.

"That's another thing. What the heck did you do to the grass? Those bare patches weren't there before."

I considered this. "It'll grow back, won't it?"

"You *stupid* girl," she shrieked. "Get out of my sight." She stalked back to the patio door.

"You still have to pay me," I called after her.

Yvonne gave me a withering look. "Pay you? Pay you? I'll ruin you. You'll never work in this village again."

Yes, she actually said that.

Spit flew as I hollered what sounded in my head like a devastating retort. "I may be stupid, but at least I'm not an old *cow*." Startled, I took a step back. Was that Verity Hawkes, the *recluse*, who uttered that amazing comeback? Maybe it was all the exercise that pumped me up, but whatever the cause, I was certain that back in Vancouver my therapist was beaming.

Yvonne Skalding was not impressed with my fleeting triumph over anxiety. Within minutes, I was in my aunt's truck, heading home with the words, "You're fired," ringing in my ears.

But my first day in Leafy Hollow wasn't over yet. Not even close.

CHAPTER 4

I GRUMBLED ALL the way back to Rose Cottage, reliving my argument with Yvonne while pushing tangled hair off my forehead and trying to ignore the itch caused by my grubby clothes. Visions of a shower, comfy housecoat, and home-cooked meal were the only things keeping exhaustion at bay.

Then I remembered I hadn't checked the fridge before heading out. What were the chances of finding the makings for a decent meal in my aunt's kitchen? Or even fresh milk? Which meant my only choices were to buy groceries or pick up takeout.

Takeout would be faster.

Rose Cottage was on the outskirts of the village, so I turned the truck around and headed for Main Street. In the taxi, Leafy Hollow's main drag had been a blur. This time, I forced myself to look around, if only to keep awake.

Not much had changed from my last visit. I passed the century-old limestone Village Hall, the white-porticoed library, two organic groceries, a free-range butcher, and a handful of ethnic restaurants. Most of the two- and three-story brick buildings lining the street had a store or office on the ground floor, with apartments upstairs.

Twice, I slowed for pedestrians who ignored the street's two stoplights in favor of ambling across mid-block with a jaunty wave to the drivers. I shrieked to a halt when a white-haired woman in a pink pantsuit wheeled her walker onto the road in front of me. While she labored across, I tapped my fingers on the wheel, forcing a friendly smile and muttering to myself. She should be more careful. If Katsuro happened by, she'd get a lecture on jaywalking.

Assuming that was even illegal in this placid backwater.

I pulled the truck into a parking spot on Main Street. While plugging coins into the meter, I scanned the nearby storefronts hoping for pizza. Or chocolate. Either would do.

A few doors down, a painted sign—5X Bakery—topped a red door. Perfect. As I stepped through the entrance, a bell tinkled overhead. Mouth-watering aromas of vanilla and cardamom wafted toward me, but there was no one behind the glass-fronted counter. The place was empty, front and back. I bent to scan the elaborate confections on display. *Look, but don't touch?* Didn't they realize this was an emergency?

I stuck my head back out the entrance. Only steps away, in the same compact two-story building, was a vegan takeout. Not my first choice, but preferable to expiring right there on the sidewalk.

Outside the shop, I paused to pet a lethargic beagle lying on the sidewalk. "Nitro" was stamped on a brass name tag attached to his collar. This dog didn't look like a Nitro. More like a Chill, or even a Prozac.

Beside him, a folding chalkboard advertised grilled vegetable sandwiches as the takeout's daily special. I pushed open the blue door, and a bell tinkled overhead. The interior was just large enough for a polished driftwood counter, a glass-front cooler, and an ancient rotating floor fan that ruffled the stack of recycled-paper napkins on the counter each time it made a rasping circuit.

A young black man stood at the counter, wearing a royal blue spandex unitard and expensive hiking boots. He pushed his Ray-Bans up from his nose and over his shorn head to study the food behind the glass. "I'll have the cold Thai sweet potato burger, if you're sure it has no tamari. I can't eat soy."

"You know it doesn't, Terence," said the young woman behind the counter. "You've been eating it here for months."

Smile lines crinkled beside his brown eyes. "Just checking."

I shifted impatiently on my feet. How long was this going to take?

"How's the high-tech world?" the woman asked while reaching into the refrigerated case for a wrapped burger.

"Same as always." He pulled a handful of toonies from the fanny pack around his waist and handed them over. The cash register rang as the woman deposited the two-dollar coins into the till and gave him the change. He dropped it into the tip jar on the counter.

The fan made another wheezing rotation. It was still moving faster than these two.

"Most of the time, we're too busy to eat. Which reminds

me." He pointed to a shelf behind her. "I need more powdered protein shakes."

Was all this gossip really necessary? I bounced on my heels.

"A two-four?" she asked.

"Yeah, that's good."

"How come you're off today? It's not a holiday."

Oh, come on. I puffed air out my lips. These sandwiches better be the best ones ever made.

"Holiday? What's that?" He gave his head a bemused shake while dropping two twenty-dollar bills on the counter. "They're retooling the system. We took the day off to give the techies room to work." He held up his wrapped burger and bottle of Green Goddess juice. "Mind if I sit outside? Nitro and I are sprinting up to the Peak after this."

His words sparked childhood memories of hiking with my aunt up Pine Hill Peak to admire the valley hundreds of feet below. If we were lucky, a tiny freight train would chug along the track that snaked through the village. It was difficult to picture Nitro making the climb.

"Is he outside?" the young woman asked.

"Yes, and he's raring to go," I broke in, hoping to jar them out of their Mayberry moment.

The young man pivoted at the sound of my voice, sloshing Green Goddess on me. "Oh, sorry." He grabbed a napkin and zeroed in on my chest. "Let me—"

"No, please, I'm fine." I took the napkin from him and dabbed my T-shirt, gritting my teeth. "It's nothing."

"Let me have that dry-cleaned for you."

I looked up in surprise. "My T-shirt?"

He held out a hand. "Terence Oliver. I have an account with Hewitt's, across the street. They could do it while you wait."

I shook his hand. "Verity Hawkes. And thank you, but no. It was my fault. I startled you."

I handed the used napkin to the woman behind the counter. She threw it into the recycling bin, but not before giving me a quick look with her tongue poked firmly into her cheek. Dark curls framed a heart-shaped face that looked to be about the same age as mine. She was five-foot-two and couldn't have weighed more than a hundred pounds soaking wet and fully dressed.

"It's nobody's fault," she said.

Terence brushed past me with an apologetic shrug. The bell tinkled again as I held the door open for him. Outside, he bent over the beagle. "How about a little sweet potato, Nitro?"

The dog lifted his head from the pavement for an exploratory sniff, and then lowered it again in resignation.

"Can I help you?" came a voice from behind me.

I closed the door and turned. The young woman behind the counter grinned at me. Her white chef's apron trailed almost to the floor and enveloped her tiny body, but her radiant smile took up half the room. It was impossible not to smile back.

"I'm considering the special. Is it good?"

"It's my bestseller. And for an extra loonie, you can have iced herb tea."

"Sold." I dropped change on the table.

She shot me a look while making my sandwich. I could tell she had questions for me, but I wasn't in the mood for chitchat. I'd spent the afternoon trying to make enough money to start repairs on Rose Cottage, and I had nothing to show for it—other than blisters, filthy clothes, and a bad case of heat rash. My goal for the rest of the day was to have a long shower, not make new friends.

"I'm Emy Dionne."

I looked up from my daze, startled. "Excuse me?"

She handed over my sandwich and tea. "Emy Dionne. That's my name. You're Verity Hawkes, right?"

I nodded. Later, I intended to rip off my T-shirt to see if there was a note pinned to the back that read, "Adeline's niece," with an arrow pointing to my head.

"My aunt seems to have made quite an impression here," I said.

"Oh, it's not that. I mean, we loved your aunt, but you're notorious for arguing with Yvonne Skalding."

My jaw dropped. It had been barely twenty minutes since I'd escaped Yvonne's clutches. "You heard about that?"

She scrunched up her face in delight and leaned over the counter. "Did you really call her an old cow?"

"Ah..." I glanced around, desperate to change the topic or leave the premises. "Do you have desserts?"

Emy pointed to the entrance, crooking her finger to the left. "Next door."

"Thanks." I backed away. "Have a good day."

Out on the sidewalk, I walked four steps to the left and

pushed open the red door to the bakery, hoping the proprietor had returned.

"The maple-bacon cupcake with cream-cheese icing is my bestseller," said a familiar voice. "But the lavender-lemon is a close second."

Emy Dionne grinned at me from the interior doorway that connected the two shops.

It took a few seconds before I clued in. "Wait a minute," I said. "Next door, you're vegan, but on this side it's all bacon and cream cheese?"

She shrugged. "It's a small town. We have to double up." She leaned on the counter with her chin resting on her fists. "What'll it be?"

"Maple-bacon, I guess."

"Good choice."

Emy placed the cupcake on a plate and carried it to a table for two tucked into the back of the tiny shop. She pulled out a chair and, with a wave of her arm, said, "Sit, and then I'll get you some real tea." With a wink, she walked back behind the counter for cups and saucers.

I sat at the table, shoved aside my roasted vegetables and iced herb tea, and peeled the wrapper off the cupcake. By the time Emy returned with a teapot in a crocheted cozy, I'd eaten half my dessert.

"Oh my God," I said through the last of the crumbs. "This is fabulous."

"Thank you." She beamed while pouring two cups of Darjeeling. "It's on the house."

"No, no. I must pay."

She gave me a conspiratorial wink before sitting opposite me and picking up her cup. "You will, don't worry." After taking a sip, she replaced her cup on the saucer. "Start at the beginning. I want to hear everything."

I contemplated the tea cooling in my cup. Was everyone in Leafy Hollow this nosy? Yes, they must be. How else had my squabble with Yvonne made the rounds at supersonic speed?

I picked up my cup and sipped, trying to look nonchalant. "Why did you name this the 5X Bakery?"

My host held out her hands. "Emy Dionne?"

"I don't get it."

"The quintuplets?"

"Ohhh, of course." I mock-slapped my forehead. "But wasn't that Depression-era?"

"God, yes. Nineteen-thirty-four. But my mother's obsessed with them. She has the books, the documentaries, everything. And since she loaned me the funds to open the bakery, I thought the least I could do was indulge her hobby." She pointed to a framed photo on the wall.

I walked over and peered at the blurry image of five little girls in matching overalls.

Emy rose to refill the teapot. "The past is always with us, Mom likes to say."

I ran a finger along the frame. *It certainly is.* I scanned the other photos on the wall. "So you rent this place, then?" I asked.

"No, I own it. The whole building." At my surprised look, she added, "It was a gift from a former boyfriend. He was... older than me."

I walked back to the table and dropped into my chair. "An inheritance?"

Emy laughed, tossing her hair. "He wasn't that old. But the jerk threw me over for a younger woman, and I guess he felt guilty."

I gazed at her with barely repressed awe. "That's a lot of guilt."

"I'm a lot of woman." She twisted her shoulder and simpered over it with puckered lips.

We both collapsed into helpless laughter. Once I'd wiped the tears from my eyes, I polished off the rest of my cupcake.

"Anyway," Emy continued. "Mom advanced me the cash to buy my bakery equipment and set up shop. I live in an apartment upstairs." She walked back to the table with the refilled teapot. "Mom works at the library. She's a literacy tutor, too."

"Your mother teaches adults to read?"

"She loves it," she said, replacing the teapot on its trivet and taking a seat. "Now, come on. Spill. What happened at Yvonne's?"

I wasn't sure if it was the maple-bacon that did it, the coconut-cream that followed, or Emy's infectious grin, but I told her about my encounter with Yvonne Skalding. I even told her about meeting Ryker Fields.

She leaned in and raised her eyebrows. "Did he hit on you?"

"No," I said indignantly.

"Too bad." Emy sat back in her chair with a smirk, fingering the tablecloth. "But that sounds like Yvonne. She is an old cow. Do you know"—she leaned over the table and

dropped her voice, even though we were alone in the shop
—"she's reported me twice to Bobbi Côté for building code
infractions? She claims my connecting door isn't legal. In fact,
the case is due up in court again this month."

"Who's Bobbi Côté?"

"The town's bylaw officer. Poor Bobbi. She hates
Yvonne."

"Why?"

"She makes so much extra work for her. Yvonne detests
noise, especially fireworks. And power tools. She hates
animals roaming about, and people driving too fast past her
house. You name it, Yvonne complains about it. Bobbi has to
go out there every time, fill out the forms in triplicate, and
then register the complaints. And they always get thrown out
of court later." Emy brightened. "Ryker knows Bobbi."

"Let me guess. He and Bobbi have a thing?"

"Fudge, yes," she said. "Or at least, they did. It ended
during our senior year in high school after Ryker got arrested
for fraud."

"He has a record?"

"He was under eighteen, so it's a juvenile record and
sealed. We're not supposed to mention it. Not only that, but
most people think he didn't do it, that he took the rap for
Bobbi."

"What does he say?"

"He won't talk about it. Listen, Mom will kill me if I don't
rope you into the book club. They meet once a month. Are
you interested?"

"I can't. I'm not staying in Leafy Hollow for long."

"Oh, I hope you change your mind. Wait..." She wrinkled her brow. "Is it the workload? Because I bet you haven't met Lorne yet."

"Lorne?"

"He used to help your aunt out. Lorne is terrific. He'll do the heavy work for you—cut lawns, shovel mulch, dig up roots, everything. You must call him," she said, snatching up my cell phone from the table. "Here, I'll add his number to your contacts list. Lorne Lewins."

Before I could reach out a hand to stop her, she had slapped my phone back on the table with a grin.

"Done. Call Lorne. Your troubles will be over."

I didn't have the heart to tell her I couldn't pay this Lorne person. Not at the moment, anyway.

"Now," Emy continued, "the book club. Mom won't want you to fall into the clutches of the breakaway group."

"There's a breakaway book club? What did they break up over?"

"Margaret Atwood." The bell tinkled in the vegan shop next door, and Emy rose. The corners of her mouth twitched as she added, "It's a long tale, best left for another time. See you around, Verity." At the door, she looked over her shoulder. "You'll need *Anna Karenina*, this month's assigned reading. You can buy a copy at Harvey's Hardbacks up the street."

"No, I'm not—"

But Emy was gone, leaving only an intoxicating aroma of warm gingerbread and lemon peel drifting from the kitchen in the back.

I bundled up the rest of my sandwich and headed for the exit and a six-pack. My first day in Leafy Hollow had been long and painful, and I was ready to kick back with a few cold ones.

After all, what else could happen?

CHAPTER 5

ROSE COTTAGE WAS SHROUDED in twilight when hammering on the front door woke me from an alcohol-induced slumber. I winced as my stiff legs swung over the sofa's edge and made contact with the floor. "Coming," I shouted.

The hammering stopped.

Brushing hair off my forehead and groaning, I staggered to the front window. A police car was parked outside the house. I ran a quick mental review as I walked to the door. I had driven home slowly from the bakery, coming to a complete halt at each stop sign and signaling every turn—including the one that led to the beer store and a refrigerated six-pack. Then I left the truck in the driveway, intending to unload it later, and slogged into the house. After putting most of the beer in the fridge, I wrapped a damp tea towel around my neck. Sometime during my second beverage, I had fallen asleep on the sofa with the cold bottle pressed between my blistered palms. And I'd been there ever since.

So, I was in the clear. Maybe this was a charity drive.

With my head pounding, I opened the front door and blearily eyed the officer standing on the doorstep. It was the same cop who had lectured me about rolling stops. The good-looking one.

"Miss Hawkes? May I come in?"

"Did I do something wrong?"

He didn't smile. "We should discuss this indoors."

Under his cool professional gaze, I turned to the mirror in the foyer. My muddy T-shirt was hiked up well above my waist, my sunburned face bore creases from the sofa cushions, and I had serious bed head. I tugged at my shirt and stood up straight in a belated, and probably pointless, attempt at dignity.

"May I see some identification?" I asked.

I thought I detected a slight smile, but I could have been wrong. It was dark in the foyer. I leaned over and switched on the light—grateful I'd screwed in a new bulb before leaving for Mrs. Skalding's—while he pulled out his ID wallet.

I peered at the photo and badge.

Jeffrey Katsuro. Detective Constable. Ontario Provincial Police.

I stepped back and gestured at the living room. "Be my guest." Closing the door behind him, I pointed to the armchair, then walked to the sofa and sat down. "What's this about?"

"You were at Yvonne Skalding's this afternoon to cut her lawn and do yard work. Is that correct?"

Great. That shrew had complained about me to the police. "I don't see how—"

"In what condition was Mrs. Skalding when you left her?"

"Condition? Has something happened to her?" With alarm, I recalled her red-flushed, contorted expression. Maybe I should have called nine-one-one after all. "Did she have a heart attack?"

"Mrs. Skalding fell from a wooden ladder in her garden. She sustained a broken wrist and a concussion. Her book club members found her after you left."

I stared at him, taking this in. "What was she doing on a ladder?"

"I thought you might know."

"Me? How would I know?"

"Something about a wisteria?"

I considered this. *Drats*. "Nope, doesn't ring a bell."

Katsuro gave me one of those intense *Law and Order* stares. I tried not to squirm.

"There's more," he said.

I raised my eyebrows.

"After Mrs. Skalding returned from the hospital, she walked into a coyote trap embedded in her lawn."

"She did... what?" I envisioned a saw-toothed mantrap like the ones in horror movies—or my aunt's garage.

"It was a six-inch one, spring-loaded. Broke her ankle." He looked at me, obviously expecting a comment.

"Ahhh..." I had nothing.

Katsuro pulled out a small notebook and flipped it open. "You were overheard having a loud and violent argument with Mrs. Skalding before her accidents."

"No... well, yes... I mean, yes, we had a difference of opinion, but no, it wasn't violent."

"Did Mrs. Skalding say...?" He checked his notes again. "'Your business is finished. I'll ruin you?'" He looked up from the notebook.

"Sort of."

"Was there a shoving match?"

"I didn't shove anybody. We had a verbal disagreement."

He regarded me with the same chilly gaze I'd squirmed under at that stop sign. Surely he didn't suspect me of pushing Yvonne Skalding off a ladder?

"Why is this a police investigation?" I asked. "These sound like unavoidable mishaps."

What did I know? Maybe everybody in Leafy Hollow had coyote traps in their lawn.

"Someone tampered with the ladder."

"Tampered? How?"

"Did you like Mrs. Skalding?"

I kept my expression neutral. "I didn't know her very well, but she seemed like a nice woman."

"Where did you go after leaving Mrs. Skalding's?"

"Are you accusing me of something?"

"These are routine questions, Verity."

Verity? What happened to "Miss Hawkes"?

"I did some shopping."

"I stopped you earlier today for driving erratically. Do you normally drive that way?"

I gave an indignant gasp and slapped my hand on the coffee table. "That is so unfair. I was not driving erratically."

Wincing, I lifted my hand from the table. I'd forgotten the blisters.

"You seemed agitated when you were talking to me in your truck—and now, as well."

"I was not."

He scribbled a note in his pad.

I craned my neck. "What are you writing?"

"Where did you go after your shopping?"

"Right here. I came home, and I... fell asleep on the sofa."

"Do you always drink in the afternoon?"

"Is there a law against it? Because—"

A knock on the door interrupted me. Before I could get up to answer it, the door opened.

An officer stuck his head in. "Jeff, we found something."

I rose and looked out the window. A second cruiser was parked outside the house, and another cop was bent over the bed of my aunt's pickup truck.

Katsuro put his notebook away and joined the officers outside. I hurried after him. The second officer pointed to the truck bed.

I peered around Katsuro's back. A hacksaw lay next to my aunt's lawnmower. I'd never seen it before. I leaned in closer. Sawdust clung to the teeth. "That's not mine," I blurted.

"Then you won't mind if we take it into evidence?"

"I don't care." I narrowed my eyes. "Don't you need a warrant?"

"Not if we have your permission."

It seemed pointless to debate it. "Okay. Take it."

"When did you last use it?"

"Never. It's not mine. I just told you."

"Did you put it in the truck this morning?" he pressed.

"No. It's. Not. Mine."

"Your aunt has dozens of tools. Can you recognize every one?"

I was putting the pieces together, and I didn't like the snapshot they made: wooden ladder, hacksaw, and tampered. This was like an IQ test—what came next in this series? I might be paranoid, but it seemed as if "attempted murder" was one possible conclusion.

"I'm telling you, I've never seen that saw."

"Do you mind if we check the garage?"

"Why?"

"We like to be thorough."

I assumed they needed my permission for that, too, and wondered if I should withhold it. But I hadn't done anything wrong—apart from calling Yvonne Skalding an old cow, which wasn't a crime. The truth was always an acceptable defense.

"Go ahead," I said. "There's nothing to see."

Katsuro rolled up the garage door and walked to the back, where he scanned my aunt's pegboard wall of tools. He flicked his hand at the constable by the truck. The constable brought in the hacksaw—now sealed in a plastic evidence bag. Katsuro pointed to an outline drawn on the pegboard, and the constable pressed the saw up against it.

It was a perfect fit.

My heart did a double-thump. How was that possible? That saw was not in the garage when I loaded the truck.

At a gesture from Katsuro, the constable returned the saw to the cruiser.

Katsuro turned to me. "Do you want to change your story, Verity?"

"It's not a story," I spluttered. "I said I'd never seen that hacksaw, and I haven't. I'm sure it wasn't there this morning. Even if I used it to tamper with Mrs. Skalding's ladder, would I be stupid enough to leave it in my truck?"

He scanned the overhead trap lines while replying. "You had a fair bit to drink today. Maybe you forgot about it." Katsuro gestured to a third officer, who stepped up to photograph the rusty hanging chains.

My eyes widened, but this time, I kept my mouth shut.

I followed Katsuro as he walked back to his cruiser.

"Could you come to the station tomorrow morning to give a statement?" he asked. "It's routine."

He handed me a business card and parroted rapid-fire directions while I read it. I looked up from the card and caught him contemplating Rose Cottage.

"What is it?" I asked.

"I'm sorry about your aunt."

"Thank you."

"You're her heir, correct?"

"I guess. There's not much to inherit, though. I mean, look at the place." I tried to chuckle, but my throat was dry. "Besides, she's not dead."

Katsuro studied me for a moment. Then, with a few steps, he closed the gap between us and leaned in.

Definitely Old Spice.

He gave me a tight smile. I assumed it was his interpretation of somebody who gave a damn.

"If you have information about your aunt's accident and don't disclose it," he said, "that could be seen as impeding a police investigation."

Excuse me? This pin-the-rap-on-Verity game was getting old fast.

"What investigation?" I stuck out my chin. "As far as I can tell, the police aren't even looking for my aunt."

Katsuro stepped back with the same tight smile and opened his cruiser door. "Miss Hawkes' car has been released by the accident investigators," he said. "They'll tow it back here in a day or two."

Then he drove off.

I watched as the second OPP cruiser followed. I thought my problems were limited to repairing Rose Cottage and finding my aunt. I never expected to be drawn into an attempted murder case.

Back inside, I yanked the curtains closed, flicked on a light, and collapsed into an armchair.

Why would I want to hurt Yvonne Skalding? Because she fired me? Unlikely. And even if I wanted to harm her, I had no way to know when she might use her ladder. I pictured her scampering up the rungs with her acrylic nails and four-inch stilettos. Impossible. Yvonne would never use a ladder, no matter how desperate her wisteria situation.

Personally, I would have gone for something more foolproof. I mentally scanned the arsenal of tools in my aunt's garage—shovels, sharp-edged hoes, pruning shears, serrated garden knives—and the possibilities they suggested. A flimsy hacksaw didn't even make the list.

Anyway, my fingerprints couldn't be on that saw, because I'd never seen it before. The whole idea was ridiculous.

With a shudder, I recalled the look in Katsuro's eyes when he mentioned my aunt. I must have misinterpreted his expression because the implication that I might have something to do with her disappearance was even more ridiculous.

I was headed to the kitchen and the rest of the beer—a slight detour on my way to that overdue shower—as a thought struck me. When the police dragged my aunt's submerged car from the river, I was in my Vancouver apartment. So I couldn't be under suspicion. Except that I had been alone, as usual, with no one to vouch for me. Tomorrow, when I called my aunt's lawyer to check in, I should ask for his advice on criminal charges. Just to be thorough.

A thunderclap shattered my train of thought, followed by the splatter of rain against the windows. I cast an anxious glance at the aluminum pail in the living room, hoping I didn't come halfway across the country to become a squatter in Noah's Ark. As the *drip-drip-drip* of water into the pail intensified, the vein in my neck throbbed, a sure sign of an anxiety attack on the way.

Food usually helped. If necessary, I would eat it in the tub. But I had been too tired to pick up anything other than essentials on my way home from Emy's bakery, so I had nothing but beer. No groceries.

While rummaging in the kitchen, I found a half-empty bag of peas in the freezer. It had been thawed and refrozen so often it could have originated in the Pleistocene era. I dumped the peas into a bowl and stuck them in the microwave. Then I pulled a bag of egg noodles, a jar of Dijon mustard, and a tin of tuna from the cupboard. Leafy Hollow must be working its magic after all. I'd never been this happy to see canned fish.

After mixing the cooked noodles with the tuna, mustard, and wrinkled peas, I took my plate to the table while considering my next moves. Yvonne Skalding was bound to spread the word about my lack of gardening skills, so Coming Up Roses was doomed. It wouldn't take long for bankruptcy news to get around. How many paid-up clients did my aunt have? What if they all turned up, demanding refunds before her business folded?

My vein throbbed again, and I jabbed my fork into the noodles.

Meeooww.

I strained to hear over the rain.

Meeooww.

It was louder this time, and coming from the back porch. After placing my plate on the counter next to the sink, I opened the kitchen door.

A bedraggled silver gray tabby sat before me. His tattered ears stuck out at odd angles, and one eye was gone—either from birth or backyard skirmishes in the years since. He raised a paw for a delicate lick, and then settled his foot back on the porch floor. His one eye fixed me with a woeful, yet somehow accusing, stare.

I remembered the tuna with a pang of guilt.

The tabby craned his neck, wrinkling his nose in an obvious sniff of the kitchen.

With a sigh, I stepped back, out of his path.

He swished past me, his tail undulating, and settled himself by the counter, looking up at my plate. *"Mrack?"*

I closed the door, reached for the plate, and placed it on the floor. It wasn't like Tuna Pleistocene Surprise was actually worth eating.

The cat sniffed at the tuna and pasta, then meticulously picked out every scrap of fish and chewed it thoroughly. Next, he ate the noodles. The shriveled peas he left marooned on the plate. After an elaborate face wash, he strolled back to the door where he gave me another one-eyed stare.

"You're kidding. Now you want to leave?"

His gaze did not change.

"It's rude to eat and run, Tom," I muttered as I opened the door.

I paused on the threshold to listen to water dripping from the sodden spruce branches beside Rose Cottage. The rain had slowed, and the humid night air was fragrant with lavender. My anxiety faded as I stood there, breathing it in.

The cat walked out into the night without a backward glance.

I had to envy his sangfroid. After all, I planned to leave Leafy Hollow in exactly the same way.

CHAPTER 6

YVONNE SKALDING SAT up and reached for the prescription drug bottle on her nightstand. After shaking two pills into her hand, she picked up the carafe to fill her glass. It was empty.

"Imogen," she hollered. "Water."

No reply.

"Imogen," she hollered again.

Yvonne clicked her fingernails against the nightstand. The clock on her bedside table said eight-ten. Her housekeeper must be outside, feeding that damn rooster. *Typical.* Here was her employer, in terrible pain, suffering, wanting nothing more than water, and where was Imogen? Looking after a bird.

With an exasperated roll of her shoulders, she pushed back the duvet, slid her legs over the side of the bed, and reached for the housecoat tossed over the armchair. She slid it onto one arm and staggered up, dropping back onto the mattress when a wave of dizziness hit her.

She waited for the vertigo to pass.

Still no sign of the housekeeper.

Yvonne rose and slipped the housecoat over her other shoulder. With one arm in a sling, she couldn't manage the fabric belt, so she let it hang loose. After a moment of balancing herself with her hand gripping the bedpost, she pushed off and started along the hall, the housecoat draped over one shoulder and the belt dragging behind her. Her bare foot sank into the plush carpet as she thumped along on the cast that immobilized her other foot.

And where was Zander? What kind of son left his mother to suffer alone? He and Kate only arrived yesterday, and now that sorry excuse for a wife had taken him shopping? Still, if Kate had been here, she wouldn't forget to fill the water jug. Kate would wait on her hand and foot.

Yvonne snickered as she thought of her daughter-in-law. More than once, she had surprised Kate while she was fingering the china, or the silver, or studying the framed Audubon in the living room, her eyes bright with the covetous glint Yvonne recognized all too well. She knew the younger woman was mentally totaling the value of her mother-in-law's possessions, as well as the time remaining until they would be hers to sell.

Occasionally, a figurine disappeared, its absence concealed by a clumsy rearrangement of the objects left behind. Yvonne noticed these petty thefts, but she never mentioned them, instead picturing Kate's shock at the eventual reading of her mother-in-law's will. Meanwhile, she intended to make the skinny bitch work for the objects she would never possess.

At the top of the staircase, Yvonne paused to look down. Dizziness overcame her again. She closed her eyes with a hand pressed to her forehead, swaying.

Where the heck was that woman? She squinted at the landing below, which shimmered in the light coming through the transom over the door. Should she chance it, or go back to bed and wait for her housekeeper to return from the garden? The thought was tempting, but the chance to make Imogen feel guilty was more tempting still. No, she would make her way downstairs alone and unaided.

Yvonne reached out with her good hand to grip the newel post before starting down the carpeted stairs. She thumped onto each step, fighting vertigo, her good hand sliding along the banister. The trailing housecoat belt tangled around her bare foot, wrenching her off balance.

She slid down the last three steps, landing on her rear with a gasp.

"Help," she wailed.

Blast. That English tart didn't give a rat's toss about her employer. Yvonne could be dead for all Imogen cared. She rolled her lips, realizing that wasn't fair. Imogen saved her life once. Kept her from choking on a chunk of prime rib, right here in the dining room, which was why she hired her full time.

Yvonne scowled as she pulled herself up with her good hand on the banister. If she had been alone that day as usual —or with Kate—she would have died. Kate didn't know the Heimlich maneuver. Or if she did, she wouldn't waste it on her mother-in-law.

The side door slammed shut. Footsteps hurried up the

steps to the mudroom and through the kitchen. Imogen burst into the hall.

"Mrs. Skalding, what's wrong?" she called, panting as she trotted up the hall. "I heard you shouting. What are you doing downstairs?"

Yvonne flattened her mouth as she regarded the housekeeper. "Tea. I want tea."

Imogen cupped Yvonne's good arm under the elbow. "Let's get you settled in the living room now that you're out of bed. Then I'll make you tea."

They trudged to the living room with Imogen supporting her employer's arm. Yvonne shuffled to stress her struggle. Once or twice, she groaned, so she could enjoy Imogen's guilty glances. In truth, with all the drugs she'd taken, she could barely feel her arms and legs at all, never mind pain.

"Sit here," Imogen said, guiding her into a wingback chair. "Let's get that foot up." She slid over the matching chintz footstool and helped Yvonne swing her cast onto it. "There." She patted the leg. "I'll be right back."

Before leaving the room, Imogen pulled the cord that opened the brocade curtains. Yvonne shaded her eyes as sunshine streamed in, and then settled back against the chair. She swept her gaze around the room, relishing the objects she'd collected over the years. A huge china breakfront rose to the ceiling, dominating the space. Antique Dresden figurines, blue china, and Meissen boys jammed its shelves. Her collection had been appraised in the tens of thousands and was worth every penny. She smiled at the delicate statuettes and translucent plates, and, on the top shelf, under a spotlight, her pièce de résistance: "Julia," a Commedia Dell'Arte figurine from the Nymphenburg porcelain factory in Germany. It cost as much as a compact car, but the eight-inch statuette of the flirtatious actress would hold its value. It was—

Yvonne started, and her mouth fell open. *What the...?* She swung her cast off the footstool and thumped up to the breakfront for a closer look. Something crunched under her foot. She peered down at a white china arm, three inches long, embedded in the carpet.

Julia's arm.

"Nooooooo," Yvonne wailed, a hand clasped to her chest.

She bent over to pluck the broken appendage from the Aubusson, staring at it with her mouth open. Then she turned her gaze to the cabinet's top shelf. The china figurine was snapped in two at the waist and lay in pieces on the shelf.

"Imogen," Yvonne shrieked while shoving the footstool over to the cabinet. "Imogen, get in here."

Yvonne scrambled onto the footstool. Her feet sank into the tufted upholstery as she opened the cabinet's glass door. Vertigo overcame her, and she grabbed the top shelf with her good hand.

The broken pieces mocked her, still out of reach. She stretched her arm toward them, her fingernails scrabbling along the wooden shelf as she swore under her breath. Another inch or so—

The breakfront rocked, gently at first, but then gained momentum.

Yvonne screamed and flailed her arms, trying to back away. China slid from the shelves and crashed onto the floor. The cabinet toppled, its huge weight crushing the footstool, the coffee table—and Yvonne.

Imogen raced into the living room with the teapot in her hand. As she stared open-mouthed at the destruction, the teapot dropped. It bounced across the carpet until it came to a rest against the red-lacquered fingernails of a hand sticking out from under the cabinet's edge.

The hand twitched. Once. Twice. And never again.

CHAPTER 7

"GOOD GRIEF," I said, the phone pressed to my ear as I sat at the kitchen table. "That's terrible. When did this happen?"

"Early this morning," Emy replied. "I thought you would have heard by now. The police have been at the Skalding place for hours."

"But it must have been an accident. Was anyone else in the room when it happened?"

"Yvonne was alone. Imogen was in the kitchen making tea and heard the crash. Imogen's in quite the state, apparently."

Well, naturally, I thought. It wasn't every day you found your employer under the china cabinet.

I rose to refill my coffee mug. "So, an accidental death."

"I'm not sure the police would agree. First the ladder, then the trap, and now this? That's a lot of mishaps for one person."

"True." Either Yvonne Skalding had been the most accident-prone person in Leafy Hollow, poor woman, or somebody had it in for her. "I still don't understand how she walked into a coyote trap."

"That was yesterday, after she got home from the hospital. Imogen said that Yvonne was heavily medicated and never should have gone outside. But someone moved the lawn furniture out of alignment, and Yvonne wasn't happy about it. Imogen was in the basement doing laundry when it happened. She thought Yvonne was upstairs asleep."

"But why was there a coyote trap on her lawn?"

"No idea."

I winced, remembering the traps hanging in my aunt's garage. At least today's china cabinet tragedy couldn't be linked to Rose Cottage—or me. "I've never been inside her house, you know."

Emy's tone was reassuring. "Everybody knows that, Verity. Yvonne never let the hired gardeners go indoors. Too much mud. Zander could testify to that."

"Zander?"

"Yvonne's son. He lives in Strathcona with his wife, Kate, but they drove out yesterday after Yvonne's accidents. I think they're staying at the house, although it's still a crime scene. Imogen says the police have fingerprinted everything, including the cabinet."

"But how could a big, heavy thing like a china cabinet fall over? Wasn't it anchored to the wall?"

"Imogen said the police think somebody tampered with it."

"Like the ladder?"

"Exactly. Hold on, I'm getting a text."

The silver gray tabby had been meowing outside during

my conversation with Emy. I reached over the kitchen counter to open the door for him. He swished past and sat by the cabinets, fixing his one-eye glare on me.

I reached into the cupboard for a tin of tuna.

"Ooh, this is interesting," Emy said. "Guess what?"

I tucked the phone against my shoulder, so I could wield the can opener. "Tell me."

"The police have moved on to Henry Upton's place next door to Yvonne's. Three cars."

"That's odd." I placed the tuna-filled bowl before Tom, who tucked in without looking at me. Perhaps he objected to the name I'd given him. "Tom" was a little utilitarian. Well, he could take that up with his next owner.

I walked into the living room where I settled on the sofa with my feet up on the coffee table. "Where are you getting these updates, Emy?"

"From Mom. She's faster than Twitter."

"But she's not there, is she?"

"No, but a breakaway book club member lives on Peppermint Lane."

"But if it's the breakaway club, how would—"

"Mom's group has a mole."

I made a mental note to never tick off Thérèse Dionne—and to finish reading *Anna Karenina* tout de suite.

"Why would the police want to talk to Upton?"

"There's history between him and Yvonne. When Henry wanted to build that huge house—well, it was his ex, Candace, who wanted it— Yvonne was dead set against it. She caused a lot of trouble. Objections at the planning committee, letters to the editor, lawsuits—she threw everything at him."

I thought about the enormous three-story Upton home with its acres of grass. "Then how did it—"

"Get built? Nobody knows. One day, Yvonne simply withdrew her objections, the lawsuits, everything. She wasn't even in Leafy Hollow at the time."

"Where was she?"

"Yvonne went south every winter. Said it was too cold here, and she could afford it, so she took off, usually for Myrtle Beach, although sometimes she went to Orlando. I think she had a condo there, but I could be wrong about that. Anyway, her house in Leafy Hollow was empty for months at a time."

"If Yvonne agreed to Upton's project, why would he be a suspect in her death?"

"I don't know that he is, but village gossip holds that building the house ruined him financially. The dispute with Yvonne took up so much time that he lost a few construction contracts as well. Then, to top it off, Candace walked out on him."

"And demanded alimony, I bet."

"Naturally. I heard he blamed Yvonne for the whole mess. He claimed that if she hadn't held up the project for so long, and cost him so much in legal fees and price increases while they battled over it, that everything would have been fine."

"Is that likely?"

"Who knows? Wait, I have another text from Mom. The

police have moved on, although they left a cruiser outside the Skalding place."

"So Upton's off the hook?"

"No idea. Oh, they're headed your way. Probably taking a shortcut to the highway."

A vehicle crunched over the gravel driveway outside. I rose to my feet and peered through the window. "Nope, not a shortcut. Talk to you later, Emy." I clicked off the call and opened the front door.

"Detective Constable Katsuro," I said. "What a surprise."

"I told you. I've never been inside that house. I've never even seen this china cabinet everybody's talking about."

Jeff leaned over the coffee table and fixed his dark eyes on me. "Who's everybody?"

"Oh, come on. This place is a hotbed of gossip."

He gave me one of those intense looks of his, and I caved. Must have been the cheekbones. "Emy Dionne called to tell me about it."

"This is a police investigation, Miss Hawkes, not entertainment."

I did my best to bristle. "That's completely unfair. How is it my fault if someone chooses to call me with news about a community tragedy? Am I not allowed to answer my phone?" I got to my feet and walked to the front door. "Unless you intend to search my home for deadly furniture, I don't think there's much more to say."

With a twitch of his lip, Jeff flipped his notebook shut

and rose to leave. "These are routine inquiries. Thanks for your time."

I rubbed the back of my neck as I watched him drive away. Three accidents in two days, one of them fatal? That was more than coincidence. That was murder.

I headed out to buy cat food, figuring it had to be cheaper than tuna. On the way, I dropped by the 5X Bakery. That vein in my neck was throbbing again, so I craved a friendly voice. And pastry.

Emy nodded gravely while I filled her in on events and consumed a coconut cupcake with seven-minute frosting. She refused to let me pay for it.

"I can't believe the trouble you've gotten into in only two days," she said. "On behalf of Leafy Hollow, I apologize." After pouring me another cup of tea, she walked to the cooler, put a banana cupcake with honey-cinnamon glaze on a plate, and set it before me. "Maybe this will help."

I eyed the cupcake, mentally toting the baked-goods calories I had eaten since arriving. Oh, what the heck. I was doing outdoor work now.

"None of it's your fault, Emy." I peeled back the cupcake wrapper and took a bite.

"It's not yours, either."

I nodded, chewing several times before adding, "Is it awful that I'm thinking this lets me off the hook? I've never been in Yvonne's house, and I know nothing about coyote traps. Except that they sound mean."

"I thought the same. Although"—Emy winced—"there is one little problem."

I eyed her suspiciously. "Go on."

"Your aunt hated traps. When Adeline was out hiking, she confiscated every trap she found, even the legal ones. She stored them in her garage. Nobody was ever brave enough to ask for them back."

I closed my eyes a moment, recalling the rusting chains that hung from the garage rafters. "I've seen them, and so have the police."

"I know. Jeff told me."

"Jeff?"

"Katsuro, the investigating officer. The one who was at your house. He dropped in here just before you."

"Is he planning to impound the traps as evidence?"

"I doubt it. He didn't seem worried. The only reason I even know about it is because I like to grill him when he comes in for his lemon cupcake. Jeff's wife was a cousin of my mom's, so we've known each other for ages."

Katsuro was married? To my surprise, I felt a twinge of disappointment. I shook my head. *Get a grip, Verity.*

"I don't think anybody believes you killed Yvonne Skalding," Emy said. "The woman had a lot of enemies. It should be easy to widen the suspect pool and take the heat off you."

"How?"

"By figuring out who profits from Yvonne's death. Let's make a list." Emy pulled a napkin over and took the pencil from behind her ear. "First, her son, Zander, because he'll inherit everything." She wrote his name. "And his wife, Kate, because she'll share it." She added Kate's name. "And then..."

We contemplated the napkin for a while.

"Well, we'll start with them," Emy said, replacing the pencil behind her ear.

"Weren't they out of town when Yvonne fell off the ladder? Didn't you say they live in the city?"

"Yes, but Zander visits all the time. That rung could have been damaged months ago, even years. Yvonne rarely did yard work herself. Whoever tampered with the ladder must have been willing to wait until she used it again."

"Which didn't happen until I came along and messed up her wisteria. How could anyone know I would do that?"

"They couldn't," Emy said, "but don't forget the coyote trap. The killer might have set up a whole series of booby traps for Yvonne."

"None of which were triggered until I arrived two days ago. You have to admit, it looks suspicious."

"Yep. I'm expecting to see your name on wanted posters all around the village."

I chuckled, but the thought had occurred. Although, I was sure those posters were on Twitter now.

"I bet if you went out to the Skalding house, you could find more booby traps and clear your name. You could question Imogen, too. Maybe she saw somebody."

"Yes, she saw *me*, arguing with Yvonne. She must have told the police, too, because Jeff Katsuro knew all about it." I recalled the look on Imogen's face when she described Yvonne as *disagreeable*. "Imogen didn't like Yvonne much," I added.

"Nobody liked Yvonne. That doesn't prove anything. Imogen had nothing to gain from her death. In fact, she'll likely lose her job. Kate will hire somebody from the city. Probably one of those bonded services with the fancy pink trucks and the websites." Emy pointed at the two names penciled on the napkin. "No, our strongest suspects are right here."

"Didn't Jeff interview them?"

"I don't know. Did he mention it?"

I shook my head, remembering our last encounter, and the time before that, when he lectured me at the stop sign. "Emy, do you remember a fatal hit-and-run accident on that country road near Leafy Hollow? Jeff seemed to be fixated on it."

She grimaced, running a finger across the napkin. "Well, he would be, because his wife was one of the victims. Jeff never talks about it. Wendy was with a friend, coming back from dinner."

"His wife is dead?"

Emy nodded. "It's been five years, but he's never gotten over it. The women were out in the rain for hours before they were found. The coroner thought they might have survived if the accident had been reported right away." She held up a finger. "Wait. I have some of Mom's book club papers here. I think her scrapbook on Leafy Hollow is with them. I'll get it."

After rummaging behind the counter, Emy returned with a large scrapbook, its coiled wire spine bulging with papers. She sat at the table and leafed through it. Then she twisted the book around to face me and tapped her finger on it.

I read the headline on the newspaper clipping glued to the page.

"Police Search for Driver in Fatal Hit and Run."

And under the headline:

"Leafy Hollow residents Wendy Katsuro and Lily Reynolds, both 26, were found dead after their vehicle was hit by another on Wednesday evening during a blinding rainstorm. Police have no leads on the other vehicle involved in the accident, which occurred at a four-way stop at Wellington Road and Concession Nine. The investigation continues."

The article quoted friends and relatives and included two head-and-shoulder photos. Wendy Katsuro had been blonde, petite, and pretty. I closed the scrapbook and handed it back to Emy.

"Poor Jeff."

"No kidding. Imagine being a cop and unable to find your wife's killer. Next time you see him, for goodness' sake, don't let on that you know."

"Never. Don't worry."

I knew the burden of unwanted pity. Jeffrey Katsuro wouldn't get any of that from me.

CHAPTER 8

BACK AT ROSE COTTAGE, I put away the groceries I bought after my visit to Emy's bakery. Milk and cereal, coffee, bread and eggs, hamburger, potatoes, bananas, and vegetables. Along with the peanut butter and tuna already in the cupboard, that should do for a week or so. No use stocking up since I didn't intend to stay long.

Surprisingly, I enjoyed my trip to the grocery. I read the backs of cereal boxes, checked out the specials, even chatted with other shoppers lined up at the checkout. Shopping was a calm, even soothing experience in Leafy Hollow. I assumed childhood memories of my time here were tamping down my usual anxiety.

Or it might simply be that the village shop was a far cry from the multi-aisled extravaganza at home and its thousands of items. On my last visit, I left a half-full grocery cart in the middle of an aisle and barreled out, barely able to breathe.

After that, I ordered my food through an online grocery service that delivered orders in a fleet of refrigerated trucks with giant vegetables painted on their sides. If such a service existed in Leafy Hollow, it would drive an aging pickup truck and be called Larry. Or maybe Francine.

I had an hour before my appointment with Wilfred Mullins, my aunt's lawyer, so I decided to make a toasted peanut butter and banana sandwich, with crudités. That way I could eat a healthy lunch as I scrolled through my aunt's laptop.

While peeling carrots at the kitchen sink, I looked out at the back garden. Overgrown plants choked the flagstone walks, and dead blooms weighted the branches of unpruned shrubs. I'd never known my aunt to neglect her beloved plants. And what about her business, Coming Up Roses Landscaping? Mullins had left an ominous message on my voicemail that the company was "in the red." How was that possible? What had Aunt Adeline been doing in the years since my mother's death?

As I stared out the kitchen window, I remembered puttering in that garden the summer I turned seven. I had been left in my aunt's care while my parents "worked on their marriage." One day, I skittered away with a shriek at the sight of a fat black spider.

Aunt Adeline smiled at me from under her wide-brimmed hat. "It's more scared of us, Verity," she said.

I crept back to her side and watched, fascinated, as the spider crawled across her hand and onto the flagstone path. I reached out a tentative finger to touch it as a beam of sunlight, filtered through the vines of the pergola overhead, lit up its back.

The expression on my aunt's face changed. She whipped

a knife from the holster at her waist, spun it twice in her hand like a gunslinger, and brought it down with a thwack on the stone. The blade sliced the spider neatly in half, four legs on either side.

With my extended finger frozen in place, I stared at the bright red hourglass—now two half-hour glasses—on its back.

"Black Widow," my aunt said, shoving her knife into its holster. "Poisonous." She grabbed my arm and pulled me to my feet. "That shouldn't be here," she muttered, scanning the ground while hustling me into Rose Cottage.

We spent the rest of the afternoon indoors.

That evening, Aunt Adeline handed me a picture book of the world's deadliest spiders and insects. It included a full-color photo of a three-inch-long hornet that shoots acid into its victims' eyes. That picture gave me nightmares to this day.

I shook my head at the memory, returning to the carrots. Other people's aunts baked cookies. Mine severed insects.

At a furious bang-bang-bang on the front door, I gave a start, dropping the vegetables into the sink. I wiped my hands on a tea towel and went to open the door.

On the threshold stood the same gray-haired man who had watched me arrive a day earlier.

"You're Verity," he said. "Adeline's niece." He stepped into the living room and brushed past me to place a knapsack on the coffee table.

I walked over to him. "And you are...?"

He grasped my hand in a hearty shake. "Gideon Picard. Neighbor." He strode over to my aunt's desk, where he peered at her papers through his blue-tinted glasses. I reviewed my conversations with Aunt Adeline, trying to remember if she ever mentioned the name Gideon Picard. The blue glasses and gray samurai topknot finally coalesced into a single image. I remembered where I'd seen him.

"You're the neighbor," I blurted.

He picked up a page for a closer look. "I just said."

So much for the platitude that boomers have better manners than my generation. This old codger could give Kanye West lessons.

I walked over, slipped the document from his grasp, and placed it face down on the desk.

"Sorry," he said, and then smiled.

In that moment, I recalled our earlier meeting. This same man—younger, with fewer gray hairs—had come through the back door, waved at me as I sat over my books in the kitchen, and headed to the basement to look for my aunt. Aunt Adeline spent a lot of time in her basement "rearranging the shelves." So, I figured they were discussing storage strategies.

Fifteen minutes later, they came up the stairs together, arguing. Gideon was trying to convince her of something.

When they reached the top of the stairs, my aunt saw me seated at the kitchen table. She stopped and smoothed her hair. "Verity?" she asked with a smile. "Could you bring my cardigan from the bedroom?"

While I searched for the sweater, I heard low voices in the kitchen. When I returned, holding the garment, Gideon was gone.

It was a vivid memory, but it didn't help me decide whether the man who stood before me was friend or foe.

"I haven't had time to go over my aunt's records," I said. "If you could come back later, when—"

He turned away to scan the bookcases.

I stepped between him and the books. "I haven't looked at those, either. In fact, I haven't done much of anything. I only arrived yesterday."

"I know. I live next door, remember?" He was on the other side of the room, running his hands over the knick-knacks on the mantel. He turned to face me with a vintage china figurine in his hand.

I walked over and took the nodding-head spaniel from his hand, returning it to its spot on the mantel next to a small, wooden keepsake box. I was tempted to kick Gideon out on his butt, but he knew my aunt. Maybe he could help me find her. I pressed my lips together, mulling my choices. Then, "Tea?" I asked.

"Thanks. I brought you something," he said, reaching for his knapsack.

I trailed after him into the kitchen. He pulled a Tim Hortons box from his knapsack and flipped it open to display a dozen donuts.

I leaned in to inhale their delicious burnt-sugar aroma. Friend or foe, Gideon displayed good taste in baked goods. "You didn't need to make a Tim's run for me," I said, switching on the burner under the kettle. I retrieved two mugs from the cupboard and tossed in tea bags from the metal canister on the same shelf.

He settled into a kitchen chair with his back to me and picked up my aunt's moose salt and pepper shakers, examining them minutely before setting them back on the table. "Didn't have to. I work there part time. Since I retired."

The kettle boiled, and I poured hot water over the tea

bags in the mugs. When I lifted the tin canister of tea to return it to the cupboard, it slipped from my hand and fell. Without turning his head to look, Gideon flung out a sinewy arm and caught the canister before it hit the floor. I gaped at the container in his hand and raised my eyes to his.

"Force of habit," he said, placing the canister on the table.

That must be some donut shop he worked at.

I picked up the two mugs and sat at the table, weighing my next words. "What type of job did you retire from, exactly?"

"This and that." He accepted a mug, added milk, and took a swallow.

I doubted I'd get the truth if I persisted. So I picked up a maple donut and tried another tack. "You knew my aunt."

"Yep."

"Any idea what might have—"

"Nope."

Obviously, Gideon was not a man to be lured into idle chatter. I bit into the donut. Given the dullness of our conversation, the ensuing hit of sugar was a welcome distraction. In my head, I practiced escape clauses. *Sorry, I have to wash my... feet.*

Gideon drained his mug and rose to deposit it in the sink. Leaning his hands on the counter, he looked through the window at my aunt's ragged back garden. From the sag in his shoulders, I suspected that he missed her. *Friend*, I decided— too hastily, as it turned out.

"Adeline is a good woman," he said. He returned to the table and sat down. "She was always bragging about you.

Hoped you'd follow her into the business one day. You're an accountant, right?"

He reached for an old-fashioned glazed, no doubt famished by that lengthy speech. And it was an excellent choice since it left the Boston cream for me.

"Not exactly. I do freelance bookkeeping, but I'm not certified. The exams make me antsy."

Not to mention I'd have to leave my apartment to write them.

He nodded. "Adeline is like that. Always wants to be up and doing."

I licked the last of the maple glaze from my fingers and picked up the Boston cream—with barely a thought for the carrots lying half-peeled in the sink. "That would explain the state of her desk. She's a little behind in her paperwork."

"That's a front," Gideon said, waving his hand. "Control wanted her to..." He dropped his donut on the plate and leaned in. "How much do you know about the business?"

"I know it's almost bankrupt, according to her lawyer." Immediately, I regretted letting that slip. "Don't repeat that, please."

"Bankrupt?" Gideon scratched his cheek, looking puzzled. "Oh, you mean the landscaping business." He picked up his donut again.

My stomach lurched. "What did *you* mean?"

"Nothing. Forget it." He took a bite of the donut and chewed it without looking at me.

Anger flared in my gut, jostling out the heartburn. "If you know what happened to my aunt, for God's sake, why don't you tell me?"

He gave me a penetrating look.

I stared back, but those blue lenses made it impossible to gauge his sincerity.

"You're right," he said.

I moved my chair closer.

"Adeline worked for a... large client."

"Large, as in physically?" I asked. "Or large as in—"

"I can't say."

I fidgeted in my chair with a murmur of irritation.

Gideon raised a hand. "But I can say that she helped safe-guard the national interest on occasion."

My breathing quickened. "She worked for the government?"

"Those idiots?" He gave a snort of disgust. "Certainly not."

"But aren't they in charge of the national interest?"

"Superficially. The real work goes on behind the scenes."

I gaped at him. *Secrets?* Like what, nuclear launch codes? No, that couldn't be it, because Canada didn't have any.

"Real work? Such as?" I asked suspiciously.

"Remember when the price of maple syrup soared a few years back?"

"Sure. Tim Hortons had to suspend its maple glazed line —donuts, Timbits, the works."

"Dark days," he agreed. "Most people don't know this, but there's a stockpile of maple syrup hidden in a solitary Quebec warehouse. Thousands of barrels. And those barrels were disappearing."

"No," I whispered.

"Operatives took out the thieves, and the price of maple syrup returned to normal."

I struggled to grasp the implications. "Took them out... where?"

"I can't say."

My brow wrinkled. "Wait a minute—was my aunt one of those operatives?"

Gideon barked out a laugh. "What an idea." He swept up his knapsack and headed for the door. "Gotta go. Thanks for the tea."

By the time I caught up with him, he had the front door open and was on the porch, the knapsack trailing from his hand.

"But Gideon—" I said, anxious for more details.

He gave an impatient wave. "We'll talk again." Then he looked intently at me. "Don't repeat any of this. The consequences for your aunt would be... extreme."

"Can I tell—"

"No."

I wouldn't get any more out of him for now. But next time we met, I'd have better questions. Like, who the heck was "Control?"

"Would you care to take the donuts home?" I asked.

"Nah. Throw 'em out if you don't want to eat them."

I rolled my eyes. Not much chance of that.

Gideon disappeared into the hedge.

I still had no idea what my aunt had been up to before her accident, but at least curiosity had replaced anxiety. I chuckled at the thought of the Maple Syrup Caper.

The moment I shut the door, two heavy deadbolts

thudded into place. I took a step back in surprise. I could have sworn I hadn't touched either one of those locks.

That was impossible. It must be jet lag. Or temporary insanity. Either would explain why I'd forgotten to ask Gideon the most important question—where was my aunt?

Something on the mantel caught my eye as I walked back into the room. I scanned the porcelain dogs, Tibetan prayer wheels, Las Vegas shot glasses, and miniature Star Trek vessels until I came to a rectangular gap in the dust. The wooden keepsake box was gone.

My irritation fled when I recalled how Gideon's shoulders sagged when he talked about my aunt. I didn't begrudge him a token, but why didn't he just ask for it? And why that box?

Was there something in it he didn't want me to see?

CHAPTER 9

AFTER GIDEON'S VISIT, I left the carrots in the sink and headed downtown for my appointment with Wilf Mullins. I parked the truck on Main Street, two doors from his office. A gold-lettered sign filled the plate-glass window.

I read the left side:

Wilfred Mullins, LL.B
Wills & Estate Planning
Title Searches
Notary Public
Divorce Cases by Appointment
Bylaw Disputes

And then the right:

Wilfred Mullins, Leafy Hollow Councilor
Property Taxes
Fish/Game Licenses

Bylaw Disputes

No wonder that bylaw officer Emy mentioned was overworked.

I pushed open the door into a carpeted waiting room with royal blue furnishings. Blue carpet, blue walls, blue uphol-stered chairs. Muzak played in the background.

An elegantly dressed woman with gray hair swept back in a bun looked up from her keyboard. "Can I help you?"

"Verity Hawkes to see Mr. Mullins."

"He's expecting you. Come right in."

I followed her through a blue door into an office at the back.

Wilfred Mullins was talking on the phone, seated in a high-backed leather executive chair. He waved me in from behind a massive mahogany desk that nearly spanned the room. "That must have been difficult for you," he said into the phone in soothing tones. "It's your decision, but I suggest you listen to him."

Mullins pointed to an armchair that faced his desk. I dropped into it with my satchel on my lap.

He flashed me a big grin. "I have someone in my office, Zander. We'll talk later." He hung up the phone. "Verity. It's great to meet you in person."

With the whirr of an electric motor, his executive chair slowly descended until his chin reached the desktop. He smiled at me the entire time as if he didn't notice his descent. When he slid from the chair to walk around the desk, I real-ized he was barely four feet tall. I swallowed my surprise. *Dynamite comes in small packages*, my aunt would say.

"You, too, Mr. Mullins." I shook his outstretched hand.

"Call me Wilf. Everybody else does."

"Even the other councilors?"

"No." He chuckled. "I won't repeat the names they use." He hopped onto the chair opposite mine and scooted up against the back. Resting his shortened arms on his thighs, he leaned forward with a smile.

"So, Verity. Are you enjoying Leafy Hollow? It must be great to be back."

"Well, yes and no." I clutched a hand to my stomach to curb my queasiness. "Here's the thing. I can't do it. Look after my aunt's affairs, that is."

Wilf's eyes widened. "I see. Which part is giving you trouble?"

"Which part? All parts." I rolled my eyes to one side and whispered, "Especially the Control part." I repeated it for emphasis. "You know, *Control?*"

Wilf nodded his head thoughtfully, not picking up on my obvious hint. "Your aunt was a bit controlling. Wonderful woman, though."

"No, I meant—"

"I'm sure you're up to the job, Verity." He slapped his hands on his thighs and gave me one of those faux-sympathetic lawyer faces. "In fact, I'm glad you're here because we need to start the process to have your aunt declared legally dead."

I sat back, speechless, as Wilf regarded me with an unblinking expression. Seriously, the man didn't blink.

"Doesn't that take seven years?" I asked.

"Not necessarily. If we can prove that your aunt disappeared"—he held up his fingers to indicate air-quotes—"'in circumstances of peril,' we can get the court to rule that she's dead." He rolled his lips. "Probably."

"She's not dead, Wilf. I know she's not."

"Have you heard from her?"

"No, but—"

"Has anyone else heard from her?"

"No, but—" I intended to tell him about Gideon's disclosure, the mysterious "Control," and my suspicions about Aunt Adeline's fate. In a few short sentences, I could alert my aunt's lawyer to her possible predicament and wrap up my familial responsibilities at the same time.

"Yes?" he asked.

As I stood there with my mouth hanging open, I recalled Gideon's warning. *The consequences for your aunt would be extreme.* I suspected the Maple Syrup Caper was a joke, but Gideon had looked serious when he mentioned "The Business."

"Nothing," I said.

Wilf pressed his lips together, nodding sadly. "Did your aunt ever mention suicide?"

My mouth sagged open again as I stared at him.

"Well, well." He reached over with a slight grunt and patted my thigh. "We can talk about that later. Now, what exactly is the problem? Is it the house, or the landscaping business? It can't be the paperwork, because—now, correct me if I'm wrong—you're an accountant, right? Who better to do paperwork than an accountant? You'll have it done in no time. Easy-peasy." He sat back and slapped his thighs again.

Easy-peasy?

I slumped in my chair, weighed down by the stone in my chest, as insight dawned. Mullins had railroaded me. He knew my aunt's business affairs would be a huge headache, and he wanted someone to take it off his hands. Hence his call to gullible Verity Hawkes and that touching appeal to my childhood memories. I'd been an idiot. This man knew nothing of my aunt's mystery employer. Nor did he care. He only wanted me to take the whole mess out of his office and dump it where he couldn't smell it.

Well, I wasn't giving up without a fight.

"I'm not an accountant, Wilf, not exactly."

"No? I thought your aunt said—"

I cut him off by raising my hand. "I don't know anything about landscaping, either, and even if my aunt's business was worth saving—which it's not—her house is about to fall down. You didn't tell me that on the phone."

His head darted back, eyes wide, like a wounded deer. Well, a wounded mouse. Deer mouse. I shook my head to clear the image.

"That's not fair, Verity. I said that your aunt's property presented a few challenges. We had a long talk about it on the phone." He gave me a hangdog look. "And you agreed to take it on. I wish there was someone else"—he shrugged —"but there isn't." His face brightened, and he hopped off the chair to shuffle back around his desk. "I know. You should call Lorne."

"If you mean Lorne Lewins, I have his number."

"Well, there you are, then. Problem solved."

"Not if there's no money to pay him. Besides, what about the house? It's a wreck."

Wilf sat on his executive chair and activated the motor before reaching for his phone. The leather seat whirred upward. I watched, transfixed, until it stopped with a whine. This must be the Ferrari of little-people furniture.

"Lorne and your aunt had an arrangement. You won't have to pay him right away. As for the house..." He leafed through a card file beside the phone with one hand and punched in a number with the other. "I know a real estate agent who can help with that."

"But what about—"

He held up a finger to silence me as he raised the handset to his ear.

"Nellie? It's Wilf. I know, but I'm calling you now, aren't I?" With a chuckle, he spun his chair to face the wall with his back to me. Wilf muttered something I couldn't make out and then swiveled back, still chuckling, and winked at me. "Stop that, Nellie, you're making me blush." He paused to listen, and then broke out in a guffaw so loud I expected the gray-haired receptionist to come bursting in with a video camera. But the door remained closed. I guessed she was used to this.

Wilf wiped his face with one hand, still shaking with laughter, and then straightened up. "Listen, Nellie, I have Verity Hawkes with me. That's right, Adeline's niece. She needs advice on the old girl's house. Let me put her on."

He gestured at me to stand and handed me the handset over the desk.

"Hello?" I said.

"Do you want to sell?" Nellie asked.

"Well, I don't think—"

"Your aunt's place is a challenge."

"Yes, I know, and—"

"Let me put you on hold while I check my calendar." After a few bars of *Sugar, Sugar*, Nellie was back on the line. "Good news. I've had a cancellation tomorrow. Late afternoon. I'll be at your place by five."

"Okay. I'll see you then."

"Ciao." She hung up, and I handed the phone to Wilf.

"All set?" he asked.

"I guess." I wasn't positive what had happened, but I felt tire treads on my back.

The door opened behind me with a sudden gust of air, and I turned. A man's huge frame took up the entire doorway. A bushy black beard extended over his chest, and his shaved head gleamed in the overhead lights. Since he was at least fifty, I surmised that his baldness wasn't a fashion choice. His shirtsleeves were folded up to his elbows, displaying impressive tattooed forearms.

Wilf flicked his gaze upward in a gesture of annoyance. "*Hen-reee*," he whined. "I have a client here, bozo."

The newcomer gestured with his thumb to the outer office. "I heard. Adeline's niece, right?" He held out a beefy hand to me. "I'm Henry Upton. Fourteen Peppermint Lane."

I must have looked surprised, because he added, "One of your aunt's landscaping clients."

"Ah," I said. "That's... nice?"

"I'm afraid I owe Adeline some money." He pursed his lips, looking thoughtful. "Tell you what. Come out to the house to cut the lawn, and I'll write you a check."

Fourteen Peppermint Lane was the house next door to Yvonne Skalding's. I recalled the acres of bright green grass that surrounded the huge house perched on the hill. The thought of pushing my aunt's mower over an expanse that rivaled Versailles was not a welcome one. Besides, my plan was to collect my aunt's overdue accounts, not accumulate more.

"I'm not doing any lawns at the moment."

Behind me, Wilf cleared his throat. "Verity, I'm telling you, call Lorne."

I closed my eyes a second to regroup. When I opened them, I found both men staring at me. "No, seriously, I don't—"

"Can you do it this afternoon?" Upton checked his watch.

Would anyone in Leafy Hollow let me finish a sentence?

Given the size of his lawn, I suspected the total on Upton's unpaid invoice was a sizable sum, too much to leave on the table. "Let me call this Lewins person first. Then I'll try for tomorrow."

"Great. Well..." Upton held open the office door with a pointed look.

"*Hen-reee,*" Wilf whined again.

"Sorry, weren't you done?" Upton asked, looking innocent. As innocent as a tattooed man who weighed at least three hundred pounds—most of it muscle—could look.

I gathered up my satchel and headed for the door. Outside, I glared at the parked yellow Hummer that blotted out the sun. I was defeated for now, but I'd be back.

CHAPTER 10

I COLLECTED a beer from my aunt's fridge and sat at her desk to consider my options.

When I boarded the plane in Vancouver, I expected my aunt to be back home from her latest adventure before I even set foot in Leafy Hollow. In my fantasy, she greeted me at the door and we buried the hatchet over tea and scones in the garden. I never expected to be faced with the impossible task of finding a woman whom—judging from Gideon's revelations—I barely knew.

Even my smokescreen was doomed to fail. How could anyone believe I intended to resurrect my aunt's landscaping business when I could barely start a lawnmower?

I reached for my aunt's laptop and flipped it open. It beeped on with a password request. I scanned the cluttered roll-top desk for stick-on notes that might contain the password. No luck. Then I typed in family names, followed by birthdays. Also no luck. I tried vacation spots, names of plants, even my aunt's alma mater. Nothing. Eventually, I pushed the laptop away. If there were answers buried there, they would stay buried. Yet another thing I couldn't do.

What could I do, then?

Counting off on my fingers, I reviewed my skills.

Bookkeeping wasn't likely to be much help. Ditto for jigsaw mastery. Years of Krav Maga classes meant I could throw a grown man over my shoulder and kick him in the groin, but, so far, there hadn't been much call for that in Leafy Hollow. I learned some Latin as a child—my mother was a professor of ancient languages—but I couldn't see any relevance there. And my only other ability... I snapped my fingers.

I trotted into the bedroom to retrieve *Organize Your Way to a Better Life*.

Flipping through to the chapter on pantries, I scanned the color-coded lists and diagrams. My aunt spent a lot of time rearranging her shelves. Time to take a look in the basement and find out why. The cellar was bound to be dusty, moldy, and even—I grimaced—full of mouse droppings, but it was my best option to find information about my aunt. Maybe my only option.

Might as well get started.

As I dropped the self-help book on my aunt's roll-top desk, a black book wedged in a cubbyhole caught my eye. I pulled it out and rubbed my fingers across the worn leather binding. On the frontispiece was printed in gold letters, *The Journal of Adeline Hawkes*.

I thumbed through the pages until I came to a section titled "Clients." I opened the *Journal* to "Yvonne Skalding, 12 Peppermint Lane," and set it on the desk to read. Along with notations about appointment times and services, my aunt had penned a note that read, "Charge Yvonne double. Bitch Tariff."

Normally, I would have snorted beer through my nose at that. But the poor woman was dead, so I allowed myself only the briefest of smirks before reading the rest of the page dedicated to Yvonne.

Near the bottom, a curious phrase was scrawled in red ink. *Watch her.* And later, also in red, *Evil.*

Whoa. I closed the notebook and tapped a nervous finger on its cover. Yvonne Skalding had been obnoxious, definitely, but "evil?" That was harsh, and unlike the aunt I remembered. I pushed the journal to one side. Had I known Aunt Adeline at all?

I could read the rest of the journal later, but for now, I was on a mission. I turned to the basement.

My first obstacle was the wooden door. Although the doorknob turned in my hand, the door itself was stuck. When I yanked harder, my fingers slipped off the handle. I staggered back, nearly losing my balance.

The second time, I grasped the doorknob with both hands and braced one foot against the frame. I tugged as hard as I could. The door scraped free and bounced off my leg, narrowly missing my head. Wincing, I rubbed my battered shin. That was going to leave a mark.

The heavy door creaked as I pushed it back against the kitchen wall. Its solid wood panels were overkill for a basement. But Rose Cottage had been built over a hundred years ago, so I guessed fiberboard wasn't available.

I flicked the wall switch inside the doorframe, and a

naked bulb came on at the bottom of the stairwell. After brushing cobwebs away with one hand, I started down the worn treads of the steep stairs. I pictured generations of women trudging up and down these narrow steps, clutching armloads of preserves—and mousetraps.

The basement air was humid, musty, and close. A vintage push-button light switch at the bottom of the stairs looked dubious, but when I flicked it, a lone bulb came on in the middle of the ceiling. I ducked under a low-lying wooden beam and stepped into the room. The basement was smaller than I'd expected, given the footprint of the cottage overhead. A crawl space would account for the discrepancy. I shuddered, imagining snakes. I wouldn't be checking any crawl spaces.

Dusty pipes crisscrossed overhead. An ancient furnace and hot water heater took up most of the available floor space, and a washer and dryer lined one wall. I crossed my fingers, hoping they worked.

The opposite wall caught my immediate attention. It was lined with floor-to-ceiling shelving units jammed with goods. Huge boxes of detergent stood next to dozens of paint cans, several cases of Molson Canadian beer, and enormous plastic-wrapped bales of toilet paper that could have serviced a battalion. Clearly, my aunt was a Costco member.

I stepped toward the shelves, hoping to find tins of soup or spaghetti sauce. Even canned ravioli would be welcome. I reached out a hand to push aside the detergent.

A crack of thunder shook the house, rocking the floor under me and sifting dust down from the beams. The overhead light went out, wicking the windowless basement into utter blackness.

My heart hammered in my chest, my breath quickened, and the vein in my throat throbbed. I started to panic. Nobody knew I was here. If I couldn't find my way out, I would starve. Alone. In the dark.

I mentally slapped myself. Oh, for goodness' sake, stop being ridiculous. *Breathe.* In, out. In, out. My heartbeat slowed.

I turned in what I thought was the direction of the stairs, and crept with my head down, hoping to avoid the low-hanging pipes. As my toes stubbed up against the first step, I let out a deep breath and a small prayer of thanks. I climbed the worn wooden stairs, skimming my hands along the wall until I reached the top.

But instead of murky twilight, my surroundings were still blackest night. The basement door had swung shut.

I ran my fingers along its heavy wooden panels, searching for the doorknob. Once I felt its smooth porcelain surface, I tried to turn it. Nothing happened. I used both hands, and then rattled it as hard as I could. Still nothing.

It was pitch black in the narrow stairwell. I couldn't even see the edges of the narrow steps. The walls were closing in.

Breathe.

There was no landing at the top, and I risked pitching down the entire flight of stairs in the dark if I wasn't careful. I paused to get my bearings. With both hands on the knob, I shoved my shoulder against the door, trying not to lose my footing on the steep wooden stairs.

The door didn't budge.

I shoved it again, harder. One foot slipped out from under me, and I flailed in the dark for the railing. When my hand slammed against it, I clung to its reassuring presence and held on tight.

My breath came in ragged gusts, and my heart raced as I clutched at the doorknob with one hand and the railing with the other. I could sense the stairwell in the blackness. It felt as if a chasm had opened under me, and my toes were gripping the edge.

I really would die alone in the dark.

Stop it.

I took a deep breath and slammed my entire body against the door, no longer caring if I slid down the stairs.

The door burst open, pitching me onto my hands and knees on the kitchen floor. Gasping, I stared at the faded starbursts in the linoleum inches from my nose. The rational part of my mind wondered how I could see them during a violent thunderstorm that should have darkened the sky, but my primitive brain didn't care. It was just glad not to be dead.

Lights flashed on throughout the cottage, accompanied by a hiccup or two from the feeble air conditioning unit and a beep-beep from the microwave on the counter. I rose to my feet and staggered to the kitchen window. It wasn't raining, and the flagstone in the garden was dry. How could I have heard thunder?

I knew about heat lightning—I'd even experienced it on humid summer nights. But heat *thunder*? Was that even a thing? Other than in the NBA, I meant? It didn't matter, because I wasn't going back into that basement.

Determined to shower before the lights went out again, I

hunted through the kitchen drawers for a flashlight—to be safe—and headed for the bathroom.

As I passed my aunt's desk, a document stamped with a big red "unpaid" caught my gaze. Curious, I pulled it from the pile of junk mail, unopened envelopes, and official-looking documents.

It was a carbon copy of a Coming Up Roses invoice addressed to Henry Upton, 14 Peppermint Lane. I had been right. It was a sizable sum. I recalled the enormous home that perched on a hill three hundred feet from the road. Hard to believe its occupants weren't able to pay their bills. My aunt must have let the account lapse.

Small businesses can be lax about their accounts receivable—I knew that from my bookkeeping jobs. If a thirty-second search turned up one unpaid invoice, there must be more. Which meant I might not have to cut any more lawns to pay for the repairs on Rose Cottage. Collecting unpaid invoices was more my style, anyway.

I allowed myself a moment of elation.

I shouldn't have gotten so cocky. Halfway through my shower, the hot water ran out. Shivering, I wrapped myself in a towel, grateful the air conditioning had called it quits after those halfhearted hiccups when the power returned. I rubbed my hair with another towel before slipping into my pajamas.

I walked into the living room on bare feet, pulled up a chair at my aunt's desk, and set to work. Hours later, I had a dozen stacked piles of paper, each of which I'd labeled with a stick-on note. I pulled the closest pile—unpaid invoices— toward me and straightened the edges.

The thought of confronting total strangers and asking

them to pay their bills made my heart race. It's not personal, I told myself. *Pretend you're Aunt Adeline.* She would never shrink from a task like this.

Taking a deep breath, I tapped the top of the pile. Starting tomorrow, every one of these deadbeats would get a home visit from Verity Hawkes.

CHAPTER 11

THE FIRST ADDRESS on my Deadbeats list was Henry Upton's, the monster home on the hill next to the Skalding place. I had reconsidered my promise to cut his lawn that afternoon. He should pay his outstanding bill first.

I drove the truck up the winding driveway and stopped at the top of the hill. The view was magnificent. I could see Young River Creek meandering for miles through the forested hills of Pine Hill Valley. The conservation lands started right at Upton's rear property line.

I walked to the door to ring the buzzer.

No answer. I stepped back to scrutinize the soaring three-story windows of the great room at the front. No one peered back. I slid the overdue invoice into the mailbox before walking back to the truck.

Sliding the gearshift into drive, I pulled out of the winding driveway and back onto Peppermint Lane, intending to return later. As I passed Yvonne Skalding's ranch house, I slowed, my gaze caught by a shiny black pickup with the "Fields' Land-scaping" logo on the side. Ryker Fields was out front, reseeding the bare patches I'd left in the lawn. I narrowed my eyes. He didn't waste any time in poaching new clients, did he?

Ryker waved, then pushed his safety glasses up his fore-head and gave me a big wink.

Pretending I hadn't seen him, I sped off to the next address on my list.

⸻

I knocked at the door of a tiny bungalow with turquoise aluminum siding.

An elderly woman with rheumy eyes squinted at me through the screen door. "Girl Guide cookies already?" she asked.

"No," I said, trying for a jolly tone. "I'm not selling—"

"Do you have those nice little mint ones?"

"No mint. In fact—"

"My sister in Milwaukee says the Girl Scout cookies in the States are better. She likes the shortbread and caramel ones. Do you have those?"

"I'm afraid not, because—"

She looked at me sadly. "That's a shame. Come back when you get those, dear, and I'll take two boxes."

She closed the door in my face.

At the next house, a worn-looking woman answered my knock. She might have been thirty, but the gray in her hair added at least ten years. A mixing bowl was tucked into one arm and a cell phone was pressed against her ear. She slipped the phone into her apron pocket.

"Yes?"

"Hello, my name is Verity Hawkes—"

Screams erupted behind her, followed by the sound of running feet thudding on the stairs.

She shouted over her shoulder, "Leave your brother alone! And go outside!" and then turned back with her shoulders slumped in exhaustion. "I'm counting the days until summer holidays end."

I nodded. "Yes. Well, I have this invoice." I pulled it from my satchel and handed it to her. "I was wondering—"

She scanned the paper with a flour-covered finger, wrinkling her brow. "Adeline said I could have more time to pay."

"This invoice is two years old—" I stopped at the tears in her eyes.

"My husband left us." She sniffed, looked down, sniffed again, and then wailed, "I don't know where he is."

I leaned over and patted her arm. "I'm so sorry. Of course you can't pay right now. We'll discuss this some other time."

"Okay," she said, still sniffling, and closed the door.

Client Number Three was positive she mailed the check the previous week. The post office must have lost it. If it didn't turn up, she asked me to make sure to let her know.

At the fourth house, a forty-something woman with a big grin opened the door. A cloud of crimson hair spilled out from her crocheted hairband, and her white, full-length apron bore liberal dabs of a rainbow of paint.

"Verity. What a pleasure to meet you at last," she said, flinging open the door.

I stepped over the threshold as she ushered me in. "You know who I am?"

"I'd recognize that truck anywhere. Adeline and I are old friends." Screwing up her face, she added, "Were old friends, I guess. Sorry. It's hard to believe, isn't it? Come through to the back. Lemonade?"

I followed her through the cluttered house, trying not to knock anything over. Colorful paintings hung frame to frame on every wall, stacks of coffee-table books teetered on sideboards, and knickknacks were jammed in two antique china cabinets. In the sunroom at the back, floor-to-ceiling windows had been thrown open to the breeze that tousled the branches of a huge weeping willow in the backyard. An unfinished canvas stood on a six-foot-high easel, next to a battered table filled with water glasses, brushes, and oil paint tubes.

I nodded in recognition. Leafy Hollow was a picturesque country village. Naturally, it had a resident artist.

My host returned with two brimming glasses of lemonade. "I'm Madeline Stuart, by the way."

I accepted a glass and took a sip. I'd expected to taste my usual store-bought beverage from a paper carton, but this was the real thing, made from squeezed juice and shaved ice, with delicate lemon slices floating on top. Delicious. I placed the glass on the paint table and reached for my satchel.

"Yes, I know your name, because"—I pulled out the invoice and held it up—"it's on this." I handed it over.

Madeline took the invoice, giving me a quizzical look, and looked at it. "Oh," she said with an airy wave, "I never pay those." She handed it back. "Would you like more ice?"

"No, thanks. I'm fine. What do you mean, you never—"

"Your aunt," Madeline interrupted, looking solemn, "was a wonderful woman. A real supporter of the arts. A credit to her community." With moist eyes, she watched the willow branches sway in the breeze. "Adeline would never take a penny from me. She always said it's impossible to make a living as an artist in this country."

I gave a sideways look at the unrecognizable smears that covered the canvas on the easel. Or any other country, I imagined. But I held my tongue since I knew nothing of modern art. This could be a masterpiece.

"If you never paid the invoices, why did my aunt write them?"

"No idea. But Adeline had a tidy mind. She liked to keep track." She took a sip of her lemonade. "You know, my back lawn is a little ragged. Do you think you could...?" She smiled and gave a sheepish shrug. "Only if you have time."

"I'll try to fit it in." With a sigh, I finished my lemonade.

Outside, a woman in tight khaki pants and a white shirt was leaning against my aunt's truck with her arms crossed. A white sedan with a coat of arms on the door was parked behind the truck.

"You Verity Hawkes?" she asked as I walked nearer.

"Yes. Can I help you?"

She pushed off from the truck with an apathetic shrug. "We've had complaints."

"About me?"

"You're soliciting, correct?"

My eyes widened. "Excuse me? I'm doing what?"

"Soliciting." She flipped her straggly, blonde ponytail. "Asking for money. Is that correct?"

Judging from her shirt's unbuttoned top half and the overflowing red lace bra it amply revealed, she was the one soliciting.

"Who are you?" I asked.

"Bobbi Côté. I'm the bylaw officer here." She gestured with her thumb at the coat of arms on her car.

Squinting at it, I made out a grinning beaver, a thunderbolt, and some sort of hat. I recognized the county crest from the property tax bills I'd found on my aunt's desk.

"I'm collecting debts owed to my aunt's landscaping business. I don't think that counts as soliciting."

"Oh, yes." Bobbi rolled her eyes. "The saintly Adeline Hawkes. Who could forget her? Well, I don't care whose niece you are. I'll be the judge of whether you're breaking the law."

It could have been the lemonade talking, but I wasn't backing off.

"You may be a bylaw officer, but you're not the police. You can't tell me what to do. I'm entitled to call on people with whom I or my aunt had a previous business relationship."

She took a step nearer and drew herself up. "Oh, you're a lawyer now? Watch your step, Hawkes," she hissed. "Or—"

Whatever else she intended to say was lost in the sound of a truck crunching over the gravel shoulder behind us. A door slammed shut, and Ryker Fields strode over, beaming.

"What are you ladies up to on such a fine day?"

Good grief. How small was this village?

"Nothing. Miss Côté was explaining a few legal issues," I said, trying to appease her.

But Miss Côté wasn't listening. She was too busy sidling up to Ryker like a cat in heat.

"How've you been, Ryker?" she purred, placing a hand on his arm and leaning in as if he were the only thing holding her up. "Long time no see."

To give Ryker credit, he looked slightly embarrassed. He shrugged off her arm with another of his trademark smiles. "Hi, Bobbi. Good to see you again."

"Free for coffee, Ryker? Or—" She slid off her sunglasses and tilted her head, letting the invitation hang in the sultry mid-afternoon air.

I cleared my throat. "I'll let you two get reacquainted." I gave a brief wave over my shoulder while walking back to my aunt's truck.

"Verity, wait." Ryker jogged up beside me. "Why don't you give me your number? I can call you later and give you a few pointers on the neighborhood. Or I can drop by and show you how to adjust your wheels."

Adjust my wheels? These Leafy Hollow gigolos were smooth.

"Thanks," I said, opening the truck door, "but I'm fine. Please don't bother."

After I climbed into the cab and started the engine, I checked the rearview mirror. A smiling Ryker stood behind me, his arm raised in a finger wave. Behind him, Bobbi's attention was also focused on me, but with an expression that could curdle milk. She slid her sunglasses onto her face and turned back to her county vehicle.

My chest tightened as I steered my aunt's truck off the shoulder. Leafy Hollow's bylaw officer seemed a tad unhinged, but what did I know? Her behavior could be normal for a country village. I glanced again in the rearview mirror as I sped up.

Even so, I planned to stay out of Bobbi Côté's way in the future.

CHAPTER 12

BOBBI CÔTÉ SLID onto a bar stool in Kirby's and glanced around the crowded room. Patrons waiting for a table in the steak house jammed the lobby, but only a few customers sat at the dimly lit bar. Despite the hot and humid midsummer weather, Kirby's air-conditioned interior raised goosebumps on her arms.

"Miller Lite please, Andy," she said to the bartender, whose starched white apron stretched tight across his middle-aged spread.

"Haven't seen you in here for a while, Bobbi," he said, grabbing a beer glass and pulling on the tap. He slid a card-board coaster in front of her and set the filled glass on it.

"Been busy. The town should hire a second bylaw officer, but you know how cheap they are."

"Same story everywhere. Do more with less."

"Too true. Business here is good, I see."

"Yep. A liquor license is always a good way to make money."

Bobbi winked over the rim of her glass as she drained it, then replaced it on the coaster and pushed it forward on the counter with a nod.

Andy filled her glass again before moving off to serve a waitress who beckoned at him over her empty tray at the other end of the bar.

Bobbi twisted on her stool and faced the restaurant, scanning the patrons as she sipped her second beer. The booths and tables were filled with families as well as boisterous hockey players from the triple rinks two miles up the road. A few high-school couples mooned at each other over shared plates of gravy-drenched poutine. And there was the odd single, willing to exchange the loneliness of eating alone at home for the embarrassment of eating alone in public.

She was about to drain her glass and leave when the vivid red dress of a woman sitting alone in a booth near the back caught her gaze. Blonde bangs were feathered over her dark eyes, and a heavy gold necklace gleamed atop her ample breasts.

Henry Upton's ex-wife was the last person Bobbi expected to see in Kirby's.

Bobbi eased off her stool and walked up to the table. "Can-dace Up-ton," she said, drawing out the syllables. "Long time no see."

The woman gaped up at her before jumping to her feet and reaching over the table to wrap Bobbi in a hug. Her breath reeked of alcohol. "Good to see you, girl," she shrieked. "Siddown."

Bobbi slid onto the leatherette bench opposite Candace

and tossed her purse on the table. "I didn't expect to see you in Leafy Hollow. What brings you back?"

Candace made a face. "Divorce stuff." She signaled the waitress for a refill. "That jerk's making it difficult."

"That's not surprising. We both knew Henry wouldn't give up his cash without a fight."

"That's just it, though. He claims he has no cash."

"That's BS, right?"

"Naturally." Candace handed her empty glass to the waitress standing by their booth. "Another Caesar, hon, and one for my friend here." As the waitress walked away, Candace leaned over the table and whispered, "He doesn't know it, but I have him by the balls."

Bobbi swiped her fingers down the condensation on her beer glass and flicked it onto the coaster. "More than usual, you mean?"

Candace threw her head back in a cackle. "You have no idea."

"Details?"

"Sorry." Candace tapped the side of her nose with a wink. "It has to be hush-hush for now."

The waitress reappeared with two Caesars and placed them on the table. When Bobbi pulled her wallet from her purse, Candace waved it away.

"No, no, it's on me."

Bobbi put her wallet away. "Thanks. I thought you stopped working. Are you dancing again?"

Candace took a long swallow of her drink and set it on the table with a knowing smile. "No need for that."

Bobbi squinted at her companion. "Does that mean you and Henry are getting back together?"

"What?" Candace snorted in amusement. "That buffoon? No chance."

"Is there somebody else?"

"Are you kidding? There's always somebody else. In fact"—Candace craned her neck to check the door—"my gentleman friend should have been here by now."

Bobbi grinned as she abandoned her beer for the Caesar. "I'm definitely hanging around to meet your new meal ticket."

Candace leaned her elbows on the table, leering. "Denny's many fine assets do not lie in the financial arena." She winked again, a little slower this time. "Henry's still my main meal ticket. I have him dead to rights this time."

Candace's slurred words made little sense. "Are you talking alimony?" Bobbi asked, taking a long pull of the Caesar.

"No." Candace leaned so far over the table that her face almost hit the top. "It's some kinda land deal. My lawyer found out about it. Thass why we're waiting to serve the divorce papers. To give Henry time to sign the deal. Then I'll get half."

"Half of what?"

"That land behind our house." Candace sank back against the bench and tapped her nose again, but this time, her finger slid off the bridge of her nose and into her eye. "They're building a subdivision," she said, blinking and trying to dislodge the fake eyelash now pasted to her cheek.

Bobbi sat back against the booth, puzzled. "That's impossible. No one's allowed to disturb the creek bed in Pine Hill

Valley. And even if they got permission to build, there's nowhere to put in an access road. A subdivision isn't any good if you can't reach it."

"Thass what I thought. But Henry found a way."

"Who did he bribe to get the approvals?"

"I dunno." Candace glanced at the nearby booths. "Listen, thiss between us, right? Can't tell you anymore."

"Of course." Bobbi beckoned the waitress. "Another round, please. On me."

Once Candace had drunk most of her new beverage, Bobbi made another try. "That tract in Pine Hill Valley is over a hundred acres. Henry doesn't have the money to buy that much land, so who's footing the bill?"

Candace ran her fingers through her hair, leaving it tangled. "Some syndicate."

"But Henry's the front man?"

"Thass right." She tossed back her drink.

Bobbi stared at her, her mind racing. Henry Upton was a well-known local builder. If he could smooth the way for a subdivision in Pine Hill Valley, he'd receive a hefty finder's fee. And he'd be first in line for the contracts to build it.

But he'd have to overcome a significant hurdle.

That tract in Pine Hill Valley was circled by untouchable conservation lands. Only three private properties cut through those lands and could be used for a road.

One, the Upton place, was crisscrossed by Paradise Creek, which was also off limits. That left the Skalding property next door, and Rose Cottage on the valley's other side. But neither Yvonne Skalding nor Adeline Hawkes would sell their land to enable a subdivision in Pine Hill Valley.

Bobbi twirled her glass on the table, suppressing a smile. Adeline Hawkes was no longer around. That meant Rose Cottage was available. She could sense there was money to be made, and she intended to get her cut. She merely had to make Henry an offer he couldn't refuse.

But first, she'd have to visit Adeline's mouthy niece.

Across the table, Candace shoved her glass aside. "Goin' to the washroom." She stumbled to her feet with her hands pressed on the table, but tipped over before she could take a step.

Bobbi caught her before she hit the floor. "Let me help you," she said, waving away the waitress who was hurrying over. With Candace leaning on her, Bobbi walked to the washroom and backed her friend through the door. Inside, she pushed open a stall door and twisted Candace onto the toilet seat. Bobbi bent over and patted her arm. "Why don't you wait here, hon?"

As she closed the door, she glanced over her shoulder. Candace was out cold, slumped on the seat with her head and shoulder leaning against the wall.

Bobbi walked through the restaurant to retrieve her handbag from the table, and then continued straight out the front door.

CHAPTER 13

FOR ONCE, the hammering on Rose Cottage's front door involved an actual hammer.

"Hold on," I yelled, walking through the living room in my bare feet, a mug of coffee in my hand. I opened the door and found Bobbi Côté holding a hammer. Thumbtacks stuck out from between her lips.

I read the poster she was attaching to my door.

CONDEMNED
By order of the Leafy Hollow Health Department.
This property has been deemed
unfit for human habitation.

On the bottom was a date, and an illegible stamped signature.

"What are you doing? What is this?" I asked, ripping the notice from the door.

Bobbi tried to grab it from me. After a brief pulling

match, the paper tore in two, and we each tumbled back onto the floor.

Regaining my feet first, I waved the fragment grasped in my fingers. "This isn't legal. You have to serve notice first."

Bobbi scrambled to her feet and spit out thumbtacks. "Your aunt was warned multiple times." Another button popped off her shirt, leaving only two as far as I could see.

"My aunt isn't here," I said.

"Irrelevant."

I opened my mouth to speak before realizing I had nothing to say to that.

Bobbi pulled another paper from her briefcase. "Luckily," she said with a sneer, "I brought a copy." She picked up her hammer.

I dashed back into the house for my cell phone, yelling over my shoulder, "I'm calling my lawyer."

"Go ahead." Bobbi hammered in more thumbtacks while I listened to the phone ring.

"Good morning. This is Wilf Mullins, LL.B.—"

"Wilf," I shouted, "it's Verity Hawkes—"

"—and Leafy Hollow Councilor. Sorry to have missed your call. Please press 'one' if you need a fishing license, 'two' if—"

Oh, for God's sake. I clicked off the call and returned to the front door, where Bobbi had hammered in enough thumbtacks to upholster a sofa.

I scowled at her.

She scowled at me.

This was getting us nowhere, so I swallowed my pride. "Bobbi? Can we talk about this?"

"What is there to say?"

"Well, for starters, you could explain how this happened. This is the first I've heard of health issues."

"I told you. Your aunt had multiple warnings."

"I understand that, but no one told me, so you can see why I'm having a difficult time with this."

She shrugged.

I was grinding my teeth so hard I expected a molar to crack at any moment. "Why don't you come in for a coffee? Ten minutes, that's all I ask."

She gave me a puzzled look. Perhaps I was the first victim to offer her a beverage. She shrugged again. "Okay."

Bobbi followed me into the kitchen, where I poured her a mug. "Cream and sugar?"

She nodded, and I opened the fridge. I refrained from pointing out that if this place was condemned for health reasons, could she trust the cream? I handed her the carton with another forced smile, and then slid the moose-head cream and sugar bowls across the table. I bought them at the gift shop after leaving Wilf's because they matched my aunt's salt and pepper shakers. I felt the herd should be together.

Bobbi and I leaned back against the facing counters, sipping our coffee, unwilling to yield the field and sit.

I settled my mug on the counter. "So. Tell me what this is about."

"The inspector who came here found numerous health code violations."

"Such as?"

"Your roof leaks, several pipes are clogged, your well shows signs of contamination, and vermin are present. Not only that, but your septic tank is too close to the house, according to the current code."

I zeroed in on the last. "I don't know much about septic tanks, but I'm sure they don't move around. Which means my aunt's septic tank must be in the same place it's always been."

"So?"

"It would be grandfathered, wouldn't it?"

"Possibly."

"If I got the roof fixed, the pipes upgraded, and the well disinfected, everything but the septic tank would meet the code, right?"

"That would be up to the health inspector who filed the initial report."

A light went on. "Bobbi, are you the health inspector here, too?"

"I fill in for them from time to time."

"Was this one of those times?"

She shrugged.

"I see. Well, you were only doing your job." I heard a crack that could have been a shingle falling off the roof or one of my molars. I ignored it and sipped my coffee. "I'm not interested in him, you know," I said.

"What?"

"Ryker Fields. He's not my type. Besides, he's into you. Too much competition."

"I don't know what you mean. Ryker and I are just friends. I've known him since grade school."

"Uh-huh. I saw him looking at you. Didn't look like a

friendly glance to me." I shook out my wrist in a "hot-stuff" gesture.

Bobbi's face brightened. "Really?"

"Oh, yeah. When I saw you two together, I assumed you had a... thing." I wasn't sure how graphic I should be. I didn't want to overplay my hand.

"We did once, in high school. But then Ryker had a little trouble. When he came back, he was... different." She bit her lip as she studied the linoleum.

"Men," I agreed, nodding grimly.

She looked up. "What about you? Any prospects?"

"My husband died two years ago." I was surprised at how easy that was to say. Usually, I choked up. Was I getting on with my life, finally? There was a time when I yearned to go where Matthew had gone, to give up, to... I stared at the wall, startled by the memory. That was unthinkable now. When did that change?

"I'm sorry," Bobbi said, interrupting my trance. She pushed off from the counter, giving her shirt a tug. "I can give you a week."

"What?"

"To get the work done. You're probably right about the septic tank, but you'll have to do the rest. One week."

"That's not much time."

"It's all you're getting." She put her mug in the sink. "Thanks for the coffee."

"Bobbi, I can't possibly—"

She turned on me with a sudden black look, and I stepped back in surprise.

"Do you think that's your biggest problem?" she asked.

"I don't know what you mean."

"Everybody in town suspects you booby trapped Yvonne Skalding's home. I'd be worried about that if I were you."

I took another step back. "That's ridiculous. I had nothing to do with it."

"And who would believe you, a stranger with no ties?"

"I'm not a stranger. My aunt—"

"Your aunt made enemies."

I hesitated. Did Bobbi know about my aunt's other job? I decided to brazen it out. "That's impossible."

"Is it? Do you know who her least favorite person in the village was?"

I stiffened as she glared at me.

"Yvonne Skalding. They hated each other," Bobbi continued. "But you knew that, didn't you?"

A flash of annoyance overcame me. "I have no idea what you're talking about."

"Well, let's see." She counted on her fingers. "Your aunt disappears, and you turn up within days to claim your inheritance. Then you have a fight with Yvonne, and now she's dead. Sounds fishy to me."

I swallowed, but not hard enough to stem the bile rising in my throat. "I know nothing about Yvonne's accidents."

"So the accounts of your temper have been exaggerated?" Bobbi crossed her arms. "Tell me, Verity. What happened to your aunt? Did you kill her, too?"

My hands shook as I fought the impulse to wrap them around her neck. "Out," I said, pointing to the entrance. "Get out before I throw you out."

She laughed on her way through the door. "Good luck with that."

I ripped off the second "condemned" notice, crumpled it in my hand, and tossed it after her before slamming the door shut. I leaned my forehead against the door, tears stinging my eyes.

CHAPTER 14

ALONE IN ROSE COTTAGE, I crumpled to the floor with my back against the front door, staring at the floor's worn pine planks and fighting back tears. I had been in Leafy Hollow for two days. Forty-eight hours. My plan was to find my aunt, revisit a warm childhood memory, and return home to my solitary life.

Instead, I'd been yelled at, insulted, soaked, sunburned, and blistered. I'd been rebuffed by deadbeat clients and suspected of murder. My aunt's business was on the verge of bankruptcy, her home was about to be condemned, and I could go to jail.

And worst, I still didn't know if Aunt Adeline was alive or dead.

I sniffed. Then I sniffed again. The tears I had been holding back burst forth in a fit of weeping that left me as damp as a run-in with Yvonne's hose nozzle. At last, my tears ran dry, leaving painful hiccups in their wake.

Wiping my face, I got to my feet and walked to the

kitchen where I poured another coffee and sat at the table. I slid the moose salt and pepper shakers back and forth with trembling fingers. I could call my dad, but he'd made it clear he wasn't interested in Aunt Adeline's problems. He wasn't much interested in mine, either, and hadn't been since he'd walked out on my mom and me ten years earlier. He hadn't even returned for her funeral. Or Matthew's.

Anyway—I glanced at the clock over the sink—it was the middle of the night in Sydney. Not the best time for a sympathy call.

Besides, the person I most needed to talk to was Aunt Adeline. I picked up my mug and went into the dining nook to take a look at her bookcases. One by one, I read the titles.

Landscaping with Native Trees.

The English Garden, a Social History.

Risk Mitigation and Threat Assessment. I wrinkled my brow at that one before deciding it must be about garden pests.

Twelve Plants for the Lazy Gardener. Ooh. I should definitely read that.

Reader's Digest A-Z Encyclopedia of Garden Plants.

That one was huge. I slid the encyclopedia from its shelf, heaved it onto the dining table, and pulled up a chair.

I ruffled the stick-on notes that formed a small forest down the side and opened one at random. In the margin next to *Convallaria majalis,* lily of the valley, my aunt had written, "A thug that muscles out other plants while sending buried shoots as far as Texas. If you like the scent that much, buy the perfume."

Classic Adeline.

As I hefted the encyclopedia back into the bookcase, a calendar dropped out and hit the floor. I bent to pick it up. A hardware store logo blazed across the cover, and photos of impossibly perfect blooms marked the months. I flipped through to July, where lawn and garden appointments were penciled in tiny print.

I ran a finger down the notations in the calendar. If I completed these jobs, I might make enough money to hire someone to fix Rose Cottage. Then I could stay on in Leafy Hollow long enough to solve the mystery of my aunt's disappearance. With a start, I recalled promising Henry Upton that I'd cut his lawn today.

I picked up the phone to call Lorne Lewins.

A half hour later, a lanky young man in jeans and T-shirt, with tousled brown hair and a gap between his front teeth, stood on my porch, twisting a trucker's cap in his hands.

"I'd be happy to help out, Miss Hawkth," he said, his tongue catching softly on each s. "I did a lot of work for your aunt."

I gestured him into the cottage and closed the door behind him. "Call me Verity, please. And I do need your help. But..."

He raised his eyebrows, and I plunged ahead.

"I can't pay you right away, Lorne. I'm sorry." I shifted uneasily as he studied the floor, rolling his lips before looking up.

"When you say 'right away,' what exactly does that mean?" he asked.

Sometimes, it's best to just rip off the Band-Aid. "I have no money. If I gave you a check today, it would bounce. But I have a stack of unpaid invoices. Eventually, those deadbeats will pay up." The word *hopefully* hung in the air between us, unspoken.

"Do you have appointments for more work?"

"Yes. That's why I need your help."

His face brightened. "Then you can pay me after all."

"Ah..." I didn't want to tell him the next bit, but no point holding back now. "Most of those are prepaid customers, so they won't be handing over any cash. But I hope to find new clients soon."

With a nod, Lorne slapped the baseball cap onto his head and turned to the door.

"I'm sorry," I said, reaching for the handle. "I shouldn't have called you."

"When do you want me to start?"

"Excuse me?"

"The lawn cutting—when do we start?" When he saw the look on my face, he added, "Your aunt was always behind, too. I have a part-time job, so I can wait. You'll pay when you can." He raised his eyebrows. "So, where to first?"

"I promised to cut Henry Upton's lawn today."

"I'll get the whipper snipper."

"Thanks." I followed him to the garage, blinking back a tear. I was also mystified—whipper snipper?

━━━

I drove the truck up 14 Peppermint Lane's winding driveway and parked outside Upton's three-car garage, next to his yellow Hummer. When I stepped out of the cab and pulled my scribbled instruction sheet from my pocket to recheck it, a gust of wind blew it out of my hand. I darted after it, but it was halfway across the lawn.

Behind me, Lorne rolled the mower down the extended ramp. "Don't worry about the instructions," he called. "I don't need them."

I watched the paper twist through the air until it landed in the creek that ran between Upton's property and Yvonne Skalding's. "Yeah, but I do," I muttered, surveying the three acres of flawless grass that surrounded Upton's monster home. Too flawless, I thought. "Lorne? My aunt wrote in her journal that weed killer is illegal here." I pointed at the lawn.

He followed my outstretched finger. "Adeline used an organic compound. Corn gluten, maybe."

"It's not in her notes."

He shrugged, and then revved the mower, which roared to life. I stepped out of the way as he started down the hill. Then I returned to the truck to write up Upton's bill.

On a fresh page in my aunt's invoice book, I wrote his name and address, then "Past Due," followed by the unpaid amount. After a moment's deliberation, I added, "Interest on Outstanding Account," and calculated two percent. Farther down the page, I wrote today's date, "Lawn Cut & Trimmed" and the amount, totaled it, added in the sales tax, totaled it again, and ripped off the page with a flourish, leaving a carbon copy.

I decided to show it to Lorne in case I'd missed something.

He shut down the mower engine and gave the paper a puzzled stare as I waved it at him.

"Lorne, can you check this over? I want to make sure I got everything."

"I don't have anything to do with the bills."

I pushed it into his hand. "I know, but give this a quick look. It's my first invoice for Coming Up Roses Landscaping, and I want to get it right."

Lorne took the paper and squinted at it. "Looks okay." He handed it back, revved the engine, and moved away.

"Thanks," I muttered, looking at the invoice. It was right side up, which meant Lorne had been reading it upside down. An unusual skill.

With the invoice in my hand, I marched up to Upton's front door and slammed the brass lion's head knocker a few times. No answer.

I tried the buzzer, with no result. Then I lifted the flap on the brass mailbox that stood next to the door, hoping Upton had left my promised check in it. Nothing. I slammed the front door knocker again.

This time, the door opened a sliver. Henry Upton's sizable bulk blocked the opening.

"Verity. What can I do for you?"

The high-pitched whine of the whipper snipper—an electric trimmer that lopped off grass ends with deadly accuracy —filled the air.

"I came to pick up my check," I yelled over the noise.

"I'm a little busy." Upton frowned at Lorne, who was snipping off the grassy bits nearest the front walk. "Why don't I drop it off later?"

"You asked me to cut your lawn, Mr. Upton, and I have.

I'd like my check now, if it's not too much trouble. At least enough to cover your arrears."

Upton pointed to Lorne. "Last time, he hacked off some hosta leaves with that thing," Upton said. "Made quite a mess."

I turned my head to study the massive leaves hanging over the edge of the lawn. They didn't seem to be in any danger. When I turned back, the front door was shut.

Son of a... I puffed out a breath and slammed the knocker again. No answer. I slipped the invoice into the mailbox and walked back to the truck, where Lorne was packing up.

"Did he pay you?"

"No."

"He owes money all over the village."

"How do you know that?"

Lorne slammed the pickup's back panel shut. "Heard talk."

"Isn't it a little late to mention this?"

"Sorry," he said with another shrug.

At our next job, a modest lawn on Thyme Circle, I wrote up an invoice, ripped it from the book, and handed it to the homeowner—a trim woman in stretch capris and an outmoded pixie cut. I had no expectation of payment.

"I'll write you a check," she said. "Hang on a sec."

I grinned all the way back to the truck, where I tucked the check behind a clip on the sunshade and gave it a self-satisfied pat. On to appointment number three, Mrs. Waters.

A Fields Landscaping truck was parked in her driveway. Ryker Fields was on the front porch, chatting to the homeowner.

I hopped from the cab and walked up to the porch, where I held out my hand. "Verity Hawkes, here to cut your lawn."

Mrs. Waters gave me an uneasy look while patting the back of her bouffant gray hairdo. "I'm sorry, dear, but I've hired someone else. I didn't think your aunt's business was still in operation."

"I'm sorry you had to wait, but—"

She held up a hand to stop me. "I've made up my mind."

I cast a glance at Ryker, whose blond head was bent, studying the porch floor. *Call me if you need any help*, he'd said. Backstabber.

I stalked across the lawn to the truck, where Lorne had unloaded the mower.

"You can put that back," I said, opening the door to climb into the cab.

"Verity, wait," a voice called behind me.

I whirled to face Ryker, who hurried across the lawn and halted before me. He stared at my face, and the corners of his lips twitched. Too late, I remembered the blazing white zinc oxide I'd slathered over my nose. The heck with it. I thrust out my chin.

"Nice work, Ryker. How many of my aunt's clients have you poached so far?"

"It's not what it looks like."

"Original."

"No, I mean it. Mrs. Waters called me because no one showed up to cut her lawn. You should have contacted your aunt's clients to let them know what was going on instead of leaving them in the dark."

He had some nerve. What was it about Leafy Hollow that transformed the men into cranky schoolteachers?

"Is that what you did, Ryker? Call my aunt's clients?"

He rubbed a hand across his forehead and looked back at the homeowner. She stood on her porch, watching us.

"Verity, I told Mrs. Waters you were perfectly competent to carry on your aunt's business and that she should give you a chance."

"I bet you did. That must be why she fired me." Turning to the truck, I climbed into the driver's seat and slammed the door. "Do me a favor," I said through the open window. "Stop singing my praises. I can't afford it."

"You're wrong, Verity."

Lorne climbed into the seat beside me, and I started the engine. Before pulling out, I added, "And tell your girlfriend to leave Rose Cottage the heck alone."

Ryker wrinkled his brow. "My what?"

"Bobbi Côté. She condemned my aunt's house this morning. Your name came up."

"I have no idea what you're talking about."

Waving dismissively, I swerved off the shoulder and onto the road. In the rearview mirror, I saw Ryker staring after me, his mouth open. I felt a twinge of guilt. But I couldn't go back to make nice because I didn't want to alienate Bobbi Côté more than I already had.

I clenched my teeth, hoping a few molars were still intact. Was one day without drama too much to ask? Leafy Hollow owed me that much.

"You're going the wrong way."

"What?"

Lorne pointed at the road behind us. "You should have turned back there."

I slapped a hand against my forehead and made a U-turn. "Thanks."

At the stop sign, I recognized the intersection where Jeff Katsuro pulled me over for his *Welcome to Leafy Hollow* lecture. Two white wooden crosses were wedged into the shoulder of the road.

I pointed the crosses out to Lorne. "Are those from that hit and run a few years back?"

"Yeah."

"When was it, exactly?"

"Five or six years ago. My mom would know."

"I'll ask Emy at the bakery. She seems to know everything. She or her mother."

"Yeah, Emy knows a lot." He clammed up and gazed out the window. I could have sworn he was blushing.

After dropping Lorne off at his parents' house, I started for home. My chest was tight, and I was having trouble breathing. I planned to hole up in Rose Cottage and ignore anyone who knocked at the door.

On my way, I passed the carved wooden sign for Paradise Falls Park. On impulse, I swung into the parking lot. On picnics with my aunt as a child, I loved to wade in the river. I could still feel the slippery stones underfoot, the cool water between my toes, and the sunlight warming my bare arms.

I strolled across the grass to the curved fieldstone bridge that had watched over the park for generations. As I leaned over the side to gaze at the water rushing to the edge of the falls, a man climbed up a set of metal stairs from the whirlpool at the base of the falls. When he crested the top, I recognized Terence. He wore a black unitard this time, but his hiking shoes and Ray-Bans looked the same as they had when I'd met him in Emy's vegan takeout. He had Nitro slung around his shoulders.

When he reached the top, Terence lowered the beagle to the ground. Nitro rolled on the grass, twisting on his back, tongue lolling.

A young woman, so thin she was nearly emaciated, puffed up the stairs behind them. She walked up to Terence and poked a finger at his chest. The wind carried their words away, but they were arguing. Terence held up his hands and backed away from her. The woman stepped forward and grabbed his arm, still berating him.

With a shrug, he pulled his arm free and turned to jog across the grass to the woods, where the trail started up again. Nitro followed at a more leisurely pace.

The woman shouted after them, her hands on her hips, and then started back down the stairs.

I couldn't help speculating. Terence had seemed like an easygoing guy to me, but he must have done something to anger this woman. Could it be it a lover's tiff? Or did he refuse to pick up her dry-cleaning bill? With a snicker, I turned back to the truck.

In Rose Cottage, I threw open the windows, hoping for a breeze to cool the house. A plaintive *meeooww* came through the open kitchen window. When I opened the door, one-eyed Tom looked up at me.

"Dinner?" I asked.

He brushed past me with a slight pressure against my leg

that might have been gratitude. Either that, or he was scratching an itch. Hard to tell. He sat at the counter and wrapped his tail around his feet.

I snapped open a newly purchased tin of *Feline Fritters* and spooned it into a saucer. "Just don't ask me where our next meal is coming from," I said, placing the dish on the floor, "because I don't know."

CHAPTER 15

THE REALTOR, Nellie Quintero, muttered for forty-five minutes straight during our tour of Rose Cottage before turning to me by the porch and lowering the boom.

"I'm sorry, Verity, but you'll never be able to sell this place. It's falling apart."

I hadn't intended to sell anything, but I had hoped to present Aunt Adeline with options when—or if—she returned. She couldn't run a money-losing business forever. "Isn't the land worth something?"

"Well, yes, but..."

"A developer could buy it, couldn't they? Tear it down, build a bigger house?"

"New homes aren't approved anymore unless they have two acres of land. Even then, current building codes require an upgraded septic system, which costs at least twenty grand, and a new well, which would be another three thousand or more. Not to mention a new electric pump and water tank."

So much for carefree country living, I thought. "None of those need replacing in the meantime, do they?" My voice sounded anxious even to me.

"I don't know. You'd have to get an inspector out here to look them over. That's not your only challenge. I'm not an engineer, but it looks as if you might have foundation problems. You'll also need a new roof, or at least good patchwork, before the winter."

"That sounds expensive."

"I'm afraid so."

"Couldn't Rose Cottage be sold as a fixer-upper?"

Nellie tapped her finger on her chin, sweeping her gaze around the yard. "Not with your aunt's mortgage. If you sell this as it is, you won't clear enough to pay off the lien."

"What would happen then?"

"Her estate would be bankrupt and her belongings auctioned off to make up the difference." Nellie pointed to my aunt's truck. "You could get a few thousand for that, and another thousand for her mower and tools."

"But then I couldn't run the landscaping business."

"I thought you didn't want to."

I regarded the porch's peeling paint. Selling my aunt's house might be the expedient route, but bankruptcy wasn't right. Aunt Adeline worked hard during her life. Assuming she was dead—still a big "if" in my mind—she wouldn't want to go out like that.

"Thanks for viewing the house," I said. "I'll think about it some more."

Nellie swept her long, blonde hair over her shoulder with

one hand and fixed her crystal blue eyes on me. "There's another obstacle, Verity. It sounds ridiculous, but some people think Rose Cottage is... haunted."

"Haunted? You must be kidding. Who would—"

"Not me," Nellie broke in with a nervous laugh, glancing over her shoulder at the cottage while stepping farther away. "I don't believe that. It does seem to have a mind of its own though."

I recalled the weird deadbolts, the sticky basement door, the whirs and clicks in the ceiling, the faulty water heater, and the wonky lights. "I can't imagine why anyone would think that," I said. "It seems like a normal house to me. Charming, even."

I was catching on to this real estate business. I might make it my next career.

Nellie hiked her eyebrows with a playful smile. I got the impression she'd heard similar patter before. "You're right. Rose Cottage is charming. And we often get requests for houses like this from young professional couples who want to leave the city. They love anything they can attach a heritage plaque to." She chuckled. "And maybe add a chicken or two." Her expression grew serious, and she let out a long sigh. "Verity, I'd love to sell your aunt's house and collect the commission. I could use the cash. But I'd be lying if I said you'd make any money. We can list it, sure, but I don't recommend it. Fix it up first, and then we can talk."

As we contemplated the cottage, a cracked shingle slid off the roof and shattered into splinters at our feet. I narrowed my eyes at it. *Traitor.*

"If it's not saleable," I asked, "why did Wilf recommend you come out to see it?"

Nellie swept her gaze over the cottage's roof, frowning. "I don't know. Maybe he thought..." She shrugged. "He probably hasn't been out here for a while. Listen, if you're staying, you need to fix a few things. Especially that roof. It will never make it through the winter without repairs."

She rummaged through her shoulder bag, pulled out a white business card, and handed it to me. It had been torn from a perforated sheet of do-it-yourself stationery. I read the spidery longhand.

Carson Breuer
Carpentry & Odd Jobs

I handed the card back to her. "I can't pay anyone at the moment."

Nellie waved it away. "Don't worry. You and Carson can come to an arrangement. Believe me; he'll be happy to get the work."

There was a tone to her voice that worried me.

"Why? Doesn't he get hired much?"

"He's a bit eccentric. But he'll do a good job, and he'll work within your budget." Nellie climbed into her car. "Ciao." With a brisk wave, she drove away.

My budget? Until I pried some cash out of my aunt's freeloader clients, my budget was zero. Who would work within that? I ran a hand through my hair and drew my head back to appraise the roof. "Eccentric," on the other hand, was good—downright reassuring, in fact. You'd have to be a little eccentric to take on a project like this.

I went into the house for another crack at my aunt's laptop. As I heaved aside a book on perennials to make room on the desk, a flattened rosebud slipped from the pages and fell to the floor. I bent to pick it up and twirled it between my fingers. It was curled at the edges, its fragile papery petals turning brown. I set it on the mantel, next to the china spaniel, and walked into the kitchen. A caffeine hit might spark some password ideas.

As I turned on the coffeemaker, a movement in the garden caught my eye. I peered through the window. A man was in the yard, holding a spade. His back was to me, but I recognized his gray topknot. I walked out onto the porch.

"Gideon," I yelled. "Are you looking for something?"

He turned to face me. "You're home," he said in his usual garrulous manner.

"I hope that's gold you're digging up. I could use good news."

He raised the spade in one hand and walked toward me, chuckling. "I'm returning this." He gestured at the garage with the spade.

That didn't explain his presence in my aunt's garden—or the freshly dug holes in the ground.

I took the spade from him. "Thanks."

He turned to go.

"Gideon?"

"Yes?"

"Did you take a keepsake box from my aunt's mantel?"

He spluttered, and I held up a hand.

"I don't mind, although you could have asked me. But while I'm posing questions—what are those for?" I pointed at the holes. "What are you looking for?"

"Nothing."

Did I look stupid? Wait, scratch that.

"You're not searching for land mines, are you?"

"What? Why would you... never mind." He dug into the pocket of his jeans and pulled out a scrap of paper, which he held out. "That box had a message in it."

"A message? From who?"

"Adeline." He stepped closer and pressed the scrap of paper into my hand.

I stared at the word on it:

AVE

I looked up at him. "This doesn't make sense."

"In Spanish, *ave* means bird."

I thought of the computer's elusive password. "Let's try this on my aunt's laptop."

When *ave* didn't work, we typed in every bird species native to Leafy Hollow and dozens that weren't. Then we typed them again, in Spanish. No luck. I closed the laptop and dropped the scrap of paper on top, tapping my fingers on the metallic surface.

When I was a child, my mother taught me dozens of Latin words and phrases. So many that Latin became our secret language, a habit that infuriated my auto-mechanic father, who felt shut out by our circle of two. I pushed the laptop away.

"It's Latin, Gideon. I should have guessed it right off."

"What does it mean?"

"It's a simple greeting, usually translated as *hail* or *hello*." I sank back in my chair with a hollow feeling in my stomach. "But it can also mean *farewell*."

"Well, crud," he said.

I nodded miserably. "You can say that again."

Gideon got to his feet. "Let's get the box."

I trailed him to his bungalow and waited on the front porch while he went inside. He came back out and handed me the empty keepsake. Then he dropped into a rocker by the front door and slammed the newel post with one foot, muttering a curse. Gideon leaned his elbows on his knees and pressed his fingers against his eyes under his blue-tinted glasses.

I settled into the other rocker, listening to the red squirrels chirrup in the spruce branches above us.

When Gideon slumped back against the chair, I held out the wooden box. "I think my aunt would want you to have this."

Pressing his lips together, he took it from my hand and curled his fingers over it. "Thanks."

"You miss her, don't you?"

He shrugged.

We were silent for a while, contemplating the twilight.

"Gideon, why didn't they find my aunt's body?"

"You should ask the police that."

"But don't you think it's odd?"

"She might have been carried downstream and into the bay. The driver's door was open."

"You saw the police report?"

He nodded.

"Do you think something happened to her before the accident?"

"Dunno. There's no evidence of it."

"Okay, then. What if—"

"Let's not talk about it."

The squirrels' chattering filled the silence while I mulled this over. "That's not good enough," I said. "I came to Leafy Hollow because I don't believe my aunt is dead. But everyone here thinks it's true. Even the police. I have to talk about it, Gideon, or I'll go crazy. Tell me what you know. And why did she neglect Rose Cottage?"

He leaned forward with his elbows on his knees and clasped his hands together, staring at the ground. "Adeline was on one of her crusades."

"Was Control involved?"

"Shouldn't have told you about that," he muttered.

"Was it?"

"That was years ago."

"Then what made you think she'd left a message? That's why you took the box, isn't it?"

"Adeline mentioned a group called the Syndicate. So, when she disappeared..." He straightened up with a shrug.

"You don't think it was an accident," I said dully. "You think this 'Syndicate' was responsible."

He exhaled heavily and sat back, one foot tapping on the floor. "Adeline went everywhere with that laptop under her arm. We have to break the password."

My heart sank. "But we have no idea how."

He nodded glumly.

I slumped back in my chair. We were still there when the

soft cries of mourning doves replaced the squirrels' chattering, and hundreds of stars winked on in the midnight
blue sky.

Surprisingly, Gideon was the first to break the silence. "I
saw Nellie Quintero's car," he said. "Are you selling Rose
Cottage?"

"Nellie says it's haunted. Could be a sales deterrent."

"Ridiculous," he said with a snort, rising to his feet. "I've
got donuts. You can take them home."

Welcoming the diversion, I followed him into the darkened living room. Gideon switched on a light, and my jaw
dropped. I expected shabby furniture, bare floors, and a
vintage turntable—not the command deck of television's Star-
ship Enterprise.

A sleek wooden console arched up from the floor on
either side of the room, curving around the backs of three
leather recliners. The chairs had remote controls and LCD
screens embedded in their arms. On the opposite wall, more
LCD screens blinked on either side of a huge flat-screen TV.

"You're kidding," I said, gazing around the room like a
twelve-year-old. Aunt Adeline loved *Star Trek*, so my childhood was filled with endless reruns of the original sci-fi series
—not to mention the reboots. "This is great."

With a grin, Gideon headed for the kitchen. "Don't take
the captain's chair," he called over his shoulder. "That's
mine."

I slid into a recliner and pushed buttons on the control
panels in the arms. The *whirr-whirr-whirr* of a Red Alert
filled the room, and I giggled.

I was still fiddling with the controls when Gideon

returned with snacks and coffee. I accepted the proffered mug, and, with a grin, reached for a Boston cream. "How long did it take you to build this?"

"A few years. I worked on it bit by bit. Adeline insisted I redo the tactical station. Twice." He pointed to the console behind the chairs.

I chuckled. "Sounds like my aunt. She's always been a stickler for detail. The cup holders are a nice touch, by the way."

Gideon sat in the middle chair and settled his coffee into the arm. "We used to watch the shows together. Her favorite was—"

"Khan," I broke in. "The original and the remakes."

"Right."

We stared at the blank screen, lost in our own thoughts.

"We should try *Star Trek* names on the laptop," I said, turning to look at him. "Tomorrow?"

"Good idea."

I settled back into my chair. "Can we watch one of the Khans?"

"Sure." He tapped the embedded remote.

One query still begged an answer. "Is Gideon Picard your real name?"

"That's an odd question."

"Does that mean you won't answer it?"

He shrugged, which I was recognizing as his signature move. I gave it one last try.

"You have the uniforms, too, don't you?"

"Oh, yeah. With phasers."

With a smile, I faced the screen and bit into my donut as

the opening sequence appeared. Memories of my aunt filled my head while I watched the Enterprise streak through the future.

Tackling the laptop wasn't my only plan for the next day. There was another mystery to solve. Emy was right. I should search Yvonne Skalding's home for booby traps.

CHAPTER 16

FROM HIS PERCH in the Hummer at the top of his driveway, Henry Upton watched the police cruiser turn out of the
Skalding driveway and onto Peppermint Lane. He put his
cell phone on speaker and tossed it onto the front passenger
seat. "I'm making a run across the border next week," he said.
"You'll have to wait until then."

The voice coming from the phone was high pitched and
whiny. "I need it now."

Henry had a clear view of Yvonne Skalding's red-brick
ranch house. The sedan parked in the driveway belonged to
her son and his wife, Zander and Kate. Henry mentally
rehearsed his pitch. He had to get it right. The Syndicate was
becoming impatient. "One more week," they insisted during
his last conference call to the Caymans. That had been two
days ago.

"I can't wait any longer," the voice from the phone
continued. "It's July. We should have had the stuff months
ago."

With a burst of irritation, Henry reached out a beefy, tattooed arm and picked up the phone. "Don't you think I have more important things to do?" he barked.

"Like what?"

Henry swung his sight to the hundred-acre field behind the Skalding house. *Like that*, he thought, although he kept the notion to himself. Too many people knew about this deal already. He must strike before Zander Skalding realized what was at stake, while he and his wife were still grief-stricken.

His lip curled in a sneer as he pictured Kate Skalding's sour face. Kate wouldn't grieve her mother-in-law, not in private anyway. Zander was the only real hurdle to Henry's landing a deal that could make him millions.

"Are you listening to me?" the voice asked.

Henry fingered his bushy, black beard. "Tomorrow. That's the best I can do." He clicked off the call and slipped the cell phone into his shirt pocket.

Cock-a-doodle-doo.

Henry grimaced at the rooster's cry. That stupid bird set his teeth on edge. It would be bad enough if it only crowed at dawn, but Skalding's fowl screeched whenever the notion took it. Much like its former owner.

A movement in the bushes that led to the river caught his eye. He reached for his binoculars in time to make out a flash of tawny brown in the thicket. Unusual to see a coyote in daylight. "Chicken dinner twenty paces to the left, boy," he muttered. "Easy pickings." But the flash of brown had disappeared.

Henry snorted. He wouldn't give up so easily. He leveled his binoculars on the Skalding house. The door onto the back patio opened, and Kate Skalding walked out. She wore shorts, a tube top, and sandals—none of it in black, Henry smirked at the thought—and carried a tall, frosted glass in her hand. After placing the glass on an end table, she stretched out on a chaise with her skinny arms over her head, lifted her face to the sun, and closed her eyes.

Perfect. Henry shifted the Hummer into drive and drove down the hill. He swerved the vehicle onto the road, and then up the Skalding driveway. Leaving the binoculars on the front seat, he walked around the house until he saw Kate Skalding's bony legs stretched out on the chaise.

"Hello," he said, coming around the corner. "Anybody home?"

Kate jerked upright and whirled around, a guilty look on her face.

"I rang the doorbell, but..." Henry shrugged, giving her beverage a pointed stare.

"I'm sorry, I didn't hear you." She flung her skeletal frame from the chaise and held out a hand. "Nice to see you again, Mr. Upton."

"Call me Henry, please. My condolences on the loss of your mother-in-law. Is your husband—"

"He's inside. Why don't you come in?"

He followed her into the house, past cabinets and tables filled with delicate china figurines of young women in billowing dresses, and into the living room.

The wood floor was bare, with a shiny rectangle in the middle to mark what must have been a large rug, since removed. An enormous antique china breakfront leaned against the far wall. The glass doors were smashed and cracked. Some were missing. Henry averted his eyes from the fingerprint dust on the sides and back of the damaged cabinet.

Zander Skalding, who was collecting broken china from the edges of the room and throwing it into a plastic bucket, rose from the floor. His round face was puffy, and his eyes were red.

"I'm sorry about your mother's passing," Henry said.

"Thank you." Zander dropped into the nearest chair.

"She was a wonderful woman," Henry added.

They nodded at each other until Kate broke the silence. "Can I get you a beverage, Henry? Coffee?"

"That sounds great." With a grunt, he settled his solid heft into an armchair. "Thank you."

Once Kate had left the room, Henry leaned toward Zander. "My associates are anxious to hear your decision. Have you thought any more about their proposal?"

"For heaven's sake, Henry. My mother isn't even buried yet."

"I'm sure Yvonne wouldn't object if her only son made a little cash, funeral or not. She had a head for figures as I recall."

She was a spiteful skinflint actually, Henry thought.

Kate returned with his coffee in a ceramic mug. At least it wasn't a stupid little cup-and-saucer thing. He could never get his fingers into the handles on those. He sipped the coffee, making appreciative noises, and then he put it on the end table beside him.

"It's a limited-time offer, you know," he said.

Kate perched on the arm of her husband's chair and

leaned in to caress the back of his neck. Henry thought he detected a shudder on Zander's part. Could have been his imagination.

"What are we talking about?" Kate asked.

"The land deal," Zander said. "The syndicate that wanted Mom to sever her property and sell them a strip on the east lawn. Their offer's still on the table, apparently."

Kate slid her fingers up his neck. "I think it's a good idea."

Both men looked at her. Kate had never expressed such an opinion when Mrs. Skalding was alive. Not in her hearing, anyway. Henry recalled the last time he visited the Skalding home to plead with Yvonne, once again, to reconsider the sale. She showed him the door.

But Kate followed him into the driveway where she leaned over his Hummer's open window. "Zander and his mother won't even consider selling that land," she said, watching the front door. "But the old harpy won't be around forever." Then she turned to him and smiled.

He studied her face while shifting the Hummer into drive. "Noted," he said, before driving away.

Now, amid the shattered china and broken furniture, Zander stared at his wife. "Mom hated the idea. You know she did."

"Darling." Kate leaned in, twisting her fingers in his hair. "Mom isn't here anymore."

Henry seized the opportunity. "Life is for the living, Zander. Your mother knew that."

Zander shook off his wife's hand and got to his feet. He trudged to the window and stared out over the front lawn. "Did she?" he asked.

Henry thought he detected bitterness in his voice. Before he could reply, Zander spoke again.

"There won't be a sale."

"Zander—" Kate said.

He held up a hand to silence her. "There won't be a sale, because we don't own this property. Mom left it to charity. The house, the car, even the damn china." He gave a disgusted glance at the bucket of shards. "What's left of it."

Kate stared at her husband with her mouth open and took a step nearer. "What did you say?" she whispered.

"The Leafy Hollow Historical Society gets the house." Zander slumped onto the sofa and leaned his head back, staring at the ceiling.

Kate looked as though she was going to be sick. "That's impossible. You have to stop it."

"We can contest it, but that will take time." Zander lowered his head into his hands and burst into tears. "I was a good son. What did I do to deserve this?"

Henry and Kate stared at him.

"For God's sake, pull yourself together and call our lawyer," Kate said, turning to the door. "I need a drink."

Henry followed her into the kitchen and watched as she poured vodka into two tumblers and pushed one to his side of the island. He downed his without comment, and she did the same.

Sobs came from the living room, followed by wailing. Kate muttered as she poured herself a second drink and slammed it back. Henry declined when she offered him another. Kate shrugged and poured her third glass, then took it to the patio doors and glared at the rooster pecking its way across the lawn.

Henry didn't give much for its chances.

He straightened up with a lusty sigh and headed for the front door. It wasn't fair. Yvonne Skalding disrupted his plans when she was alive, and she was still interfering from the grave. The Leafy Hollow Historical Society was a dusty collection of old prints and crumbling maps stored in the back room of a local rectory. Why did it need money?

But even if Zander contested his mother's will, it wouldn't happen in less than a week. That meant Henry had to find another way to fulfill his promise or kiss that finder's fee goodbye. Not to mention the construction contracts. Without those, he'd lose everything.

Rose Cottage was the only other property in town that fit the bill. Adeline Hawkes had refused to sell, but that was before she vanished. Too bad that niece showed up. Otherwise, he could have picked up the house for a song in an estate sale.

Henry climbed into the Hummer and headed down Peppermint Lane with renewed purpose. All he had to do was make sure that Verity Hawkes disappeared, too.

CHAPTER 17

I STARED in shock at the skinny woman who opened the front door of the Skalding residence. The last time I saw her, she was poking her bony finger into Terence Oliver's chest at Paradise Falls Park.

"Kate Skalding?"

"Yes?"

I stuck out my hand. "I'm Verity Hawkes, Adeline's niece."

She gave my hand a dead-fish shake. "What's this about?"

"I want to express my condolences. I'm sorry for your loss."

"Thanks." Kate jerked her head in an abbreviated nod and made a move to close the door.

"Also," I added hastily, "I wondered if you might have a few moments to discuss your mother-in-law's landscaping contract."

Her brow furrowed. "Do we owe you money?"

"Not a penny. Mrs. Skalding paid in advance. I only need

to know if you want to continue the service and if you have any special requests."

She stepped back from the door and gestured me in.

"Zander," she called. "Come here."

The man who stuck his head out of the living room door in the hall wore a sweater vest over a button-down shirt, blue jeans, and stocking feet. His hair, however, was anything but conservative. It stuck straight up in a semi-Mohawk likely intended to wrest attention from his receding hairline. It wasn't working. I had heard of moon-shaped faces, but this was the first time I'd seen one.

"This is Verity Hawkes," Kate said.

Zander stared. "Aren't you the one who—"

I cut him off with a proactive question. "Argued with your mother? I'm afraid so. But I had nothing to do with her death, obviously."

"Why obviously?" Kate asked.

"Well, I... I couldn't," I spluttered. "Surely you don't think that."

Kate didn't look convinced, but Zander stepped into the hall and extended his hand. "I'm Yvonne's son. Of course we don't think that. To be honest, I'm not convinced Mom's death was anything other than a tragic accident." He turned to his wife. "Kate, darling, might we have tea?"

After giving us both a steady look, Kate headed for the kitchen.

"Please, come in," Zander said, gesturing to the living room.

I followed him into a chintz- and china-bedecked room with framed botanical prints centered on striped wallpaper.

Except for Zander's hair, the bare floor, and the bruised and splintered breakfront, we might have traveled through a time tunnel to the eighties. I perched on the edge of an overstuffed armchair, afraid if I sank in, I might never get out again.

"I'm sorry for your loss."

"Thank you," he murmured. Zander sat on the sofa in front of the window, crossed his legs, and tented his fingers on his knee. He looked straight ahead, not at me, and his round chin quivered almost imperceptibly.

"Are you staying in Leafy Hollow?" I asked. When he didn't reply, I added, "I'm only asking because I'd like to know if you intend to continue your mother's landscaping contract. It's paid for."

He sighed, not looking at me. "Yes. Mom's property has to be cared for, at least until everything's settled."

Zander looked up as Kate entered holding a tray with a teapot, cups and saucers, milk, and sugar.

She plunked it on an end table, but made no move to serve. "What are we talking about?" she asked.

"The lawn, darling. It needs to be cut and Verity's willing to do it."

Kate knitted her brows and sank into the remaining armchair. "Not for long. I thought—"

"Let's not discuss that now," Zander broke in. "Not in front of guests." He got to his feet and poured the tea. "Milk and sugar?"

"Thank you, yes," I said, accepting a cup. After a few sips, I balanced the cup and saucer on my knee with one hand. "Zander, do the police have any idea what happened? What makes you think it was an accident?"

"We'd hardly discuss that with you, would we?" Kate said.

"Kate, please," Zander snapped without looking at her. He rubbed a hand over his forehead. "Who would want to harm my mother? She never hurt a fly. She did volunteer work, you know. Hosting the book club and so forth. Everyone loved her."

Thank goodness I wasn't drinking tea when he said that because it would have gone right out my nose. On to Plan B. I set my cup on the end table beside me. "Do you mind if I take a look in the garage? I think I forgot some tools when I left in a hurry the other day."

Zander exchanged glances with Kate, who shrugged.

"Go ahead," Zander said.

Kate got to her feet. "I'll go with you," she said with a fixed smile. "In case you need help."

I couldn't check the place for booby traps with Kate Skalding breathing down my neck, but it was too late to change my story. I followed her to the garage, where she unlocked the side door and motioned me through.

With Kate standing in the doorway, I scanned the tools above the workbench and on the back wall of the double garage. A wire rope was looped over a rafter at the back. One end was connected to a heavy-duty winch on the far wall, the kind used to haul stuff up and down. I wondered if that could be considered a booby trap. You wouldn't want to get a foot caught in it. You might end up hanging from the ceiling.

I pointed to the rope. "What's that?"

Kate followed my finger. "A clothesline. Imogen hangs

the wet deck cushions there to dry." She waved a hand at the workbench along the wall. "Are any of these tools yours?"

"Sorry, no. I must have been mistaken."

Kate's face was impassive as I brushed past her into the yard. She locked the door behind me and turned to the house.

A red-and-brown blur came out of nowhere, shooting across the path in front of her. Kate tumbled back with a shriek. I grabbed her arm to keep her from hitting the ground.

Imogen, one hand anchoring her sunhat, bolted from behind the house.

Kate regained her footing and yanked her arm away. "What the heck was that?" she yelled at Imogen, who skidded to a halt.

"I'm sorry, Mrs. Skalding," she gasped, trying to catch her breath. "He got away from me."

I watched the rooster as he tilted his head at the ground. He took two spiky steps forward, then stopped and tilted his head again. Clearly, the front yard offered better pickings than wherever he was normally kept.

Kate's voice was cold. "I told you to get rid of that damn bird. Now do it."

Imogen, bent over and puffing with her hands on her thighs, raised a hand to show that she couldn't speak yet, never mind give chase.

"Imogen—" Kate added in a warning tone.

"I'll get him for you," I broke in.

How hard could it be to corral a flightless bird?

I tiptoed up to the rooster, holding out my hand in a gesture of friendship while he pecked at a grasshopper. "Here, birdy. Good birdy."

But when I got within arm's length, he leaped out of the way with a flutter of feathers and an affronted squawk.

I dove for him again. And again. Then I picked up the pace. He couldn't fly, and his little legs were scrawny. It should have been easy to catch him.

The rooster and I darted around the yard. The bird easily maintained his lead. Finally, he zigged when he should have zagged, and I lunged with my arms wide to snatch him up.

Unfortunately, I had forgotten the muddy patches in the lawn. My feet skidded out from under me, and my back thudded against the ground with a smack. Water seeped through my jeans and T-shirt as I lay there, wincing.

The rooster, intrigued by this development, made his way to my side, spiky step by spiky step. I watched him from the corner of my eye, until, with a flutter of his wings, he leaped onto my chest to proclaim his victory.

Cock-a-doodle-doo.

I wrapped my arms around him, rolled over in the muck, and struggled to my feet. "Gotcha," I said with satisfaction.

There's no substitute for perseverance. It's number two in *Top Ten Tips for Success in Life.*

The rooster cocked his head to study my face. We had clearly established a rapport, so I leaned in to cement relations. "Nice birdy," I said.

He darted his head toward me in a lightning-fast move, his razor-sharp beak slashing my left eyebrow.

"*Dammit.*" I let go of the rooster and slapped a hand over my eye.

The bird fluttered docilely to the ground, its bloodlust sated for now.

Meanwhile, my jeans and T-shirt were soaked and muddy, my palms were scraped and grass-stained, and my eye was swelling shut. All in a day's work for Coming Up Roses Landscaping.

Kate stomped across the grass and glared at us. "Get that bloody bird out of here."

Imogen snatched up the rooster and tucked it under her elbow like a football, its thin legs dangling from her arm.

We watched Kate disappear into the house.

"Is she always like that?" I asked.

"She usually has her knickers in a twist over something. It's been worse since Yvonne"—Imogen puffed out a breath and turned her head away—"well, you know."

"Imogen, I meant to tell you how sorry I am. It must have been horrible for you."

She screwed her eyes shut behind her thick lenses. "It was awful," she whispered. "I've never seen anything like it."

I nodded, imagining the scene. "Kate's upset. People express grief in different ways, don't they?"

Imogen's bottle eyes sprang open. "Grief?" She let out a full-throated chuckle. "That woman's delighted her mother-in-law is gone. They're making plans to sell this place. Kate told me to be gone by the end of the week." Imogen ruffled the feathers on the rooster's back with her free hand as she studied the house.

"Do you live in?" I asked.

"No, I have a place in town. I'm here four days a week."

"There's no for-sale sign."

"Not yet, but there's a deal in the making. With Henry Upton, I think." She tipped her head at the house on the hill.

"He was here the other day. I couldn't hear what they said, but there was a huge row after he left."

"Between Zander and Kate?"

"Not their first, either."

I studied the Upton home.

Imogen followed my gaze. "He watches this house with binoculars. He sits in that daft vehicle of his for hours sometimes, watching us."

I felt a chill and rubbed my arms. What did Upton expect to see?

As long as Imogen was being cooperative, I decided to chance an unrelated question. "Does Kate Skalding know Terence Oliver well? The young man who hikes in the conservation area? Blue spandex and Ray-Bans?"

Imogen snorted. "Terence Oliver? I should say she does."

"Are you suggesting—"

"I'm suggesting nothing. I've said too much. Four more days and I'll be on my way. And the Skaldings can go to Hades." She ruffled the rooster's feathers again. "Well, mate, you're for the chop. Might as well get on with it." She turned to the garage.

"Wait. What do you mean... chop?"

"Kate wants him taken to the chicken farm up the road and slaughtered. They're going to eat him for dinner."

"But he's a pet."

"He's not her pet."

I looked at the rooster. He cocked his head to size up my other eyebrow.

"Let me take him," I blurted before I could stop myself. I think it was remorse over my Thanksgiving dinner flashback.

"You can buy a chicken at the supermarket. Kate won't know the difference."

Imogen grinned. "I'd enjoy that. Putting one over on her." She held out the rooster. "Hold him this way, and you'll be hunky-dory. Hang on a tic. I'll get his crate from the garage and some feed."

Ten minutes later, I was on my way home with Reuben cackling behind me in the truck bed. I hoped that Lorne could tell me how to look after a chicken.

Meanwhile, murder suspects danced through my thoughts. Were Kate and Terence lovers? Imogen seemed to think so, which upped the suspicious-person count in Yvonne Skalding's murder to three: Zander, her son and heir; Kate, her daughter-in-law; and Terence, Kate's lover, who would benefit if Kate divorced her husband and walked out with her share of the estate.

I struggled to recall my original conversation with Imogen when she said Yvonne refused to sell a section of her land.

She'll never do it. Not a chance.

They didn't need Yvonne's approval any more, did they?

CHAPTER 18

HENRY UPTON SHIFTED his bulk in the Hummer's front seat and glared at the bylaw officer leaning against his half-open side window. "You're wrong," he said. "I haven't done anything illegal."

Bobbi Côté looked up and down Main Street before replying. "Yvonne Skalding stood between you and a lucrative land deal. Now she's dead. I think the police would find that interesting, don't you?"

Henry shifted again in his seat. Blast the woman.

Bobbi leaned closer, flattening her breasts against the glass like loaves ready for the oven. "Zander doesn't know what you did, does he? What are the chances that your deal will go through if he learns about it?"

Henry rubbed a hand across his beard, scowling.

Across the street, a bevy of young women in skintight dresses emerged from the bridal shop, laughing and jostling each other under the locust trees that grew in the sidewalk's concrete containers. Henry scowled at the woman who anchored the circle of female admirers. Bitch probably had a divorce lawyer on speed dial.

"I had nothing to do with Skalding's death," he said.

A slow smile curled Bobbi's upper lip. "Liar."

Henry's desperate grip on the steering wheel echoed the clench of his gut. He needed a few more days, enough time to convince Zander to challenge his mother's will and sign Henry's purchase offer. They could make the sale conditional on Zander's challenge being approved, but the offer had to be signed.

The Syndicate had given him one week to put the deal together. He had four days left. If Bobbi spooked Zander now, it would end the whole bloody arrangement. He'd be finished. Even the Hummer would have to go.

"I'm telling you, I had nothing—"

"That's not everything, though, is it?" Bobbi broke in. "Adeline Hawkes refused to sell, didn't she?"

"I don't know what you're talking about."

Bobbi lowered her voice to a husky whisper as she ran one finger along the edge of the glass. "Do you think I'm stupid, Henry?"

He stared straight ahead, hoping if he ignored her, she would go away.

"And now Adeline Hawkes is missing. That's quite a coincidence, wouldn't you say?" Bobbi straightened up with her fingers crooked over the window glass. "I can get rid of Verity Hawkes."

He flashed her a suspicious look. "What do you mean?"

She leaned in again, smiling. "Not what you're thinking."

"You don't know what I'm thinking."

"Maybe I don't. But I was at Rose Cottage yesterday and I gave her a week to fix that rat's nest before it's condemned. She'll be gone within days, I figure."

Henry stared at her while he did rapid-fire calculations in his head. "Does anybody else know?"

"Nope. You're first in line. Although..." She swung back on her arms, her fingers still hooked over the window's edge. "There's still that other little problem. I can't ignore it."

"What are you going to do?"

"I have to go to the police. It's my civic duty." Bobbi swung back in and pressed up against the window. "Unless..."

His knuckles turned white on the wheel. "Unless what?"

"Unless you convince me to forget it."

"How much?"

She pulled a card from her hip pocket, slid it over the window, and smiled. Henry grabbed it, read it, and felt the blood drain from his face.

"You can't be serious."

"Ten o'clock. Your place."

He stared at the card, his fingers growing cold.

"By the way"—she pulled a yellow pad from her belt and scribbled on it before ripping off a ticket and handing it over —"your parking meter expired ten minutes ago."

Henry glowered as Bobbi strutted up the sidewalk and disappeared into the 5X Bakery. He tossed the ticket onto the dashboard and pulled out into traffic. One day soon, Bobbi Côté would get hers, and he'd be the first to cheer.

CHAPTER 19

MY SUSPICIONS about Zander and Kate Skalding fled when I pulled up to Rose Cottage to find a tow truck parking a ruined car in the driveway. The ancient Ford Escort looked as if it had weathered a tsunami.

I pulled the pickup over on the shoulder and hopped out. "Hello," I called to the tow-truck driver, who had unhitched the car and was getting back into his cab. "What are you doing?"

He looked up from the clipboard he was carrying. "Verity Hawkes?"

"Yes. Whose car is this?"

"Sign here." He held out the clipboard and a pen. "This vehicle was released by the police, and you're the next of kin. Sorry for your loss." He pushed the clipboard into my hand.

So, this was Aunt Adeline's car. Katsuro had said to expect it, but I'd forgotten. With a numb hand, I signed the form and returned the clipboard. The tow-truck driver ripped off a carbon duplicate and handed it to me. He jumped into his truck and backed out of the driveway.

I stared at the paper, the words blurring in front of me. My aunt's disappearance had never seemed so real. I tried to read the scrawled signatures on the release form, but they were illegible.

I walked over and peered through the car's filthy windows at the mud on the seats. Opening the doors, I rolled down the windows, although the Escort wasn't worth airing out. The front end was crushed, the windshield was cracked, and the front and rear bumpers were gone. A key jutted out from the ignition, stuck in place. Airbags hung limply from the dash.

Inside, the car was dry, but a musty aroma overwhelmed me as I bent in and opened the glove box. It held a ruined automotive manual.

As I stepped away from my aunt's derelict car, I could hear her voice: *When life hands you lemons...*

I marched into the house and headed for the roll-top desk and the stack of papers I had labeled "Insurance." Five minutes later, I was on the phone with Aunt Adeline's agent.

"I'd like to help," he said, "but your aunt had a five-thousand dollar deductible on that old car. It hasn't been worth more than five thousand for quite a while. And since there's no indication that any other vehicle was involved in the crash, there's no basis for a claim."

I swiveled the desk chair to look through the window at the ancient Ford. "Can I get it towed away at least?"

"A tow-truck driver can take it to the nearest junkyard for you. It shouldn't cost more than a hundred dollars."

I hung up the phone and chewed at a ragged cuticle. I couldn't afford to spend a hundred dollars simply to clear the driveway. My aunt's car would stay put for now.

Cock-a-doodle-doo.

I peered out the window again.

Cock-a-doodle-doo.

I had left Reuben's crate in the shade of a spruce tree beside the driveway while I determined where best to put him. Apparently, the new location agreed with him, because he was puffing up his chest for another blast. I'd better tell him to pipe down before Bobbi Côté heard him.

As I opened the front door, a battered blue pickup pulled up behind the Escort. A wiry middle-aged man in a plaid shirt and saggy-bottomed blue jeans emerged from the truck and walked up the porch steps.

"Verity Hawkes?"

"Yes. Can I help you?"

"Carson Breuer." He held out a gnarled hand, which I cautiously shook while eying his split and blackened fingernails. His nose was enormous, with spidery veins crisscrossing its bulbous bulk.

"Nellie said you needed help." He took a step back to appraise the roof and gutters. "Not a moment too soon, looks like." He grinned, displaying crooked teeth. Then he reached into his back pocket, pulled out a flask, and took a swallow. "Coffee," he said as he replaced the flask in his pocket. "I had a late start today."

I was confused for a moment, and then it sank in. "You're the handyman."

"That's correct, ma'am." He winked at me.

"Carson, I don't know if Nellie explained this to you, but I don't have any money at the moment."

"Interesting example," he said, nodding at the house.

"Excuse me?"

"Worker's cottage. Late nineteenth century. Post-and-beam construction, gable roof, built-in gutters, split fieldstone walls. A real beaut." He pulled out the flask for another swig before continuing. "But you knew that, I imagine."

"Uh, no... not all of it. I knew Rose Cottage was old though." I tilted my head back, trying to spot the "built-in gutters."

Carson pointed a twisted thumb at the tacks that made a perfect rectangle on my front door. Bits of yellow paper clung to a few. "Côté's been here," he said.

"Well, yes."

"How long did she give you?"

"A week."

"Then I better get started."

I opened my mouth to protest, but he gave a dismissive wave and turned back to the truck.

"You can pay me later." Over his shoulder, he added, "You don't mind if I park my vehicle in your drive?"

"Of course not."

"I'll go get it." He climbed into the pickup and drove away, dust rising in his wake.

I'll go get it? What was wrong with the truck he was driving? Mystified, I turned to the house. From the corner of my eye, I saw Gideon in the driveway, peering into the windows of my aunt's car.

He looked up as I approached.

I inclined my head at the Ford Escort. "They brought my aunt's car back."

He nodded, his gaze inscrutable behind those blue-tinted glasses. Bending over, he ran a hand under the back wheel well and straightened up. I could have sworn he pocketed something.

"What are you looking for?" I asked.

"Spare key holder."

"It won't do any good. This car will never start again."

"True. Don't know why I bothered."

"I'm glad you're here, Gideon, because I have something to ask. I found an unusual entry in my aunt's journal about Yvonne Skalding. Were they enemies?"

"Enemies?" He snorted. "Why would they be enemies?"

"It looked like—"

My next words were drowned out by the sound of Carson's truck as he backed into the driveway, maneuvering a pop-up tent trailer into place beside my aunt's ruined vehicle. He shut off the truck's engine and hopped out to admire his parking job. "Perfect," he said, rubbing his bulbous nose. He bent to crank open the tent trailer.

"Carson? What's this?" I asked.

He gave me a thumbs-up gesture. "She's a beaut, eh? I been out to the East Coast with this a buncha times."

"And now it's in my driveway?"

"Well, sure, you said I could park it here."

"Are you living in it?"

"Where else?"

My mouth was hanging open, but I seemed unable to close it. I looked to Gideon for assistance.

He was gone. Vanished. Fat lot of help he turned out to be.

Cock-a-doodle-doo.

"Nice rooster," Carson said.

"Thanks. It's a new arrival. He'll have to stay in that crate tonight until I can get a coop built."

"You can't leave that crate outside. Raccoons'll get into it. And then..." Carson drew a finger across his neck.

"Raccoons kill chickens?"

"Any bird they can get. Nasty little creatures. And then there are the coyotes." Carson pulled the flask from his back pocket for a swig.

Seemed a bit late in the day for a caffeine boost.

I stared helplessly around the yard. "Well, where—"

"Why don't you put it in that car?" He gestured at my aunt's ruined vehicle. "Doesn't look like you'll be driving it anywhere. You can close the windows every night to keep out the critters. Won't even need a crate."

Cock-a-doodle-doo.

Carson helped me transfer the rooster to his new home. We threw in the straw from the crate and some feed. Reuben settled right in—after clawing and pecking at my aunt's muddy upholstery. He appeared pleased with his new accommodations.

Stars had winked on in the deepening velvet blue overhead, and the evening air cooled my sunburned cheeks. Before turning in for the night, I glanced over my shoulder from Rose Cottage's porch. Carson's tent glowed yellow in the driveway. High in the walnut tree on the front lawn, beady eyes beamed down at me.

I recalled Carson's words: *Nasty little creatures.* I smiled, knowing Reuben was safe from their nasty ways. My eyes widened. Good grief. I'd adopted a rooster and named him Reuben. What would be next—goats? I paused, recalling the adorable wide eyes, floppy ears, and little-bitty heads of the miniature goats I saw at a fall fair.

With a mental slap, I cleared my mind of livestock and went indoors to make popcorn and type passwords at random.

An hour later, I closed the computer and headed out the door for my first stakeout.

CHAPTER 20

I PARKED my aunt's pickup truck in the alley behind the 5X Bakery and hopped out to join Emy, who was idling her neon yellow Fiat 500. She lowered the driver's side window and leaned her head out. "C'mon, we're late."

I bent down—way down—to reach the window, hesitating at the thought of tucking my five-foot-ten frame into the tiny vehicle. "This is your car?"

"Cute, eh? My brother gave it to me when he moved to London. It's old, but I love it. Get in."

"We could take the truck."

"We can't. It's too loud, remember? And it's too recognizable. Don't worry"—she flicked her hand at the seat beside her and grinned—"there's tons of room."

Almost true. Once I'd moved the seat back, I was nearly comfortable. I settled back for the trip. "Do you think this will work? Have you ever done it before?"

"Me?" Emy chortled. "No, but how hard can it be? I've

seen it on television often enough. Did you bring the binoculars?"

"Yes." I held up the pair I borrowed from Gideon on the pretext that I wanted to go birding. He didn't ask what I expected to see at night. "Did you get the rest?"

"In the back."

I twisted around. Three tractor caps were lined up on the backseat, green leafy foliage attached to each with duct tape.

"Why do we need three?"

"I asked Lorne to come along in case we need help."

I thought of my straight-arrow landscaping assistant with trepidation. "Isn't this a little clandestine for Lorne?"

She shrugged, her expression close to a simper. "We're not doing anything illegal."

I pondered that as Emy pulled the Fiat into the Tim Hortons drive-through lane. My concept of "legal" had been expanding of late.

"Three large double-doubles," Emy said into the microphone.

"Do you want Timbits with that?"

Before Emy could reply, I leaned over the seat toward the speaker. "Yes. The biggest box you have."

We drove through to the window, which slid open to reveal Lorne's toothy grin. So this was the location of his part-time job. I wondered if he and Gideon shared tips on donut display.

"Aren't you ready yet?" Emy asked.

"Two minutes. Meet you out front." He handed her a pressed cardboard tray with three large coffees. A box of Timbits followed.

After running Emy's rewards card through the machine, Lorne handed it back and closed the window.

Emy pulled the Fiat around front. Lorne bolted out the door, still wearing his Tim's uniform and cap. He folded himself into the backseat.

We headed for Peppermint Lane.

About three houses from Yvonne Skalding's, Emy pulled the car onto the shoulder in a spot hidden by overhanging tree branches. "We can walk from here," she said.

With our camouflage caps in place, the box of Timbits under my arm, and each of us holding a coffee, we crept through the branches and into a farmer's field. Then we back-tracked to the Skalding house. Emy led the way, our passage lit by a full moon.

Emy stopped. I ran into her. Lorne ran into me. "Sorry," we whispered to each other. "Sorry."

Emy pointed ahead. "I forgot about the creek."

We contemplated the moonlit water rushing under the bridge. On a whim, I looked about for the mower instructions that were blown from my hand on Upton's hill. No sign of them.

"Should we go back to the road and cross the bridge?" I asked.

Lorne pointed to a series of flat rocks in the water. "We can cross there."

"Good idea," Emy said.

I was dubious. "Guys, I don't think—"

But they were already heading for the rocks, so I followed.

Lorne started across first, stopping frequently to lend

Emy a hand. I kept a wary eye on the whirling eddies around me, my footing uneven on the slimy, moss-covered rocks. It was fine for Emy—she was closer to the ground—and Lorne was a guy, so he was used to derring-do, but one slip and I'd be in the water. Not to mention that I only had one good eye since the other one was still swollen from my close encounter with Reuben.

I winced as cold water sloshed over a rock and soaked my running shoe, nipping at my toes like a hungry piranha. But I couldn't help grinning, too. On a night like this, anything was possible. I hadn't felt that way in quite a while.

We reached the other side and scrambled up the grassy bank, then skulked across the lawn. Hunkering down in a bushy thicket, we sipped coffee and watched the Skaldings' front door.

The first hour was pleasant enough. We finished the coffees and most of the Timbits while chatting about Kate Skalding. I told them about spotting her with Terence Oliver at Paradise Falls Park.

Lorne looked surprised, but Emy nodded. "I've heard rumors about those two," she said. "Terence spends a lot of time here whenever Kate and Zander visit."

I licked powdered sugar from my fingers. The donut holes were delicious, but not as good as Emy's maple-bacon cupcakes. Not to mention the banana cream.

"Do you think Zander knows?"

"I doubt it. The husband's always the last to find out, isn't he?"

We nodded knowingly, even though none of us had any idea if that was true.

The second hour was less pleasant. I shifted to take the pressure off my knees, but the shrubs were so thorny I was soon covered in scratches. The leaves on our camouflage caps began to droop, blocking our vision, and the breeze coming off the creek was too cool for comfort.

"This is harder work than I thought it would be," I said, blowing on my hands to warm them. "On TV, they always do stakeouts in a car."

"Yeah, but those guys have to pee in empty coffee cups," Lorne said as he scrambled back into the thicket.

"TMI, Lorne."

"Sorry."

Emy grabbed my arm. "Look," she whispered. "There's Kate."

I rummaged through the foliage beside me for the binoculars and raised them to my eyes. Kate looked different. "Has she changed her hair?" I asked.

Emy took the binoculars from me and zeroed in on our prey. "She's definitely dolled up." She squealed in excitement. "This is it, Verity. We'll catch her red-handed."

We watched as Kate opened the driver's door of Yvonne's pale blue Volvo and climbed in.

"Come on," Emy whispered, getting to her feet. "We have to follow her."

Lorne wasn't listening. He lifted a hand, pointing with the flashlight.

We followed his gesture and saw two yellow eyes scrutinizing us from fifty feet away. Two *big*, yellow eyes.

"Oh, cheesit," Emy hissed. "It's a coyote. Move."

We burst from the thicket and raced across the lawn to

the creek. Emy and Lorne bounded over the slippery rocks like gazelles. I bounded like a lumbering seal. I was nearly across when an owl hooted in the trees. In my panicked state, it sounded like a coyote. I leaped for the last rock. My foot slipped off the edge, and my arms flailed in the air as I fell back. With a huge splash, I landed butt first in the water.

I sat in cold water up to my chest, the leaves on my camouflage cap dripping over my face. On the bank, Emy and Lorne clapped their hands over their mouths in a feeble attempt to stifle their laughter. I got to my feet with as much decorum as I could muster, waded to the bank, and climbed out. Lorne held out a hand and helped me up the embankment. Once there, I spun around to check the opposite bank.

An Eastern coyote stared back at us from the edge, the fur along his back ruffling in the breeze. I swear his lip curled in amusement. Then, he trotted soundlessly across Henry Upton's lawn and disappeared over a ridge.

Emy and Lorne were doubled over.

I drew myself up to my full height. "What's so funny? I could have been *killed*."

Emy placed a hand on my arm. "Coyotes never attack humans. Well, almost never."

"Then why were we running?"

"Because we have to catch up to Kate. C'mon."

We hustled over to the Fiat. Emy popped the trunk and reached in for a beach towel, which she tossed to me with a grin. "Let's go," she said, sliding behind the wheel.

"*Almost* never?" I muttered, wiping my face with the towel and spreading it across the front passenger seat before climbing in. I continued to mutter, while rubbing my arms to warm up, as we zoomed along the winding road.

At the next stop sign, Emy turned right, toward the village center. A quarter mile farther on, we caught sight of the blue Volvo.

Lorne pointed from the backseat. "There she is."

Emy slowed the Fiat. We followed Kate for another mile until she parked outside a red-brick two-story house on Peebles Street. Emy parked on the opposite side of the road. We watched Kate walk up the sidewalk and knock on the front door. Nudging me, Emy pointed to the bottle of wine in Kate's hand.

Someone opened the door—we couldn't see who—and Kate disappeared inside.

"Whose house is that?" I asked, leaning over the seat well to dry my dripping hair with the beach towel. I corralled my damp locks under the camouflage cap and sat up.

"I don't know. It looks familiar, though," Emy said. "Do you have any idea, Lorne?"

"Afraid not."

"We're back to square one, then. Do you think Terence opened the door?" I asked.

"Possibly, but he doesn't live here. He has a walkup on the other side of town." Emy had her cell phone in her hand, searching for the address. "A Margery Marshall lives here," she said. "Her name's familiar, but I can't remember why."

"She could be a friend who lets them use her place for their rendezvous," I suggested. "A walkup in somebody's home isn't the ideal spot for an illicit tryst."

"Could be, but how will we find out?"

"We'll have to stay here all night."

In the cramped backseat, Lorne cleared his throat. "We didn't bring the empty coffee cups."

Emy and I twisted in our seats and looked at him. He held up his hands and looked away.

"Lorne has a point," Emy said. "We can't spend the night here. There must be another way." She studied the house. "The curtains are closed, so we can't look in the windows."

"There's a window on this side, near the front, without a curtain," I said. "It's between floors, so it must face the staircase landing. I bet we could see the living room from there."

"Can you reach that high?"

"I think so."

We closed the Fiat's doors as quietly as we could and nonchalantly crossed the street one at a time, gathering under the side window of our target. By standing on my tiptoes, I reached the concrete sill with my fingertips, but there was no way I could heave myself up high enough to look through.

"Lorne, help me."

He leafed his hands together and held them out, palms up. I hesitated before placing my foot on them, recalling Emy's insistence that this wasn't illegal. We weren't breaking in, but there must be a law to discourage people from peering into their neighbors' windows. Oh, well. Katsuro could add it to my rap sheet.

I heaved myself up with my fingers gripping the sill, my left foot in Lorne's cupped hands. My other scrabbled for a foothold on the brick.

"Can you see anything?" Lorne whispered.

"Not yet." I narrowed my good eye, the one Reuben

hadn't gotten to yet, and swept my gaze along the stairs and between the balusters. I could see a door that led into the living room. Kate stood there, her back to me.

My fingers were going numb.

"Anything yet?" Lorne asked, grunting. His feet slid on the damp grass, and my foot wavered in the air.

"Hold steady," I hissed.

Kate stepped through the door and into the living room, clearing my line of sight. I saw feet, more feet, knees, and a circle of chairs. "There's a whole crowd in there," I blurted.

Lorne lost his footing and toppled back, leaving my left foot flailing in the air. My fingers lost their grip, and I let out a shriek as I fell back on the lawn.

I lay there with my eyes shut and the breath knocked out of me, wet leaves trailing over my face from the camouflage cap.

The front door burst open, and footsteps thundered along the walk. The footsteps stopped.

I opened my eyes. The fourteen members of Leafy Hollow's Original Book Club—plus Kate Skalding—stared down at me.

"I'm Verity Hawkes."

They nodded. Then fourteen voices said in unison:

"Adeline's niece."

CHAPTER 21

BOBBI CÔTÉ KILLED the lights on her candy-apple red Mustang as she drove up Henry Upton's winding driveway. She pulled onto the lawn beside the garage, out of view from the road, and checked her watch. Ten o'clock. Right on time.

She walked up to the front entrance and pushed the buzzer. It rang inside the house, a ridiculous Westminster chime that went on and on. After pushing the buzzer again, she backed up a few steps to scan the second-floor windows. They were as dark as the windows on the ground floor.

"Where the blast are you?" she muttered, and then stepped up and rang the buzzer again before slapping her palm against the doorframe in frustration.

She scanned the darkened yard. With tonight's full moon, she was visible from the road. Better to wait by the car.

Leaning up against the Mustang, she took a cigarette from the pack in her pocket and lit it while studying the Skalding house at the bottom of the hill. A light came on in the kitchen at the back, and then went out. Probably Kate, seeking a nightcap. Imogen West, Skalding's housekeeper, lived over the jewelry store downtown, next door to Bobbi's apartment over the hardware shop. Bobbi often grilled her for information on the Skalding household.

Not that she provided many answers. When Imogen moved in five years earlier, Bobbi popped over to invite her for a drink at Kirby's. Imogen turned her down. A café latte at Tim's was the most she would agree to. But while Bobbi waited for Imogen to gather up her coat and purse, she asked to use the bathroom. The ruse allowed a quick detour into Imogen's bedroom, where she scanned the photos on display and rifled through the documents on the bureau, cell phone camera at the ready.

If Imogen noticed that her papers had been disturbed, she never mentioned it. In Bobbi's experience, no one ever did. The photo of a girl holding a baby that Bobbi found on Imogen's nightstand, in a kitschy frame labeled "Souvenir of Leeds," meant nothing to her. She took a snapshot anyway. Like the pieces of a puzzle, it might fit into a larger picture someday. Imogen was clean, but her employer wasn't. Bobbi could smell it.

Bobbi exhaled a stream of smoke, then dropped the lit cigarette into the lawn and ground it out with her foot. Might as well look inside Henry's garage while she waited. She walked over to the side door, fingering a set of metal lock-picking tools in her pocket, expecting to find the door secured. But the handle rotated in her hand as she turned it. Bobbi shut the door and waited for her eyes to adjust to the moonlight coming in through the front windows. Tarpaulin-covered piles at the back cast ghostly images in the half-light, but the wooden crates closer to the front caught her eye first.

She ran a hand over the nearest crate. The lid resisted her attempt to pry it open, so she walked over to the far wall and lifted a crowbar down from the pegboard over the workbench. When she tested it against her hand, the metal came down on her palm with a satisfying thwack. Should do nicely. After grabbing a flashlight off the workbench, she returned to the crate.

The corners were nailed in place. She slid the crowbar's thinnest edge into a crack between the boards and bent it back. The wooden slats cracked and splintered. After she'd repeated the process on the other corners, she yanked out the isolated nails with the crowbar's V-shaped end.

A breeze whispered across her neck, as if someone had opened a door. With the crowbar hanging from her hand, Bobbi looked over at the side exit. "Henry?"

The door was shut, and she was alone in the garage. She hadn't heard the Hummer's engine outside, so Upton couldn't be back yet.

Rubbing the back of her neck, she swept the flashlight's beam around the room. "Anybody here?"

The flashlight lit up the tarp-covered piles that jammed the space, but nothing else. After propping the light nearby so it shone on the crate, she returned to her task. Once she freed the lid, she propped the crowbar against the box and pried up the top.

With both hands, she brushed away packing material, revealing stacked bags of weed 'n' feed. She hauled a fifteen-kilogram bag out of the way to check the next layer. More weed 'n' feed. After moving enough bags to see to the bottom, she stepped back in disgust, puffing from the exertion. Now she had to put those bags back. She directed her gaze to the stacked piles deeper in the garage. First, she'd take a look at those.

She zigzagged between the stacks with the flashlight in one hand, flipping up tarps as she passed. There was nothing interesting. Old furniture, posters, stacked paint tins, rusted lawn furniture, boxes of clothing—

Bobbi never felt the crowbar that landed on her skull with a crack. She dropped to the floor, bouncing off a crate on the way down, and lay motionless on the concrete surface.

The crowbar drew back and slammed into her head twice more.

CHAPTER 22

"BOBBI CÔTÉ IS MISSING? How do you know?" I stared at Emy from across the tiny table in 5X Bakery, a cheddar scone crumbling in my clenched fingers.

"She didn't show up for work today, and there's no answer at her apartment."

"Is that unusual for her?"

"She never misses a shift, according to Mom's friend at Town Hall. Bobbi arrives late sometimes, especially when she's hung over, but she always comes in." Emy leaned against the table and lowered her voice. "Mom's friend thinks Bobbi never books off because she's fiddling with town records and doesn't want anyone to find out."

That seemed dubious. Bobbi was a bylaw officer—not much scope for embezzlement there. "She doesn't handle money for the town, does she?"

"No idea. She drops by here for cupcakes, but we don't discuss anything other than the weather and how overworked she is." Emy gestured impatiently at the portal that connected her shops. "And my illegal door."

I had dropped by the bakery to apologize for getting Emy into trouble with her mother, but the news of Bobbi's disappearance temporarily pushed regrets over our book-club misadventure into the background.

"It makes me nervous, not knowing where she is," I said. "What if she's in Strathcona getting legal clearance to lower the boom on Rose Cottage?"

"She gave you a week, Verity. I doubt that's changed."

"She didn't put it in writing." I narrowed my eyes at Emy's dubious door. "I'd better go back to Rose Cottage and check on Carson. See how the roof's coming."

"At least tell me what you came in for." Emy made a mock-tragic face. "Unless you only like me for my cupcakes."

"Of course not. I'm fond of your scones, too."

Emy stuck out her tongue.

"I do want your mom's phone number, though."

"Sure," she said, pulling her phone from her apron pocket. "But why do you need it?"

I forged ahead with my white lie. "I want to apologize for last night." Wincing, I again relived the ten-minute tongue-lashing by Thérèse Dionne we had endured the previous evening. It only ended when I professed curiosity about the book club. I left loaded down with copies of their next three selections.

"Again? It's not necessary, you know. As soon as Mom heard that you were interested in the book club, she practically glowed. Nice work, by the way." Emy held out her phone, and I copied the number.

"Thanks. And while we're on the subject of the book club, why didn't you warn us about the meeting at Margery Marshall's? We walked into a trap last night."

Emy looked sheepish as she tucked the phone back into her pocket. "I didn't know about it. I'm not a member of the book club."

"What?" I slapped both hands on the table and leaned in. "How did I get roped in, then?"

Emy winced. "I know. I'm sorry. Mom gives me a pass because I get up at four a.m. to start baking for the day. You"—she pointed a finger—"don't have that excuse."

I spluttered a bit, but I had no comeback for that. Muttering, I pushed the scone around on my plate.

"What is it?" she asked. "Something wrong with my scones?"

"Well... they're a little dry. You should add more cream to that recipe."

"They are not dry." Emy leaned over to give my arm a playful tap. "Come on, tell me what's up."

"Okay, but I doubt I'll be able to eat more than two or three of these," I said, cramming the last of the scone into my mouth. I delicately dabbed at my lips with the napkin.

"Stop acting so prissy and tell me what's up."

"Prissy? Have you never seen ladylike behavior?"

"Not from you, that's for sure."

We grinned at each other as I settled back in my chair. "I've been thinking about Henry Upton. He's up to something, I'm sure of it. I want to check it out."

The smile that tugged at Emy's lips blossomed into a full-blown grin. She pumped a hand in the air. "Yes. Another stakeout. When?"

"Tonight."

Her shoulders sagged. "I can't. Mom made me promise to attend tonight's book club meeting."

"Wait a minute. You just said you're not a member."

"I'm not," she insisted. "But the club hasn't been able to get to the end of this month's meeting. Mom wants to keep an eye on me. To make sure they aren't interrupted this time." Her eyes flashed in merriment as she raised the teacup to her lips.

"Serves you right. If I recall correctly, that means you have to read *The Woman in White*. Six hundred pages, isn't it?"

"Not a problem." Emy settled her cup onto its saucer. "I checked out the DVD at the library this morning."

I gasped, but before I could reply, Emy held up a finger. "Not. One. Word."

We giggled through the rest of our scones.

Once my plate was empty, I pushed it away with a sigh. "It's a good thing that you can't come along, because it's a dumb idea."

"No, it's not. Stop saying that." With a sympathetic glance, Emy picked up the teapot and refilled my cup.

I'd forgotten how reassuring a confidante could be. I hadn't had a real friend since Matthew died. That wasn't surprising, since I turned my back on everyone during those two years, lost in my grief. Still, there was no one in Vancouver I missed, not really—except my neighbor Patty, who had texted me several times since my arrival:

STAY HYDRATED, VERITY!

STRANGE SMELL IN HALLWAY. PROBABLY DOPE.

SENDING RECIPE FOR MUSTARD JELLY ROLL. YUM!

I grinned at the memory of the smiley faces and emojis on those messages. Hopefully, Emy would visit me in Vancouver, so I could introduce her to Patty—and Clark, if he looked up from the television long enough. But that was in the future.

For now, something was going on in Upton's huge house, and I was itching to find out what. But I wasn't crazy enough to try it alone. Not with Yvonne's murderer on the loose.

Emy replaced the teapot on its trivet. "Why don't you ask Ryker to go with you?"

I sat back in my chair and stared at her, dumbfounded. "Ryker Fields, the landscaper?"

"Yes, Ryker Fields the landscaper. Don't act coy with me, Verity. He's perfect. You need a good strong man for this."

"He's strong, I'll give you that, but I don't think he's all that good. Anyway—"

Emy cut me off. "Ryker is good. You don't know him. Besides, it's a shame to waste those supermodel looks of yours."

"I look like a giraffe. That doesn't make me a supermodel."

"Stop being so modest. You two would get along great, and you're in the same business. It's perfect. You need to get out there, Verity."

I looked down at the tablecloth to hide the twitch in my eyes and toyed with my butter knife as the silence lengthened. When I looked up, Emy was grimacing.

"Gawd, that was insensitive," she said. "I'm sorry. I know it's only been two years. I'm an idiot."

"Don't apologize. It's fine."

She still looked stricken.

"But a scone would make it even better," I added.

Emy jumped up to retrieve yet another baked good—maple toffee this time—and placed it in front of me. I tucked in. I didn't need the extra calories, but this was an emergency.

Her face brightened. "I know. Let's ask Lorne again."

"I'm sure Lorne has sworn off investigating, after that pasting we got from your mother."

"Oh, he'll do it if I ask him," Emy said, picking up her cell phone and dialing.

I solemnly nodded. "He certainly will."

Emy pressed the phone against her chest to muffle her words. "Stop that. Lorne and I are just friends." She raised the phone to her ear. "Hi, it's me. Can you drop by the bakery? Verity and I have a proposition for you." A pause. "See you then."

She clicked off the call and gave me a thumbs-up. "He'll be here in ten minutes."

———

Lorne and I waited in Emy's Fiat up the road from the Upton house, parked under overhanging branches to shade us from the afternoon sun. I fiddled with the CD player, but the controls eluded me, even after we'd retrieved the manual from the glove box. I watched Lorne blunder through the instructions. At least he had them right side up this time.

"Let's forget the radio," I said from behind the wheel. "We should probably be quiet anyway."

With a sigh of relief, Lorne put the manual back and snapped the glove box shut.

"Lorne, do you have a driver's license?"

He chuckled, displaying the gap in his front teeth. "Not exactly."

"Did you lose it for some reason? One night you had a bit too much to—"

"No, I'd never do that." He plucked at his jeans with his fingers. "That's not why."

"Then how—"

"Look." He pointed to Upton's driveway. The yellow Hummer was almost at the road.

I switched on the Fiat's ignition, ready to swerve off the shoulder and follow as soon as Upton turned onto Peppermint Lane to head into the village.

But he went the other way, toward the highway, driving right by us. We ducked as the Hummer roared past. After waiting a few seconds, we pulled out to trail him. Upton travelled the ten miles to the turnoff at quite a clip. If he drove that much over the speed limit on the highway, we'd have trouble trailing him in the sluggish Fiat.

We bumped over the ruts and potholes in the pavement and reached the turnoff in time to see the Hummer veer onto the ramp. We followed.

I was right. Upton sped along at well over one hundred and twenty kilometers an hour, despite the posted one hundred kilometer limit. Even at that, he was far from the zippiest vehicle on the road. Cars and trucks whipped by, each one rattling the Fiat's rolled-down windows. The air conditioning controls suggested cool air was a possibility, but that was apparently a practical joke devised by some hilarious Italian engineer. Sweat trickled down my neck as I struggled to handle Emy's Fiat on the curves. More than once, I lost sight of the Hummer when I slowed to take a curve and faster traffic veered around us.

Over the next two hours, shopping malls and subdivisions gave way to orchards and vineyards. Rows of grape vines stretched off on our right, full and glossy in the summer sun. Lake Ontario's blue-gray waves sparkled on our left. It would have been a tranquil drive, except that my cramped fingers gripped the wheel so tightly my knuckles were white as I struggled to keep sight of the Hummer.

We veered right, following the Niagara River. When we reached Fort Erie, Upton took the exit for Buffalo and the U.S. border. I thumped the steering wheel in frustration. "I didn't bring my passport, did you?"

Lorne shook his head.

At the next exit, I veered off and pulled into a gas station next to a Tim Hortons for a fill-up and an early dinner. "I have to get out of this car for a while," I said. "Even my bones are rattled."

Inside, I ordered chili and a coffee, double-double, from a young server with a "trainee" tag on her uniform. When Lorne asked for the turkey soup, the server hesitated over the register.

"Third row, fifth over," Lorne said.

"Thanks." She punched in our order.

We sat by the front window with our meal.

"You're good with the order screen," I said. "How did you do that upside down?"

"I memorized it," he said, tearing his dinner roll into pieces, "when I got the job at Tim's."

I stared at him, with my spoon dripping chili. "Wrong side up? Does everybody do that?"

"No. Only me."

I kept my thoughts to myself.

After lunch, we savored our coffee, reluctant to start the cramped and overheated journey home. A flash of yellow in the parking lot caught my eye. I turned to the window. Henry Upton's Hummer was pulling up to the drive-through.

We dashed to the Fiat.

Upton travelled straight back to Leafy Hollow, parked the Hummer outside his garage, and went into the house.

Lorne and I left the Fiat near our previous spot. We scuttled through the shrubs by the creek in deepening twilight. I looked around for the coyote. No sign of him. He'd probably moved on now that Reuben was gone.

We hid in a thicket close to the house and settled in to wait. Hours later, we were still there.

"I think he's in for the night, Lorne. We should leave."

"No, we should stay. I don't think you did it, you know."

"Did what?"

"You know, the murder."

"Oh good grief, Lorne. Of course I didn't do it."

"I know. That's what I said. But Emy told me you're trying to prove your innocence, and I want to help you. So, we should wait until Upton comes out."

I focused on the middle part of his speech. "You want to help me?"

"Of course I do. I like you, Verity. So does Emy. I think Ryker does, too. And Gideon."

I blinked rapidly, trying to absorb this. That was quite a few people who liked me—a stranger "with no ties" who'd lived in their village only five days. I looked away, biting my lip.

Lorne shook my arm. "He's on the move."

Upton came out the front door, leaving it open, then walked to the garage. He clicked on the remote in his hand to open one of the bay doors. It slid up, revealing the stacked boxes and barrels I'd seen earlier when I peered in through the side window.

He disappeared inside.

A few minutes later, he came back out, guiding a motorized handcart. It held a lumpy package, five feet long and wrapped in black plastic. We watched as he dragged the package off the cart and into the Hummer through the vehicle's open back door. Part of the package dangled over the edge. Upton climbed up into the back to pull it inside, then clambered out and closed the Hummer's door. He scanned the vicinity.

We ducked, holding our breath, when he swept his gaze over our thicket.

Upton took the cart back into the garage, and the light went out.

"He's gone through into the house," Lorne said.

Two minutes after that, Upton's bulky frame blocked the light streaming out the open front door. He stuck his head out, looked around, and closed the door. The light in the living room went out.

We waited until an upstairs light came on before leaving the shrubbery.

"We have to take a look in that Hummer," I said. "That package was the right size for..." I didn't want to finish that thought, which was ridiculous. Bobbi Côté was missing, but there was no reason to think she was dead.

Lorne's voice in my ear startled me out of my reluctance. "A body?"

"So I'm not foolish to think that?"

"We should call the police."

"And tell them what? That Henry Upton has a body in his Hummer? I'm in enough trouble with Katsuro as it is."

I returned my gaze to the silent house. Even if Upton wanted Yvonne Skalding dead to smooth the way for a real estate deal, why would he kill Bobbi Côté?

The upstairs light went out, leaving the yard in semi-darkness, with only the moon to light the driveway. If we left, Upton might come out later and drive away with the body. Then the evidence would be gone. In an instant, I made up my mind. Those self-help books on procrastination must be working.

"Let's take a look."

We crept across the lawn to the Hummer and peered through the windows at the plastic-wrapped package. "Is that long enough for a body?" Lorne asked.

"Definitely." My heart raced. Feeling dizzy, I crouched behind the vehicle, hidden from anyone who might look out the house windows above us. "I still think we should look in the house, though."

We tiptoed around the garage and across the patio. The moonlight streaming through the patio windows and falling in silvery rectangles on the sunroom floor revealed an empty room. No furniture. We sidled around to the front of the house and peered into the great room's soaring windows.

They were uncurtained, affording a clear view of a forty-foot-wide space anchored by a massive stone fireplace on the far wall. A rumpled recliner, a floor lamp, and a modest TV sat in the middle of the gleaming hardwood floor. Electric cords trailed from the lamp and television, joining an extension cord plugged into the wall.

The rest of the room was empty. The passageway at the back showed that the dining room was also empty. No table, no chairs, no anything.

I ducked below the window and crawled away on my hands and knees in what I hoped was an appropriately clandestine manner.

"We're calling the police," I said over my shoulder.

CHAPTER 23

KATSURO and his friends arrived in two cruisers with flashing lights but no sirens, which I found disappointing. They roused Upton and marched him out to the driveway. His massive bulk was decked out in a faded blue T-shirt, pajama bottoms printed with big, red lips, and scuffed leather slippers.

Lorne and I watched, reluctant to reveal our hiding place until Upton was in custody. I craned my neck to see what was happening.

"They're opening the package," I whispered. I chewed on my lip as I watched. Much as I disliked Bobbi Côté, I didn't wish her dead.

Then the OPP constables stood aside. Upton closed the Hummer's back door. Katsuro shook Upton's hand, and the pajama'd hulk strode back into his house, slamming the door with a force that made me start.

Katsuro contemplated the closed door for a full minute

before training his gaze on our shrubbery. Glaring, he headed in our direction.

"I don't like the looks of this," I muttered. "We should run for it."

But there was nowhere to go. Within seconds, he was standing over us with his arms crossed. Reluctantly, we emerged from our leafy bower.

I plunged in, hoping to distract him. "What did you find? What was in the package?"

"Weed killer. Mr. Upton travels to Buffalo to purchase weed killer and other prohibited lawn products."

I gaped at him. "But that package was huge."

"He resells these products to other Leafy Hollow residents. He gave us a list."

So, it wasn't a body. But still. "That's illegal, isn't it?"

"It's illegal to use it, not buy it, which you can do in New York State, no questions asked."

A constable walked up to Katsuro. "Jeff, we're heading back."

"Right behind you." Katsuro directed his scowl at my comrade-in-sleuthing. "I'm surprised at you, Lorne. This one"—he flicked his thumb at me—"doesn't know when to stop, but you never should have agreed to this."

Lorne studied the ground. "Verity would have come alone." He looked up at Katsuro. "I didn't think that was a good idea."

I felt as if I was back in Miss Lefebvre's fifth-grade class after a scuffle with a sixth grader dumb enough to ask me, "How's the weather up there?" I sensed my excuses wouldn't work on this occasion, either, so I kept my mouth shut. Which was not easy.

Katsuro walked to his cruiser and drove away.

Beside me, Lorne chuckled. I looked at him in surprise.

"Wait till the book club hears about this," he said. "A weed-killer ring in Leafy Hollow? The names on that list will be all over town by tomorrow."

He was still chuckling when we regained the Fiat and headed for home.

After dropping Lorne off, I parked Emy's Fiat behind the bakery and climbed into my aunt's truck. At Rose Cottage, I pulled the truck into the driveway and left it there, too tired to unload it. I'd deal with it tomorrow.

Inside the house, I switched on the kettle and went into the bedroom to slip into my favorite pajamas, the ones with tabby cats marching across the butt. I thought Tom would appreciate them if he ever came back. Then I settled onto the sofa with a cup of tea on the table beside me, my feet up on the coffee table, and my aunt's laptop on my knees. I was determined to crack the password.

I opened the laptop and peered at the screen with my lips pursed. *Password, password, what is the password?* I took a sip of tea and put the cup down. For fun, I typed in tea varieties, starting with Oolong—a name I'd always considered awesome. As a child, I used to go through my aunt's house chanting *Oooooo-looong* in my deepest voice, trying to sound like a doorbell.

It didn't work. I sipped my tea. A screen saver came on, and I watched languidly as famous garden quotes floated across the laptop's screen.

The earth laughs in flowers. —Ralph Waldo Emerson

A weed is but an unloved flower. —Ella Wheeler Wilcox

If you have a garden and a library, you have everything you need. —Cicero

I snapped to attention. *Cicero.* Famous Roman orator, politician, philosopher—and creator of some of my mother's favorite word puzzles. *Ave?* I knew what it meant, and I was an idiot for not thinking of it sooner. I had even memorized it as a child so I could print it on a card and give it to my mother as a shared joke. I had mailed a similar card to my aunt, certain she would be impressed.

Ave was a rebus puzzle, a mental pictogram. *Mitto tibi navem prora puppique carentem.* In English: *I send you a ship without a bow or a stern.* The Latin word for ship, *navem*, becomes *ave* if you remove the first and last letters—the bow and the stern. Thus, *I send you greetings.* It's a terrific joke if you're ten years old and annoyingly precocious.

I pulled the laptop toward me and typed *mitto-tibi-navem*, paused to say a prayer, and then clicked the "enter" key. The laptop sprang into life. I thrust my hands in the air. "Ha," I yelled. "Gotcha."

My exhaustion forgotten, I scanned the directory that listed my aunt's thousands of files. A quick search for "Control" came up blank, but it would take me weeks to go through the files one at a time. Should I start tonight, or leave it for the morning when I would be fresher?

A brief siren blast cut my deliberation short. I slid the

laptop to one side and rose to draw the curtains. I stared in disbelief. Three police cruisers with flashing lights were parked outside Rose Cottage. Katsuro emerged from the lead vehicle and headed in my direction.

Good grief, what now?

I threw open the door. "Come to give me another scolding?"

Behind Katsuro, an officer walked over to my aunt's truck. He unlatched the back door and stepped up into the bed.

I pointed at him with a gust of irritation. "What's he doing?"

The officer straightened. "Jeff, over here."

With a loud sigh of annoyance, I followed Katsuro to the truck. Which of my aunt's tools did he intend to confiscate this time? In the driveway, I leaned over the truck bed and looked in.

Bobbi Côté lay on her back, her eyes frozen open and her lips a cold blue.

I staggered back, my hands clapped over my mouth. Then I vomited all over Jeff Katsuro's shiny black shoes.

CHAPTER 24

OUTSIDE ROSE COTTAGE, the flashing lights of five cruisers and an ambulance lit up the road like Hollywood Boulevard. Curious neighbors emerged from their houses to rubberneck at the white-suited men studying Bobbi's body in the truck bed.

Inside, I shrank into an armchair with my head in my hands. I looked up as Katsuro held out a mug of coffee and took it from him with a grateful nod. "You can't seriously think I killed Bobbi."

Katsuro sat on the sofa and took out his notebook while I sipped the coffee.

"Where were you this evening, Miss Hawkes?"

"You know that. I was with Lorne Lewins. We followed Henry Upton to the border and back and then sat outside his house. And later, we phoned you."

"Was your truck unattended at any point?"

"All evening. I parked it outside the 5X Bakery."

"And you didn't notice the body in the back?"

"I think I would have mentioned it, don't you? How did you know about it?"

"Tell me about your relationship with Bobbi Côté."

"We didn't have a relationship. She threatened to condemn my aunt's cottage, and I was angry about it, but I didn't kill her." I placed my half-empty mug on the coffee table.

"What about Ryker Fields?"

"What about him?"

"Did you and Bobbi fight over him?"

I stared at him. "That narcissistic self-righteous know-it-all? I'm not the slightest bit interested in Ryker Fields. That's ridiculous."

"That's a strong response."

I picked up the mug and raised it to my lips. "Do you have any real questions?"

He shut the notebook and got to his feet. "I'm afraid we have to confiscate your truck."

"You can't. I need it."

"I'm sorry, but forensics has to go over it."

"How did Bobbi die?"

"The coroner suspects blunt force trauma."

"What kind of weapon?"

"We don't know yet."

I followed him to the door. At the entrance, he gave me a searching look with those dark eyes.

"I don't know what you hoped to accomplish by tailing Kate Skalding and Henry Upton, but don't do anything like that again."

"I know it was stupid, and I'm sorry, but I'd never been a

suspect in so much as a shoplifting case until I got here. I haven't done anything wrong. I haven't."

Katsuro stared over my head while he collected his thoughts. He really was tall. I waited.

"Verity, you're a person of interest in two homicides. I doubt you killed Bobbi Côté, but somebody did. Then they dumped the body in your truck and reported it. Until we find out who that was, you could be in danger."

I swallowed hard. "I understand."

"No more investigating. Leave this to the police."

I followed him onto the porch and watched as the tow-truck operator hitched up my empty pickup and drove off with it. Bobbi's body had been taken away in the ambulance.

Katsuro walked back to his cruiser, stopping to stare at the pop-up trailer in my driveway. Carson stuck his head out the trailer's door with a glass in his hand and a cigarette dangling from his lips. He gave us a wave.

Glancing over his shoulder at me, Katsuro raised his eyebrows. Then he climbed into his cruiser and drove away.

I went into the house, locked the front and back doors, and headed for the bathroom to draw a hot bath. Given the state of my aunt's hot-water heater, I had to settle for luke-warm. I lowered myself into the tepid water, and leaned my head back against the claw-footed tub, trying to calm my nerves. But as soon as I closed my eyes, I saw Bobbi Côté's blue-tinged skin and vacant stare. My eyes popped open with a shudder. All these years, I pictured Leafy Hollow as a tranquil respite from the modern world when it was actually a refuge for bloodthirsty barbarians. And now my own life might be in danger, according to Katsuro.

At least he didn't think I killed Bobbi—or maybe he did, and that was a strategy to put me off my guard. I wrapped myself in a bath towel and studied my sunburned, swollen face in the mirror while the tub drained. From somewhere deep within, I heard Matthew's voice.

It had been after our first hiking expedition together when I looked almost as battered as I did today. I was counting my bruises in the bathroom mirror when Matthew brushed up against me, warm and damp from his shower, and dropped a kiss on the top of my head. I loved that he was tall enough to do that.

"You're a klutz, aren't you, Verity?"

I twisted to face him, pressing my body against his. "Are you saying I'm clumsy?"

"Not at all. The word I would use," he said, wrapping his arms around me and smiling, "is goofy." He lowered his lips to mine.

Now, alone in Rose Cottage's bathroom, a sob tore at my throat, and I slumped onto the tub's edge, wiping tears from my eyes. Nothing had been the same since Matthew. My life was upside down, and the one person who could right it was gone forever, leaving me blubbering into a hand towel in my aunt's hot water-less bathroom.

At this point in my pity party, I normally took to my bed to re-read *Life is a Jigsaw: How to Pick up the Pieces*. But not this time. The last few days in Leafy Hollow had been grim, but they'd also given me new purpose. I straightened up, rolled the towel into a ball, and slammed it into the hamper. Two points.

After climbing into a fresh pair of pajamas, I headed for

the living room. The police had put Coming Up Roses on hold by confiscating my aunt's truck and lawnmower, but I still had her laptop and journal. I pulled the worn leather volume from her desk and took it to the armchair, where I settled in with a cup of tea. I was alone, but I wouldn't be lonely as long as I could hear my aunt's voice echoing in my head.

After reading her journal for an hour, I came across a section that caused my undamaged eyebrow to hit the ceiling. The heading was succinct:

The Murder Garden

A list of plants followed, coded to a diagram of a garden bed. Next to *Aconitum napellus*, monkshood, my aunt had noted:

'Eating the roots can cause death by asphyxiation. Handling it without gloves can cause numbness and arrhythmia. Its vivid indigo-blue flowers often attract novice gardeners. Those who want to survive the novice phase should steer clear.'

For *Datura stramonium*, or Jimson weed:

'Such beautiful, six-inch, white or purple trumpet-shaped flowers! Shame about the highly toxic seeds that can cause hallucinations, coma, and death. Not called 'Devil's trumpet' for nothing.'

I studied the planting diagram, hair lifting on the back of my neck. Could these "murder garden" residents be among my aunt's plants?

I pulled a cardigan over my pajamas, walked through the kitchen, and reached out to unlock the back door. At a loud thud outside, I pulled my hand back and flipped on the porch light, my heart racing. There was a sound best described as skittering, followed by high-pitched chattering, and then a clatter. Either aliens were visiting Rose Cottage, or the raccoons had arrived.

I threw open the back door. Shriveled green peas rolled across the porch from the overturned compost pail. I bent to pick up the pail and shrieked as something brushed against my leg.

Meeoow.

"Don't scare me like that," I gasped, my hand clapped to my chest.

The one-eyed silver tabby regarded me gravely. At least he was company.

"Want to go for a walk, Tom?" I stepped off the porch and into the back garden. The cat followed as I strolled through the beds. In the moonlight's ghostly glow, the plants seemed to be animated. A vine sprang out and slapped me in the face. I stepped back in fright. Then I moved on, chuckling to myself. I was definitely overwrought. Finding a body in your truck could do that to you.

At the foot of the garden, a yew tree hedge and a rusted wrought-iron gate enclosed a square area about twenty by twenty feet. With a creak, the gate swung open at my touch, and I stepped through. My bare feet caught on a rough flagstone underfoot. I looked down, and then dropped to my knees to brush away dead leaves so I could make out the letters cut into the surface of the stone. My blood ran cold as I read the words.

THE MURDER GARDEN

Sitting back on my haunches, I looked around the

enclosed space. The most aggressive of the plants had twined to the top of their arbors and metal towers and were smothering their neighbors. Other plants were dried up and obviously dead. The Murder Garden had been abandoned some time ago.

The cat brushed against me, purring, as I brushed the dead leaves back over the name. I was certain this garden was my aunt's idea of a joke, but why take chances?

"I think we should keep this to ourselves, don't you, Tom?"

We headed back to the house.

Thirty feet from the back door, a dark shape stepped out in front of us. My heart leaped into my throat, cutting off my breath.

"Verity? What are you doing out here?" Gideon stepped out from under a lilac and into the moonlight.

"What am I doing here?" I sputtered, gasping for air. "You scared me half to death. What are you doing here?"

"Keeping an eye on you."

"Who asked you to do that?"

"Jeff Katsuro."

The cat twisted between my feet, still purring.

"You should stay indoors, especially at night," Gideon said.

"House arrest? What for? I've done nothing wrong."

He rubbed a hand across his face. "Your aunt is gone. Two people are dead. Isn't that reason enough?"

I took a quick step toward him. "Do you think my aunt's disappearance is connected to the murders?"

"No, but..." He appeared to be struggling for words. "Adeline was reckless. Always. Don't follow in her footsteps."

He strode off, parted a few branches, and, in seconds, had disappeared in the shrubs. The man was a regular stealth machine.

I turned back to the porch, where Tom was washing his face. When Bobbi threatened to condemn my aunt's house, she mentioned "vermin." At last, a problem I could solve.

I opened the back door. "What do you say, Tom? Ready to move in?"

He strolled through, tail waving, to take up his usual position by the kitchen counter.

"I'll take that as a yes," I said, closing the door and opening the cupboard where I'd stashed half a dozen cans of *Feline Fritters.*

While Tom chowed down on his midnight snack, I reviewed the murder suspects. "No more investigating," Katsuro had said. He couldn't ban thinking though. One thought kept recurring—an offhand comment by Imogen West, the Skaldings' housekeeper.

He watches this house.

What had Henry Upton seen through his binoculars? Could it have been Zander or Kate—or both—rigging the ladder? What if he came up with a blackmail scheme that would fill his empty house with furniture? But Kate didn't want to pay, hence the argument with Zander that Imogen overheard.

I was new at detecting, but it seemed like a watertight case to me. Given the night's events, however, I hesitated to call Katsuro with my theory. Also, it didn't account for Bobbi's murder.

Could two murderers be stalking Leafy Hollow citizens? I regarded the back door lock uneasily. Maybe so, but in my attempt to determine who might want both Yvonne Skalding and Bobbi Côté dead, I came up with only one name.

Verity Hawkes.

CHAPTER 25

MY PROMISE TO stop investigating the Leafy Hollow murders gave me more time to search for my aunt. The next morning I sat at her desk, equipped with a double-double, and opened the laptop.

Tom watched from the sofa, his tail twitching to show he was on the alert for vermin. After fifteen minutes of heightened vigilance, he flopped back on the cushions and closed his one eye, basking in a job well done. I pictured rodents chuckling behind the baseboards.

I combed through sub-directories for half an hour without success. Then I pushed the laptop away, unable to concentrate. I couldn't shake the memory of Bobbi Côté's cold blue body. Physical labor might help, but, for that, I'd need a functioning truck and lawnmower.

I called my aunt's insurance agent, expecting to be rebuffed again.

Instead, he told me that Aunt Adeline had business insurance. "There's enough coverage to rent any equipment you need. I'll call the rental place and tell them you're on your way."

Two hours later, Lorne and I were admiring a brand-new rental pickup—it even had air conditioning, a welcome bonus. A brand-new rental mower sat in the back. We drove the truck to Rose Cottage and loaded it with gardening tools. But we left my aunt's aluminum ladder behind so Carson could start repairs.

As we pulled out of the driveway, I glanced up at the roof.

Carson, a cigarette hanging from his lips, was chipping off broken shingles and tossing them onto the ground at a steady pace. So far, he hadn't noticed that I'd emptied his flask when he wasn't looking and filled it with real coffee.

Or maybe he had. I winced as a cedar shingle crashed onto the sole remaining azalea.

Tom, refreshed by his catnap, observed the handyman's progress from the ground. Possibly, he hoped the activity would spook a squirrel into falling prostrate at his feet. I liked his initiative if not his chances. From time to time, Tom cast a hungry glance at Reuben, who was pecking and strutting his way across the lawn. I scratched the scab on my gashed eyebrow, confident that Tom was out of luck there.

Lorne and I pulled up outside the first address on our list for the day, a ranch house with yellow siding and, along the drive, a fifty-foot-long overgrown cedar hedge in need of pruning. Silk flowers twined through a grape vine wreath on the front door. When I pushed the button, the doorbell played a jaunty reel.

A middle-aged woman with a pleasant expression opened the door. "Yes?"

"How do you do?" I extended my hand. "I'm Verity Hawkes, here to cut your lawn."

Her smile disappeared. "It doesn't need cutting."

I glanced over my shoulder. "Are you sure? It looks a little long."

"It's fine, thank you." She started to close the door but paused long enough to add, with a scowl, "Except that now, it will be full of weeds."

She shut the door in my face.

I returned to the truck and twisted the key in the ignition.

"Aren't we staying?" Lorne asked.

I shook my head and drove to the next address.

After two more refusals, my superb investigative skills detected a pattern. The day that dawned with such promise was turning to dust in my mouth. I pulled the truck onto the shoulder and rested my forehead on the steering wheel.

"It's not personal, Verity," Lorne said. "Try the next name on your list. Mrs. Farrier is a long-time client. Then we can wrap it up for today."

With a heavy heart, I pulled out onto the road.

Mrs. Farrier opened her front door before I'd even lifted the brass horse-head knocker.

"Verity Hawkes?" she asked.

I nodded, my chest tightening in anticipation of another dismissal.

"I'm glad you made it out here today. The lawn is a disaster."

"So you want us to cut it?"

She tilted her head. "You look surprised."

"No, it's not that. It's only that... some of my aunt's clients don't want me to cut their lawns."

Mrs. Farrier came out onto the patio and patted my arm. "Verity, I don't believe those stories. No relative of Adeline Hawkes' would do such a thing."

My stomach churned so hard that my morning coffee jostled for a reappearance. "Stories?" I choked out.

"About Yvonne and Bobbi?"

"Yvonne and Bobbi? Do people think that I..." My voice was a squeak by this point. Bobbi's cold blue features flashed through my mind again.

Mrs. Farrier took a step back when she saw the look on my face. "I'm so sorry." She patted my arm again. "How silly of me. Forget I mentioned it." She disappeared into the house. I stared at the closed door for long seconds, unable to move, and then returned to Lorne and the truck.

After cutting the grass and leaving an invoice in Mrs. Farrier's mailbox, we set out for home. We passed the first house on our original list, whose owner had insisted the grass was fine. Ryker Fields was out front, mowing the lawn with his head down. He didn't glance up as we passed.

After dropping off Lorne, I pulled the truck into the driveway at Rose Cottage and marched into the house, not even stopping to wave at Carson, who was sitting on a camp chair outside his trailer with Tom lounging by his side. Reuben was perched on my aunt's car. As I closed the door, I looked back at the driveway. Far from being unencumbered—my usual state—I had attracted dependents. That realization should have sent me tearing back to Vancouver with my tail between my legs, but it didn't. Instead, I felt more energized than I had in years. Things were looking up at this old stone cottage because of me. The landscaping business would take longer to turn around, unfortunately.

I took a bottled water from the fridge and sat at the table in the dining nook, sipping the water as I scanned my aunt's bookcases. I reached over to tuck *A Handbook of Poisonous Garden Plants* out of sight.

My phone rang, and I slipped it from my pocket to check the display. Wilfred Mullins. I raised the phone to my ear with a shiver of apprehension, hoping to hear news of my aunt.

After his usual artificial pleasantries—while I fidgeted in my chair—Wilf got to the point. "Verity, you're getting a reputation around town, what with two dead bodies turning up in your... vicinity."

I couldn't believe what I was hearing. "You don't—"

"No, no," he interrupted. "But input from a specialist might be a good idea."

"What kind of specialist?"

"Criminal law. It's time to call in a hired gun. Let's get ahead of this, be proactive. We can get someone from Toronto. Now, Adeline used to rely on a lawyer from—"

My head was spinning. "Hold on—criminal law? I haven't been charged with anything."

"And you won't be. But it can't hurt to be prepared."

"What would that cost?"

"Ah, well, depends on their retainer. Unless you need a full defense down the road which," he added hastily, "is doubtful, but that would be fifty thousand or more."

I drew my head back and stared at the phone. Fifty thousand? I was more likely to grow wings than to generate that sort of money.

"Wilf?"

"Yes?"

"Let's hold off on that for now."

"Whatever you want, Verity. I'm here for you."

I wondered if that meant he was timing this call so he could send me a bill for "consultation." Might as well get my money's worth. "Several of my aunt's clients don't want me to cut their lawns. Is there any contract law that might apply?"

"Not unless they ask for refunds."

"Does everybody in Leafy Hollow think I'm a murderer?"

His guffaw was so loud I had to hold the phone away from my ear. I pictured him spinning his chair around, his short legs sticking straight out, and rolling his eyes at his gray-haired assistant—while twirling a finger to his head.

"A murderer? Good heavens, Verity, hiring a specialist is a precautionary measure. Think of it as... good public relations. You have a business to run, don't forget."

"But that's just it. People are shunning me. Why would they do that unless—"

"Ah. That has more to do with Henry Upton. Turns out quite a few people in the village bought lawn products from Henry, and now they've been outed as weed killers. The local newspaper is doing a feature on it. Part of their 'Enemies of the Environment' series." He lowered his voice. "You didn't hear that from me."

I clicked off the call. After Katsuro's latest reprimand, I had vowed not to dig into any dirt that wasn't in my aunt's garden. But maybe I was wrong. I was a stranger with no ties. I'd had three visits from the police. A dead body was found in my truck. Leafy Hollow residents were afraid to let me cut their lawns.

The village was forming up into ranks. If I didn't become "proactive" on my behalf, who would?

CHAPTER 26

THE NEXT MORNING, Lorne and I were loading the rental truck when a black pickup turned into the drive. I frowned at the Fields' Landscaping logo on its door and returned to the garage. Lorne could deal with Ryker Fields. I intended to avoid any more confrontations with Leafy Hollow's self-righteous males.

With a grunt, I hoisted the electric hedge trimmers from the pegboard and twisted around to take them to the truck. They were heavier than I remembered.

"Verity?"

Ryker stood in the open garage door, his face obscured by the sunlight streaming in through the door behind him. When I shaded my eyes with one hand and saw the look on his face, my resentment vanished.

"I'm sorry, Ryker. About Bobbi."

"Thanks." He slipped off his baseball cap and twisted it in his hands. "We weren't close, not for a long time, but it's too bad. She didn't deserve that."

"Do the police know what happened?"

"If they do, they haven't shared it with me." He flashed me a weak smile. "I have a little history with the local force."

"I see."

"Nothing serious," he added. "It was a long time ago." He stepped closer and extended a hand for the trimmers. "Let me take those to the truck for you."

I handed them over, and we walked out of the garage.

I settled a baseball cap on my head. "Ryker, I understand if you don't want to talk about it, but Jeff Katsuro said Bobbi was beaten."

He swung the trimmers into the back of the truck, his lips pressed tightly together. "I heard that, too."

"From whom?"

"It's going in the weekly paper tomorrow. I know the reporter."

That would be a female reporter, obviously.

"What did she, er, this reporter say about the weapon?"

He gave me a quizzical look.

"What did the killer use?" I asked.

"A shovel, possibly." Ryker scuffed his feet on the gravel drive, looking ill.

"I'm sorry. Let's not talk about it. Why are you here, anyway?"

He flipped his cap back on with one hand and pulled a crumpled bit of paper from his jeans pocket. "To give you this." He smoothed it out and handed it over.

It was a list of names and addresses, including two places I'd visited yesterday.

"But these are—"

"Former clients of your aunt's, yes. I spoke with them, and they're willing to take you back." He motioned to the paper in my hand. "A few of my clients are on it, too. I have more than I can handle, and I recommended you. They're switching to Coming Up Roses."

Tears stung the backs of my eyes as I perused the list. I swallowed hard. "Thanks, Ryker. I—"

He shrugged off my gratitude. "No problem. Consider it a 'Welcome to Leafy Hollow' gift. This place has been way too hard on you."

As his handsome face lit up in a slow smile, my face flushed hot. Luckily, my third-degree sunburn would camouflage it.

"Still, I'm grateful. Can I buy you a coffee, at least?"

He took a step nearer, and my heartbeat accelerated.

"I'd like that," he said softly. "But why don't we make it dinner?"

"Well—"

Lorne came around the side of the truck. "We should get going, Verity."

"Yes," I said, a little too loudly. "We should." I handed the list of names to Lorne. "Especially now that we have new clients to visit, thanks to Ryker."

Lorne took the list from me but didn't read it. "That's nice of you, Mr. Fields."

"Call me Ryker, please. And it's my pleasure. Oh, and Verity." He gestured at the paper in Lorne's hands. "Try not to mention the weed-killer ring. A few of these people were customers of Henry's and they might be a little"—he stifled a chuckle—"touchy about it."

He tipped his hat to me and winked before walking back to his truck. Over his shoulder, he added, "Don't forget about that coffee."

"I won't."

Lorne looked at me with a grin on his face.

"What?" I asked.

"Nothing." He opened the truck's passenger door and climbed in.

Once his truck had disappeared, I turned to Lorne. "We're not missing any shovels, are we?"

He tugged on his ear, thinking. "Don't think so. Why?"

"No reason."

Armed with our new client list, I drove to the first house we'd visited the day before. Ryker had cut the lawn, but the fifty-foot-long cedar hedge still needed pruning. Lorne showed me how to run heavy cord from stakes in the ground at either end to serve as a guide so we could trim the sides evenly. The labor was harder than I'd anticipated, but it kept my mind off more worrisome topics. Lorne did most of the heavy work with the trimmer, but I collected up the sheared branches and heaved them into the truck for disposal at the recycling depot.

He climbed up to do the top branches while I steadied the ladder on the ground. Watching from below, I admired his precision with the trimmer. By the time he was done, the massive hedge sides were straight and even all the way to the top where they curved gently to meet in the middle.

"That's a work of art, Lorne. How long did it take you to learn that?"

He climbed down, grinning, collapsed the ladder, and

swung it back into the truck. "Your aunt taught me. She was terrific at the high work."

"I wish I had you with me when I mutilated Yvonne's wisteria. It would have saved me a lot of grief."

"You'll learn."

I looked up from writing out the invoice. "You think so?" I ran an appraising eye over the perfect hedge. "I'm afraid it's beyond me."

"No, it's not. Time, effort, and someone to show you how. That's all it takes."

"I'll keep that in mind." I ripped off the invoice and slipped it into the homeowner's mailbox. "I'll drop you off at home, Lorne, but I have to stop at Thérèse Dionne's to pick something up first."

"Emy's mom? Why?" He shifted his feet on the driveway, looking a little uneasy.

I smiled. "Don't worry. She's forgiven us for the book-club incident."

Ten minutes later, I parked the truck in front of the Dionne family home, a two-story brick house a few blocks from Town Hall. "Can you come in with me?" I asked. "I need your help with this."

The side door was unlocked, so I pushed it open and walked in, motioning to Lorne to take off his work boots. We shuffled up the stairs to the kitchen in our socks. "Thérèse?" I called out.

"In here," a voice answered.

We walked through to the dining room where Thérèse Dionne was seated at the table with a stack of notebooks and pencils. A whiteboard stood near her elbow.

Each time I saw Thérèse, I was struck by her resemblance to Emy. Same petite build, same black hair, same sparkling eyes. Except for the lines around Thérèse's eyes and mouth, and her severe chin-length bob, they might have been twins.

Thérèse looked up and smiled, gesturing to the chair opposite her. "Sit down, Lorne."

He hesitated, and then looked at me.

I pointed to the chair, with a brief nod.

Lorne pulled it out and sat down, sweeping his gaze from Thérèse to me. "What's this about?"

I squeezed his shoulder. "Thérèse is a literacy tutor. She teaches people to read."

His shoulder stiffened under my grasp. "I can read."

"Of course you can, but a coach can take you to the next level."

With a snort of disgust, Lorne tried to rise. I pushed my hand down hard on his shoulder. "Lorne, please—"

"It's none of your business," he snapped, shoving my hand away and standing up. He turned to the door.

I held up my hands to show I wouldn't try to stop him. "You said we were friends, Lorne."

"So?"

"Did you mean it?"

Thérèse watched us intently, tapping her pencil on a notebook, but she said nothing.

"What does that have to do with anything?" Lorne asked.

"You're my friend, and I want to help you. It takes a smart person to ask for help. And you're smart, Lorne."

I waited, hoping the situation wouldn't require a headlock.

Lorne sagged forward, his hands gripping the back of the chair, not looking at me. "How long have you known?"

"Since you read Henry Upton's invoice upside down."

"Does Emy know?"

Before I could answer, Thérèse gave a vigorous shake of her head. "No, and we'll never tell her," she said. "I won't even share your progress with Verity if you don't want me to."

Lorne pulled out the chair and sat down, tapping his fingers on his thighs, still not looking at me. "There wouldn't be any progress. I'm too stupid. You're wasting your time."

Thérèse leaned over the table. "I've done this for many people, Lorne. It works."

He looked unconvinced.

I pulled out a chair, turned it to face him, and sat down. "There are good reasons why some people don't learn to read in school. But because you're smart, you were able to hide it. You were too embarrassed to let your teachers know. And when you were old enough, you dropped out. Am I right?"

Lorne leaned forward on his elbows, still not meeting my eyes.

"You can do this, Lorne," Thérèse said. "I've seen this method work for hundreds of people. Every one of them thought the same—that they were too stupid. It wasn't true for them. It isn't true for you. Let me prove it." She opened a workbook and slid it across the table to him.

Lorne straightened up and ran a finger across the page, looking dubious.

I stood and leaned over his shoulder. "Time, effort, and someone to show you how. That's all it takes."

Lorne pressed his lips together.

I patted the back of his chair as I turned to the door. "Let's get an early start tomorrow. I'll pick you up at seven." Glancing back over my shoulder on my way out, I saw Lorne pick up a pencil and pull the workbook toward him.

CHAPTER 27

I LOOKED up from my roasted vegetable sandwich, regretting my vow to turn over a new leaf and wishing I had opted for the lemon meringue pie instead. Lorne had already eaten two pieces and was going for a third.

"I came by to ask your opinion, not to enlist your help," I told Emy, who had pulled up another chair to join us at the tiny table in the 5X Bakery. "You and Lorne should stay out of this. So far, I've accomplished nothing but to get you into trouble."

Lorne grinned broadly, and then raised a hand to his mouth with a self-conscious glance at Emy. He only covered that gap between his teeth when he was with her.

"We're not in trouble," he said, lowering his hand. "Hardly anything ever happens around here, so if you're going on another stakeout, I want to come along."

"Me, too," Emy said, exchanging a high-five with Lorne and holding up her other palm to me. "We're a team."

I groaned, ignoring her gesture. "That's not a good idea.

I'm a suspect in a murder case, and you shouldn't be associating with me. I'm simply here to pick your brain about Bobbi Côté." I turned to Lorne. "I didn't expect to see you here."

"I dropped in to buy cupcakes for my mom," he said, blushing.

"Uh-huh. Well, you might as well listen, since you're already here. But that's it. No stakeouts."

Emy leaned in with a serious look on her face. "What do you want to know?"

"There can't be two murderers running around in Leafy Hollow. Bobbi's death must be connected to Yvonne's, but I can't see how. Did they know each other? I mean, on a personal level?"

"They must have. They would have seen each other at village events, and they would have had acquaintances in common," Emy said.

"Like who?"

"Henry Upton, for one. Imogen said Bobbi had driven up there several times recently."

I considered this. "Did Bobbi have a lawn?"

"She lived in a walkup over the hardware store."

"Was Upton making bylaw complaints, then?"

"Doubt it. He hates paperwork."

"Could they have been having an affair?"

"They've never been seen together, and they'd have no reason to hide it now that his wife is gone."

I ran a finger along the tablecloth, thinking. "I originally suspected that Upton saw something at the Skalding place that implicated Zander and Kate in Yvonne's death, and then he blackmailed them. But Imogen told me that Yvonne refused to sell her land to developers. What if Upton was involved in that land deal and needed Yvonne out of the way to complete it? And what if Bobbi found out?"

"And blackmailed Upton?" Emy asked.

"It's possible, isn't it?"

"I guess, but I don't see how you'd prove it. And the police won't listen to any of your theories at this point. Which is their loss, obviously," she hastened to add.

"What if I had proof?"

Lorne and Emy leaned in closer.

"What's your plan?" Emy asked.

"To break into Bobbi's apartment and go through her papers."

"Wow." Lorne leaned back in his chair, letting out a low whistle. "Good idea."

I was beginning to worry that I was a bad influence on Lorne.

"I have balaclavas from last winter's ice fishing," he said. "And a bigger flashlight. We should be better prepared this time."

"There's no we," I said. "I'm doing this alone."

Neither Lorne nor Emy took any notice.

"We'll need a credit card and a screwdriver," Emy said, leaning toward him.

"And a mini crowbar," Lorne said. "Don't forget gloves, either. We don't want to leave any prints."

"No. You're not coming with me," I insisted.

Emy tossed her hair. "Fine. We'll do it without you. Should we wear running shoes, Lorne? They make less noise."

He nodded thoughtfully. "Definitely."

I tipped my head back, my jaw slack. Then I sat up and pointed to the serving platter on the table. "Pass me that lemon meringue. If we're going to jail, this might be my last chance to try it."

———

The clock on the old brick post office in the middle of town had struck two by the time we gathered in the parking lot behind the hardware store on Main Street to pull on balaclavas and gloves and synchronize our watches.

Lorne's balaclavas weren't as practical as the black ones robbers wore in the movies. Emy's was brown, with a yellow button nose and upright ears that made her look like a deer. Mine featured a bright white background with horizontal blanket stripes in Hudson Bay colors—white, yellow, green, and blue. Lorne's royal blue balaclava was topped with a fluffy wool pompom and a Maple Leafs hockey logo.

We tugged them on and leaned in for our huddle.

"All right," I said, "here's the plan. Emy will act as lookout in the parking lot until Lorne and I get the door open."

Emy handed Lorne our crowbar, screwdriver, and credit card.

"Then I will go in alone. I don't want either of you to be found inside. I'm breaking the law, and I'm doing it alone. If anybody asks, you only came along to talk me out of it."

Emy and Lorne exchanged glances.

"I'm going in with you," Emy said. "I can help sort

through Bobbi's papers. It will go a lot faster with two. You don't even know what you're looking for."

"Neither do you," I said.

"The faster we get through it, the faster we'll be gone."

"No, Emy. You're staying outside. We're not just trespassing on somebody's lawn here."

Emy put a hand on my arm. I think she was trying to look serious, but her button nose ruined the effect.

"Lorne and I are already here, Verity. It won't make any difference whether we're inside, or outside keeping watch. The best approach is to do it fast. In, out, and done. Let's get it over with."

Lorne's blue pompom wobbled as he nodded in agreement. "We're not leaving."

Comrades in arms. I blinked, trying not to sniffle. Clasping my satchel to my chest, I said, "Let's go, then. One at a time, like we rehearsed."

We darted through the parking lot, following a wire mesh fence covered in climbing weeds on the perimeter. We reconvened under the narrow metal fire escape that led to the two walkup apartments over the hardware store. Bobbi's apartment was on the third floor.

At the second floor, we ducked under the windows, although they were curtained and dark. On the third and top floor, I shrank back against the wall. In the moonlight, we were easy to spot on the fire escape. I scanned the trees and low rooftops for several blocks around us. No one was moving about at this hour.

"Quick." I motioned Lorne forward. "Try the credit card."

After ripping off the yellow police tape stretched across the door, he bent and looked at the lock. He twisted toward Emy with his hand out.

"It's a deadbolt. I need the crowbar."

She handed it over.

A second later, the wooden doorframe splintered. Cringing at the sound, I peered over the fire escape. A few buildings over, raccoons shrieked and chattered, but no one else took any notice.

"Go. I'll be on the ground," Lorne said, stepping out of the way. He brandished the crowbar. "Three taps on the railing means 'get out now.'"

We filed past him and into the narrow hallway beyond. After Lorne closed the door behind us, Emy flicked on the flashlight.

My heart sank as I looked around. Clothing, knickknacks, DVDs, and magazines cluttered the one-room apartment. Dirty dishes were stacked in the sink and along the counter of the galley kitchen. The blue plastic recycling bin was full to overflowing. Costume jewelry spilled out from a box on a dressing table that was covered with bottles, jars, and brushes. A four-foot-high mound of clothing in the middle of the room turned out to be an upholstered chair serving as a makeshift closet.

How would we find anything in this mess?

Emy gave me a sharp nudge. "Snap out of it. We're looking for documents, right? Ignore everything else."

I started in on the file folders that filled the small bookcase while Emy shuffled through a shoebox of papers she found under the bed. The front windows of Bobbi's apartment overlooked Main Street, but the moonlight coming in through the overhead skylight wasn't bright enough for us to read the papers by. We had to turn on a floor lamp. If the driver of a passing police cruiser happened to look up and notice a light on in a dead woman's sealed apartment, we'd be in big trouble.

"Let's give it fifteen minutes," I said.

"Agreed," Emy replied without looking up.

Most of the papers were receipts, old bills, letters, hand-bills, advertisements, postcards, and junk. But on the second shelf, I found a brown expanding file folder with a string fastener. I unwound the string and opened it. Inside it were plain file folders marked with initials.

The biggest, labeled H.U., contained a sheaf of paper-work, including a land survey. I unfolded it to reveal the Peppermint Lane properties of Yvonne Skalding and Henry Upton and the land that ran behind their houses. The other papers in the file were financial agreements, deeds of sale, and letters. Several documents included a reference to a numbered company that owned the land behind the Skalding and Upton properties. Could this be the elusive Syndicate?

The next folder, marked Y.S., contained two photographs. One was a late-model SUV with a computer-generated date across the bottom. The other was a young girl holding a baby. After taking snapshots of the papers and photos with my phone, I replaced them in the folder and flipped through the other folders one by one.

Gong. Gong. Gong.

Emy and I froze as the clank of metal on metal resonated

through the apartment. I dove for the lamp switch as footsteps thumped up the back stairs.

The steps stopped at the floor below.

"Wherzse key?" a man said loudly, his words slurred.

"I don't have it," a woman replied. "You have it."

"No, I dunt."

I thought I heard Emy breathing shallowly beside me,
although my heart was pounding so loud it was hard to tell.

"Check the mat," the woman said.

After some scraping and shuffling, a door opened
below us.

I tapped Emy with my finger and whispered, "Time to
leave." I felt her nod in the darkness.

I grabbed the two folders and stuffed them under my
back waistband. Emy and I tiptoed to the door. A floorboard
creaked under me, and I froze.

"What was that?" the woman said below us.

"Raccoons prolly."

"You better check. Remember what those cops said."

"It's nuthin'," the man grumbled.

"Get on with it."

Emy clutched my arm. I knew what she was thinking. If
Bobbi's neighbor checked the back door, he couldn't fail to
notice the torn police tape and splintered doorframe.

Heavy footsteps echoed on the stairs, halting at Bobbi's
door. I looked wildly about, hoping to spot another exit, and
then directed my gaze upward.

"The skylight," I whispered. "We can go out that way."

"Hey," a man said outside Bobbi's door, "it's busted."

Quick," I whispered, lacing my fingers together. "I'll give you a boost, and you open the latch."

Emy stepped into my hands, and I heaved her up. She held onto the edge of the skylight with one hand while she undid the latch with the other.

I grunted under her weight. For such a tiny thing, she weighed a lot. "Hurry up."

"It's stuck."

My hands wobbled. "I can't hold you."

"Nearly there."

More steps came up the stairs, and the woman spoke. "We better call the police."

"Nah, goin' in," the man replied, rattling the handle.

Bobbi's door cracked open as Emy pushed open the skylight. She heaved her top half through the opening and flopped onto the roof. Then she scrambled out and stuck her head into the room. *"Hurry up."*

On the fire escape, the couple argued.

"Don't go in. Wait for the police."

"Whass the matter now? You told me to go see."

A siren wailed in the distance.

There was nothing in Bobbi's room to climb onto except for the mound of clothes on the chair, so I pushed it under the skylight and clambered up. My feet were ankle deep in dresses, sweaters, and lingerie. I waved my arms wildly at the skylight while trying to keep my balance on the slippery fabric.

The man and woman at the door were still debating their next move.

"Wait for the police," she said.

"Don't be sush a wuss."

"If you get your head blown off, I'm not cleaning it up."

My hand caught the edge of the skylight. I hung there for a moment before lunging up with my other hand and gripping the edge. My feet dangled into the room as I frantically tried to scrabble onto the roof. My legs felt like lead. Eventually, I got both elbows over the edge, but the rest of me was still inside Bobbi's apartment.

"C'mon, we have to go," Emy muttered.

"You think I don't know that? My foot's caught."

She bent over the skylight. "You have a skirt or something wrapped around your legs. Shake it off."

"I'm trying."

Emy scuttled on her hands and knees to lean farther over the edge. She grabbed the waistband of my jeans with one hand and yanked while I wriggled. Together, we pulled my body flat onto the roof, although my feet were still hanging through the skylight with clothing dangling from them.

The door downstairs burst open with a loud crash.

We froze. Then, for some inexplicable reason, Emy laughed. She clapped her hands over her mouth to stifle the sound, her body shaking helplessly. I laughed, too. We shook like leaves in a storm, struggling desperately to stay quiet, our eyes wide as saucers.

"Nobody here," a man said directly under my feet. "God-awful mess, though. Clothes hangin' everywhere."

"If you think it's a mess, it must really be bad."

The door closed behind him.

I pulled my legs through the opening and collapsed onto

the roof where I lay, gulping air. The siren was louder now. We exchanged panicked glances.

"Move," Emy said.

That was when I realized we were on the front of the roof, in full view of Main Street below. If it hadn't been three in the morning, we would have attracted quite a crowd. Not only that, but the roof was slanted. I tried to stand and immediately thought better of it. Emy was upright, though, as if she had been a tightrope walker in another life.

"How are you doing that?"

"Years of gymnastics. Follow me."

Emy scampered over the connecting roofs of the hardware store, the optometrist, and the jeweler, heading for the side street. I inched along on my hands and knees, my heart in my mouth, trying not to look down. Lingerie flapped from my legs.

"There," Emy said, pointing to a terracotta drainpipe that snaked down the building's side. "We can shinny down that."

"You can't be serious," I hissed.

"Well, you can stay up here and get arrested if you want, but I think we should leave." She flipped her lower body over the edge of the roof, grabbed hold of the drainpipe, and scrambled down.

I said a quick prayer to the god of cat burglars and followed her. My knees scraped against the brick wall and the blisters on my palms peeled off in layers on the rough pipe. If the cops were looking for DNA evidence, they'd find plenty right here.

When my feet touched the sidewalk, I crossed myself. And I wasn't Catholic.

With a last whoop, the siren stopped as the police car pulled into the parking lot behind the hardware store. Its flashing rooftop lights lit up the back alley. I looked wildly around, wondering which way to run.

Emy pointed up the side street. "Look."

With gears grinding, the yellow Fiat lurched toward us and mounted the sidewalk, narrowly missing our feet. Lorne stuck his head out the driver's window. "Get in, quick."

We scrambled in, and he took off down Main Street, grinding gears the entire way. Emy and I ducked down in our seats as another police car passed us with its lights flashing. Bent over in the footwell, I peeled Bobbi's underwear off my legs and over my running shoes.

In the parking lot behind the 5X Bakery, I emerged from the Fiat on shaky legs.

"Thanks," I said hoarsely, handing Lorne my Hudson Bay balaclava. "That was awesome."

"Did you get what you needed?" Emy asked. She took over the driver's seat as Lorne moved into the passenger side. Thank goodness.

"I think so." I turned and lifted my shirt to show her the file.

Emy brightened. "That's great, then. We did it."

I waved as they drove away. I didn't want to contradict Emy after she'd risked life and limb for me, but the file I pulled from my waistband and tossed on the truck seat beside me was stolen property. Not to mention potential evidence in a murder case, one in which I was a prime suspect.

CHAPTER 28

HENRY UPTON'S Hummer chased me down a deserted Main Street, coming closer and closer with the engine's roar pounding in my ears. I ran and stumbled, desperate to escape the rumble of... purring. My eyes shot open. I saw, not Main Street, but the columns of my aunt's four-poster bed. Tom was sitting on my chest, pawing at my face. I pushed him away and glanced at the bedside clock. Ten a.m. So much for my intention to rise early and comb through my purloined file.

I'd heard another noise, though, and pushed aside the last tendrils of sleep to try to recall it. But I didn't have to because there it was again—a knock on the front door. I slipped on my robe and slippers, shuffled into the living room, and pulled back the curtains.

A police cruiser was parked outside. With a sigh, I undid the deadbolts and threw open the door. What did the local OPP detachment do with their empty days before they had Verity Hawkes to pester?

"Come in, Detective Constable. Coffee?"

Without waiting for Katsuro's reply, I headed to the kitchen. I measured out ground coffee, reached into the fridge for milk, and switched on the coffeemaker. He stood in the doorway of the kitchen, watching me, holding a plastic evidence bag in one hand.

"Late start?" he asked, indicating my attire.

I tightened the belt on my robe and waved toward my aunt's bookcases in the next room. "I was reading till all hours. I'm studying landscaping."

"Reading? Were you alone?"

"That's an impertinent question."

"And one I'd like you to answer."

"Yes, I was alone, unless you count Tom." I pointed to the cat that was twining around my feet, and poured two mugs of coffee. After handing one to Katsuro, I sat at the table, sipping my coffee and not looking at him. Which was hard to do since he was the type of man whose presence filled a room.

He pulled out the chair opposite me and sat down. "Thanks."

We sipped our coffees. Eventually, I looked up and found him studying the moose salt and pepper shakers. His dark eyes and razor-sharp cheekbones gave me a tingly feeling in the pit of my stomach.

He looked up, and our eyes met. We both looked away.

I pushed the rest of the herd to his side of the table. "Cream and sugar?"

"I like it black, thanks."

I set my mug on the table and rose to open a tin of food for Tom. He was waiting by his dish. Yes, I'd designated a bowl for the cat, but that didn't mean I planned to stay in Leafy Hollow. It made the washing up easier, that was all.

After placing the filled dish on the floor, I stood and leaned against the counter. "So, Jeff—you don't mind if I call you that?"

He smiled. "Seems appropriate, given how frequently we talk."

"Which brings me to my next question. Why are you here?"

His smile disappeared, replaced with the no-nonsense manner I'd observed several times by now. Its reappearance wasn't a good sign.

"Bobbi Côté's apartment was broken into last night. Do you know anything about that?"

"Me? How would I?" Crossing my arms over my chest, I added, "What time did this happen?"

"A little after two a.m."

"Well, there you go, then. I was in bed."

"Reading."

"Yes." I paused. "Well, I might have finished reading by then."

"Of course."

He opened the plastic evidence bag and placed an object on the table. I gave an involuntary start as I recognized the brown deer's head balaclava Emy had worn the previous night. The yellow nose was more squashed than the last time I'd seen it.

"Have you seen this before?"

"Never."

He placed a red lace bra on the table. "Or this?"

I sniffed. "That's not my size—unfortunately."

"We found it in Emy Dionne's Fiat."

I glanced uneasily at my cellphone, wondering how many text messages I'd missed while I was asleep. "Well, it must be Emy's, then."

Jeff dangled the D-cups from one hand with a bemused smile.

I shrugged as nonchalantly as possible. "I'm not familiar with Miss Dionne's lingerie."

He replaced the balaclava and bra in the evidence bag and set it aside. "Hold out your hands."

"Excuse me?"

He pointed at my crossed arms. "Let's see them."

I swallowed hard, and then flipped my hands over, displaying my red, blistered, and torn palms. "Satisfied?"

"I could arrest you right now, as well as your two friends."

"They had nothing to do with it. I'm to blame. Emy and Lorne tried to talk me out of it. They didn't do anything. Please don't arrest them." I slumped in my chair at the table and stared at the floor. If this house were haunted, now would be a good time for the ghost to help me out a little. Provide a trap door, for instance.

I raised my eyes. "Wait a minute. You said you *could* arrest me. Does that mean you're not?"

"I'll probably regret this, but I'd rather have your co-operation than your enmity." He pointed his finger at me again. "And I can always arrest you later, if you don't cooperate."

Enmity? That was a big word for a cop. "Cooperate in what way?"

"Show me what you took from Bobbi's apartment."

"What makes you think—" I broke off at his warning frown. The jig was up, so I puffed air through my cheeks and said, "Give me a minute."

In the bedroom, I changed into yoga pants and a reasonably clean T-shirt, then I retrieved the file folder from under the mattress and returned to the kitchen. I placed it on the table.

Jeff pulled it toward him and unwound the string fastener. He riffled through the folders within. "Is this everything?"

I nodded.

"Have you been through it?"

"Not all of it, but there's something there about Henry Upton and Yvonne Skalding. It's a land deal, I think." I reached for the folder. "Let me show you."

Jeffrey closed the folder and wrapped the string around the leather fastener. "Thanks. I'll read it myself later."

"Suit yourself. More coffee?" I picked up our mugs and went to the counter to fill them. "And I have cupcakes." I put two banana-filled on a plate and set them down before Jeff.

He picked one up and took a bite. "These are good. Emy's?"

"Of course." I set the filled mugs on the table and sat, watching him eat. My gut was churning too rapidly to chance even a piece of toast, never mind a custard-filled cupcake. *What did he mean—I can always arrest you later?*

"Actually," I said, trying for a casual air, "I wouldn't have pegged you as a cupcake eater."

"Oh? What do you think I like to eat?" He gave me a steady look with those dark eyes.

I nearly slid off my chair and onto his lap. "I dunno, but guys don't like sugar much, I thought."

He smiled and raised the coffee mug to his mouth.

I mentally kicked myself. *Way to go, Verity.* Time to change the subject. "Am I a murder suspect?"

Jeff choked on his coffee and put the mug down. "What you are, Verity, is a pain in the butt."

I couldn't tell if he was smiling.

"So that's good, right?"

"You tell me. Do you intend to continue disrupting this investigation?"

"That's not fair. I'm not disrupting anything."

"Oh?" Jeff picked up the expanding file folder and waggled it in the air with a knowing look.

That's what you get for "co-operating" with the police. They throw it right back in your face.

"All right," I said. "Take that folder, for example. Didn't you search Bobbi Côté's apartment? Isn't that standard practice when someone is murdered?"

"Of course we—"

"So why didn't you find that folder? It only took me five minutes."

"We haven't completed our—"

"And what about Terence Oliver? Have you questioned him about his relationship with Kate Skalding?"

"Terence Oliver? What does he—"

"And another thing." I was on a roll. No way was I letting him finish a sentence. "Gideon Picard is a friend of yours, isn't he?"

"I know Gideon, but—"

"Is that why he's never been questioned about my aunt's disappearance? He knows something about it. I'm sure he does."

I leaned back in my seat, arms crossed and chin jutted. I regretted offering up Gideon, a little, but the rest of my objections were rock solid.

Jeff Katsuro wasn't smiling now. In less than a minute, I'd demolished the police investigation into two murders and one disappearance. I should have gone into law, not accounting. I would have made a killer defense lawyer.

His face was set in that "don't mess with me" expression he'd been wearing when he pulled me over at the stop sign. I thought we'd gotten past that. I should have known that with cheekbones like that, he was bound to be shallow.

"Perhaps the official investigation isn't moving fast enough for you, Miss Hawkes, but I assure you that we take your aunt's disappearance, and the deaths of Bobbi Côté and Yvonne Skalding, seriously. We will find the killer." His words were calm, but his expression was black.

Why had it taken me so long to realize that Jeff's cool and calm exterior hid a smoldering interior? I should learn to keep my mouth shut. At this rate, I might have to learn that lesson behind bars. I wondered briefly if they'd let me read my self-help books in jail. Or I could write one of my own. *How to Win Very Close Friends and Influence the Warden.*

"I'm sorry," I said. "That was out of line. I didn't mean to criticize the investigation. I know you're doing your best." I bit my lip. That hadn't come out quite the way I'd intended. "What I meant to say is that the investigation has been first rate."

"Because you would know, with your superb investigative skills."

Ouch. I guessed I deserved that.

I gestured at the expanding file, which sat between us on the table. "Let me show you the papers I mentioned. Then I'll shut up, I promise."

With his lips set in a straight line, he pushed the folder across the table. I unwrapped the string fastener and leafed through the files, dumping a few onto the table until I found the one labeled H.U. I unfolded the survey map and pointed to the Upton property.

"See this tract of land behind Yvonne's and Henry's two houses? Imogen West says that property triggered a dispute between them."

"Upton doesn't own that land."

"Not officially, but look at this." I pulled out the document that showed the real owner. "He could be involved with this numbered company that does own the land. We should at least check it out."

He took the document from my hand and studied it.

"If anything needs to be checked out," he said without lifting his eyes from the page, "I'll do it, not you. Remember that."

Sensing a softening of hostilities, I attempted a conciliatory tone. "I certainly will."

He put the documents back into the H.U. folder. "Now, what's this about Terence Oliver? In thirty words or less, please."

"He's sleeping with Kate Skalding."

Jeff gave me a startled look. That had gotten his attention. "Kate Skalding?"

"Yes. I saw them together at Paradise Falls Park. They were arguing."

He shook his head, and I swear he suppressed a smile.

"Why not?" I asked. "It's possible. Kate strikes me as someone who likes money, and Terence seems to have plenty. He told Emy that tech startup he's involved with churns out cash."

"I'm sure he did."

"Are you telling me it's not true?"

"I'm telling you nothing."

"Oh, come on. I gave you the file, didn't I? I could have made you search for it."

"Which would have taken five minutes, I'm guessing. Under the mattress, was it?"

"Well, next time, I'll find a better hiding spot."

"I thought we agreed there wouldn't be a next time?"

"Come on, you can tell me this one thing. Please?"

He sat back against his chair and tapped his fingers on the table. "I'm only telling you this so you'll stop tailing Kate Skalding. That startup that Terence claims he works at doesn't exist."

My jaw dropped. "He's been lying about it to everybody in town?"

"That's right. He did work there, originally, but it went bust about a year ago."

"Then where does he go every day? He commutes into the city, doesn't he?"

"Yes, where he's a barista at a coffee shop." Jeff raised his finger. "This is between us. Do not repeat that."

"How did you find out?"

"I told you, Verity. The official investigation is proceeding, even if it's not moving fast enough for you. We don't jump to conclusions. We investigate."

Ouch, again. But at least we were back on first-name terms.

He pulled over the platter, reached for the second cupcake and slowly tore off the wrapper. "So, tell me about yourself," he asked.

"Are you interrogating me?"

"Nope. Chalk it up to professional curiosity." He took a bite.

"I live in Vancouver, where I do freelance bookkeeping jobs when I can get them. Wilf Mullins asked me come to Leafy Hollow to wrap up my aunt's financial affairs."

"Any family?"

"Dad's in Australia. Mom's dead. No siblings."

"But there must be someone special back in Vancouver."

"My husband died two years ago."

He looked up from the cupcake and our eyes met. "I'm sorry."

"That's okay. I'm used to it."

That wasn't true. I still sometimes woke sensing that Matthew was by my side. But my sleepy hand would encounter only the duvet, creased and rumpled from another restless night.

Jeff pushed the cupcake back and forth on the platter. "My wife died five years ago."

"I'm sorry. Was she ill?" I asked, since Emy had warned me not to let on that I already knew.

He reached for the folders and slid them back into the accordion file. "I don't talk about it."

"People treat you differently when they know, don't they?"

He gave me a sharp look and resumed shuffling the papers. "That's part of it."

I hesitated. I wanted to question him further, but it felt like an intrusion. Instead, I asked, "Does Gideon know anything about my aunt's disappearance?"

He unwound the file's string fastener. "I'm sorry, Verity, but there's no reason to suspect that it was anything other than a tragic accident, late at night, on a slippery road."

I toyed with the moose salt and peppers, prancing them around each other. "I know. I guess I don't want to accept it." If only I could tell him about my aunt's alternate job. Then Jeff could use official police resources to investigate the numbered company I'd found among Bobbi's papers. I decided to test the waters.

"Hey." I chuckled, careful to keep my tone light. "You'd tell me if my aunt had gone into a witness protection program, wouldn't you?"

Jeff wasn't listening. He was staring at the photo of the black SUV in the folder labeled Y.S.

"Jeff?"

He swept the folders back into the accordion file and rose to his feet, pausing only to grab the evidence bag before heading for the front door.

By the time I caught up, he was already at his cruiser.

With the door open, he called over his shoulder, "Thanks for your help, Verity. Stay out of trouble." Then he was gone, his vehicle churning up so much gravel and dust that Carson poked his half-shaved face out of his pop-up tent to see what was going on.

"It's nothing," I called. Carson retreated with a nod.

Which left me standing on Rose Cottage's porch, watching the dust settle, wondering what in Bobbi's file had so alarmed a hardened police officer.

CHAPTER 29

I WENT BACK INSIDE to shower and contemplate the day ahead. Lorne was at the dentist's, so I had time to read more of my aunt's laptop files. But once I was dressed, Carson's hammering on the roof drove me out of the house.

I wandered the back garden, munching toast and marmalade. A breeze rustled dead leaves on vines trailing over the pergola. In an awesome burst of knowledge, I observed that the vines needed pruning—which I had learned from the *Encyclopedia of Garden Plants*.

Cock-a-doodle-doo.

I looked up. Reuben strutted along the roof of Rose Cottage, steps away from Carson. The bird had taken quite a shine to the industrious handyman. I wondered if a rooster would be happy living in a pop-up camper. It would be a step up from a ruined Ford Escort. *Carson and Reuben.* It sounded like a folk-singer duo.

"Verity," Gideon called from the shrubbery between our houses, interrupting my reverie. He fumbled through the branches, apparently unable to use the driveway like every-body else. I should put in a gate. Maybe even charge a toll.

I walked over to meet him. "You're just in time to help me with the garden."

Gideon swept his gaze over the overgrown plots and beds with a faraway expression that suggested he saw past glories, not the faded and browning plants of today.

"We used to sit out here in the evenings," he said. "That's Pine Hill Valley back there." He pointed to the fields and woodlands behind my aunt's property line to the north—four hundred feet from where we stood. Gideon smiled, and then his expression turned more serious.

He reached into his jeans pocket and pulled out a rusted metal tin about three inches long. "Open it," he said, holding it out to me. "It's from Adeline's car."

I slid open the top, expecting to find a spare key. Instead, a small, plastic bag held a folded paper. I pulled it out, recognizing my aunt's handwriting, and read the three words on it.

LOOK AFTER HER.

I flipped the paper over, but the other side was blank. I looked up at Gideon. "What does this mean?"

"Adeline and I left notes for each other that way."

"What sort of notes?"

He smiled. "Not love notes, if that's what you're thinking. Everyday stuff—water the roses, take the mail in, there's a delivery coming Tuesday. Your aunt worked long hours and sometimes needed a favor. If I wasn't home, she'd leave the tin in the wheel well of my truck."

"But this note was in her car."

"That's why I didn't think of it before. But when I saw

her old Ford in the driveway, it hit me that she could have left it there."

I rubbed my thumbs over the paper, staring at the message. "But what does this mean? Who is 'her'?"

"That's obvious."

"Not to me."

"Adeline wants me to look after you."

All the color drained from the world as I realized what this meant. Even the blazing reds and yellows of the shrub roses turned a sickly gray. I closed my eyes and let my heartbeat slow. When I opened them, the note was still in my hands. *Look after her.*

"It wasn't an accident. She knew it would happen."

Gideon's face had turned gray, too. "It looks that way."

I folded the note, slid it into the plastic bag, and closed the tin with a heavy heart. Why had I ignored my aunt for so long? I pictured the hurt look on her face the last time we'd met. Adeline adored her younger sister. If she didn't attend her funeral—and showed up at the interment only in disguise—she must have had a compelling reason. But I didn't hang around to hear it. I was so wrapped up in my own sorrows that I made no attempt to understand hers. How could I forgive myself?

"My aunt committed suicide."

"No." He reached out to touch my arm. "Not Adeline."

"I'm wasting my time looking for her. She's gone." The tin dropped to the ground as I pressed my hands against my temples, seeing my aunt's car veer off the road in the dark, smashing through the fence and hurtling into the river. Did she close her eyes before it hit the water? No. Never. Aunt Adeline would have met death straight on, her head high.

I crumpled to my knees as the finality of that last image overwhelmed me. Jeff called it a "tragic accident," but he was trying to be kind. Mullins was blunter. *Did your aunt ever mention suicide?*

How could I have been so blind?

"She's gone," I whispered, "and it's my fault."

Gideon bent to pick up the tin. He grabbed my upper arm and pulled me to my feet. "Listen to me," he said, shaking my arm. "I knew your aunt for over thirty years. Adeline Hawkes did not commit suicide." He unclenched my fingers and forced the tin into my palm. "That's not what this means."

"Leave me alone." I turned to the house, but before I could take a step, he grabbed my arm and twisted me around. "Stop feeling sorry for yourself," he yelled.

Then he slapped me.

I didn't try to smother my anger, or pause to reflect, or even take a second to adjust my stance. I simply lashed out.

It had been a long time since I'd delivered an uppercut punch, but some things you never forget. I followed it up with a knee strike and spinning heel kick to the chest. By the time I paused to take a breath, Gideon was sprawled on the path before me.

I shook out my hand, wincing in pain. *Oh, sheep.* I forgot to drop the metal tin from my fist before delivering that punch. Rookie mistake.

I looked down. Gideon was still sprawled at my feet. No need for an elbow lock, then.

"I'm sorry," I said with a grimace. "I don't know what came over me." I did, though. To be honest, landing that one punch did more for me than two years of therapy.

Gideon moved his jaw from one side to the other with his hand as he stared at me. I hoped the gleam in his eye wasn't a desire for revenge.

"Don't worry about it," he said. "I sparred plenty with your aunt over the years."

I held out a hand and helped him to his feet.

"And I gotta say," he continued, "your uppercut is even more effective than hers. Well done."

"You're not mad?"

"No, although you may have to take me to the hospital later," he said, tentatively testing his knee. "Are those my glasses in the geraniums?"

I retrieved them for him.

"So," he said, replacing his glasses and smoothing down his shirt, "do you believe me now?"

My head was clear although my hand still hurt. I flexed my fingers as I spoke. "If you're right, then my aunt didn't commit suicide. So why did she leave those notes?"

"Dunno. A ruse, maybe."

"So that the Syndicate would think she was dead?"

"Could be."

"Which means—" I looked at the roses, now vivid reds and yellows again. A smile bloomed on my face. "Gideon," I whispered. "She's alive."

"We don't know that. Not for sure."

I clasped the tin, weighing it in my hand and ignoring his comment. If Aunt Adeline was alive, someday she'd be back.

Raising the tin in a triumphant gesture above my head, I pivoted to face the back door.

"Thanks, Gideon," I called over my shoulder, unable to stop myself from grinning. "And I don't need looking after, by the way. I can look after myself."

Back inside, I sat at my aunt's desk—with earphones on to drown out Carson's hammering—and opened my aunt's laptop, humming along to a digital copy of "We Are the Champions." If Aunt Adeline wasn't dead, then she must have left clues, or information about the mysterious Syndicate. I was determined to find it.

But her most promising files were still locked. The overall password for the laptop didn't open them, nor did any of my other attempts. I pulled a Latin dictionary from my aunt's bookcase and settled in, trying each word over six letters long. This could take days.

A while later, as I shifted in my chair, I caught movement out of the corner of my eye and turned to the window. Henry Upton's beefy face was pressed up against the glass, staring at me. I ripped the earphones from my head and sprang to my feet.

Upton tapped on the window and gestured to the front door.

I walked to the entrance, pausing with my hand on the door handle to listen for Carson's hammer overhead. I heard skittering, which could have been a squirrel, but no hammering. Carson must have gone to the hardware store for more nails.

Upton's heavy tread sounded on the steps. I jumped as he hammered his fist against the front door, inches from my head.

I hesitated, then unlocked the door and pulled it open.

"Didn't you hear my knock before?" he asked.

"I'm afraid not, Mr. Upton. I had my earphones on."

"May I come in?"

I craned my neck around the open door to check the driveway. The pop-up tent was still there, but Carson's truck was gone. "I'm a little busy at the moment."

"It won't take long." Upton crossed his tattooed arms. "I think you'll find it's worth your while." He took a step over the threshold.

I took a step back.

His conservative orange silk tie and blue shirt, sleeves rolled to the elbows, did little to distract from his imposing bulk and bushy black beard. A skull-shaped gold earring with tiny gold crossbones dangled from his right ear. I hadn't noticed that before. But then, I had never been this close to him before. And hoped never to be so again. I turned my head away, if only to avoid his cloying aftershave.

"If this is about the weed killer, I'm sorry. I had no idea—"

"No, no," he boomed. "It's not your fault some folks over-reacted. You had no way to know that it was entirely inno-cent. Merely a few favors for friends. Where would we be without our friends, eh, Verity?"

He advanced several steps while talking. I had to step out of his way as he brushed past me into the room. I couldn't stop him. He weighed well over three hundred pounds. Self-defense skills are all well and good, but few strategies are as effective as a hasty retreat.

I glanced out the front door. No sign of Carson yet. Upton was still talking.

"But you don't have any friends in Leafy Hollow, do you, Verity? Such a shame." He gestured at the armchair. "May I?"

With a last glance at the empty driveway, I reluctantly closed the door. Upton settled into the armchair, resting a foot on his knee. He beamed at me as I perched on the sofa, facing him.

"The lawn care products are not important, although several people in town are a little annoyed with you." He waggled a bloated finger at me with a chuckle. Then he lowered his hand and adopted a more serious expression. "I'm here about an entirely different matter. It could be extremely profitable for you."

"Profitable" was not a word I'd heard much since my arrival in Leafy Hollow. I was intrigued, despite my wish that Henry Upton would leave Rose Cottage and never return. "In what way, profitable?"

"It's a real estate deal. An opportunity."

Real estate? I should have kept my mouth shut, but I wanted to play a hunch. "Is this the same deal you offered Yvonne Skalding?"

Upton leaned forward, his nostrils flaring. "What are you talking about?"

Realizing that he'd called my bluff, I twisted my fingers

together in my lap as I tried to gather my thoughts. "I heard... something."

"From whom?"

"Oh, you know, around town. People... talk."

He was staring at me. Might as well go for broke.

"The Syndicate, isn't that what it's called?"

His eyes widened, but only for an instant. Then he uncrossed his legs and sprang to his feet, a surprisingly agile move for a man so large.

"But I'm forgetting the purpose of my visit," he said, his face contorted into a phony smile. "Would you show me around? It's been years since I've been in your aunt's house, and I'd like to take a look."

"What for?"

"It's going to be on the market soon, isn't it?"

Had Wilf told him that?

"Possibly," I said.

His look turned black. "Humor me. It won't take long."

I could see he wasn't going to leave until I agreed, so I stood up. "This is the living room," I said, with a sweep of my arm. "That pail will be gone soon, now that we are repairing the roof." I took care to emphasize *we*, hoping Carson would soon return.

"And over here, we have the dining area and the kitchen," I said, adopting the dulcet tones of a professional realtor. "Why don't we go out the back door to look at the garden?"

But I couldn't walk any farther, because Upton had stepped in front of me, blocking my way.

"You left out the bedroom."

I stared at him, my spine stiffening. "It's pretty standard."

I gasped as he grabbed my neck with one hand. His fingers dug into my skin. Upton sneered at me, his face way too close for comfort. "Still, I'd like to see it."

In your dreams. I slid my thumb under his hand and twisted my wrist down, taking his fingers with it. He dropped to his knees with a bellow as I yanked his hand back hard until I heard a slight pop.

I released it and backed away. "Sorry," I said, my heart racing, "but you were a little out of line."

Upton rose to his feet, cradling his sprained fingers.

"Can I get you some ice for that?" I asked, gesturing at his hand and stepping back on my right foot to position myself for a follow-up kick to the groin.

Upton stared at me for a beat, and then let out a howl of laughter. "I didn't see that coming," he said, shaking his head. "Awesome."

"Thank you. I hope I didn't do too much damage."

He laughed again, holding up his hand. "Hurts like stink, but I'll survive." He gestured at the sofa. "Mind if I sit?"

"Be my guest."

I sat in the armchair since I was certain my aunt's old sofa couldn't take any more weight. Plus, I wanted to be closest to the door. "So, why are you here?"

"I have a proposal for you."

"Which is?"

He gave a magnanimous wave around the room with his undamaged hand. "I want to buy Rose Cottage and your aunt's landscaping business. Don't look so offended. I'm not suggesting a fire sale price. I think you'll be pleased." He pulled a paper from his shirt pocket and slid it across the coffee table to me.

I read the sum he'd written. It was twice as much as Nellie, the realtor, estimated I could get for my aunt's derelict estate. I picked up the paper and handed it back. "You can't be serious."

"I am very serious indeed."

"The only way Rose Cottage would be worth that much is if you tore it down and built a monster home, but the lot's too small. You can't get the county's approval for a variance."

He ran his hand across his mouth, studying me. "You can, if you know the right people."

I couldn't tell if it was Upton's attempt to intimidate me, or the fact that Rose Cottage was finally on the mend, but as I stared at his phony face, I knew I wouldn't leave. Besides, Aunt Adeline wasn't dead, so I couldn't sell her house even if I wanted to.

I walked to the door and flung it open. "The answer is no."

"It's an incredibly generous offer. You won't get another like it."

"I understand that. It's still no."

Upton got to his feet. "They told me you were stubborn. Why don't you speak to your lawyer before dismissing my offer? Maybe he can talk some sense into you."

At the threshold, he leaned in so close that his beard brushed my neck and I heard the crossbones on his earrings jingle.

"Talk to Wilf," he said, his breath warming my ear, "before you take steps you'll regret."

CHAPTER 30

HENRY UPTON'S Hummer was barely out of sight before I was on the phone with Wilf Mullins.

"But that's terrific, Verity. It means you can sell the house and business lock, stock, and barrel and go back to Vancouver. About time, too, before those rumors become entrenched."

"I've changed my mind."

"What about?"

"I'm going to stay and revive my aunt's landscaping business."

"Hang on a sec."

I heard a muffled, "Harriet? Close the door," and then Wilf came back on the line.

"Verity," he said in his faux-hearty tone, "where did this come from? I thought you hated gardening."

"I never said that."

"You implied it. Your exact words were, 'I can't do it.'"

"I know, but—"

"And now you've received an incredibly generous offer, and you want to turn it down? Let me call Henry and tell him you've reconsidered."

An incredibly generous offer? Those were the identical words Upton used.

"Did you talk to him about this?"

"Certainly not. That would be a conflict of interest."

"How long have you known him?"

"I don't recall exactly—"

"Have you ever been to his house?"

"Let me think. No, I don't recall—"

"He doesn't have any furniture in that huge place. Don't you think that's a bit odd?"

"I never enquire about a client's domestic situation," Wilf said stiffly. "Henry might be redecorating."

"Or he has no money, in which case he couldn't pay any amount, never mind what he offered."

"You're jumping to unjustified conclusions, Verity."

"If Upton was about to go bankrupt, you would know, right?"

Wilf erupted in his trademark guffaw. "I'm quite certain that won't happen. Now, can I call him on your behalf?"

"I'll think about it and let you know. Meanwhile, I'd like you to check something for me. Do you have a pen?"

"Go ahead."

"It's a numbered company." I rattled off the number I'd copied from the document in Bobbi's file. "Can you run a search on it, or whatever lawyers do, and find out who the principals are?"

"Well..."

"You can put it on my bill."

"I'll get Harriet on it right away."

I clicked off the call and tapped the phone with my finger. Upton wanted Rose Cottage, but it wasn't to build another monster home.

I walked to the kitchen window and looked out at my aunt's garden and the field beyond it. I pictured the survey in Bobbi's folder laid over the landscape before me, and another piece of the jigsaw snapped into place. The developers' land behind the Upton and Skalding homes was bigger than I'd realized when I saw it during my first visit to Yvonne's. In fact, it ran all the way across Pine Hill Valley until it bumped into Leafy Hollow and another property, one I knew well.

Rose Cottage.

━━━

Until Wilf got back to me with those names, I couldn't confirm my suspicions. Meanwhile, I'd check in with Emy. She answered on the first ring.

"Where the Fig Newtons have you been?" she asked. "Didn't you get my texts? Jeff was here this morning to grill me. I'm so sorry, Verity, he made me tell him about our raid. I couldn't help it. He practically held a lit match to my feet. And he took the deer's head balaclava with him. Not only that"—she lowered her voice to a whisper—"but you left some of Bobbi's lingerie in the car. I didn't notice last night."

"I know," I said with a groan. "I'm sorry."

"As cat burglars, we kinda suck."

"Speak for yourself. I'm very impressed with your roof-scaling abilities."

"Thanks, but I crumbled like shortbread when Jeff pulled out that bra." Emy chuckled, and then her tone turned more serious. "He didn't charge you, did he? He promised me he wouldn't if I told him the truth."

"I'm not charged with anything. Not yet, anyway. How's Lorne?"

"He's a bit rattled. He's never driven the Fiat before."

"I had no idea."

After promising to drop by the bakery the next day, I went into the living room and sat down at my aunt's desk to sift through the unlocked files on her laptop. I lasted half an hour before giving up. My thoughts kept returning to the murders no matter how much I directed them elsewhere.

Jeff cleared Terence Oliver as a suspect in Yvonne's death, so that must mean Kate Skalding was clean, too. But what about Zander, her husband? He was bereft and suffering when I visited, but that could have been an act. I knew from experience that parents and their children don't always get along. And if Henry's land deal was all I imagined, Zander inherited a potential gold mine when that china cabinet fell on his mother.

I should talk to Imogen again. Cleaners and housekeepers were privy to all the secrets. I had a perfectly legitimate reason to visit the Skalding home, because I held the land-scaping contract. Somebody should water those bare patches in the lawn that Ryker reseeded during his temporary stewardship.

Another *cock-a-doodle-doo* pierced the air.

Besides, Imogen would appreciate an update on Reuben. They'd been close.

————

When I arrived at the Skalding house shortly after the dinner hour, I turned on the hose and cautiously twisted the brass nozzle until it emitted a delicate spray. I soaked the bare patches in the lawn one by one, casting an occasional surreptitious glance at the house.

Imogen came out the side door and headed into the garage. Lights flicked on in the front living room, and music drifted out an open window. I strained my ears to hear. It sounded like—yes, Radiohead. The raised voices that followed were easier to hear, although I couldn't make out the words. A door slammed, and then Kate Skalding marched across the flagstone path and into the garage. A moment later, the garage door opened, and Yvonne's pale blue Volvo drove down the driveway with Kate at the wheel.

I turned off the nozzle and returned the hose to the patio, where I wound it back around its cradle and wiped my hands on my jeans. I strolled over to the garage. Imogen was crouched on the floor inside, separating recyclables into plastic containers.

"I'm leaving now," I said. "Thought I'd say hi."

She rose to her feet, stripping off her plastic gloves and draping them over the containers. "Don't. It's nice to see a friendly face for once."

I inclined my head at the garage door. "Kate didn't seem too friendly this evening."

Imogen wiggled her nose in disgust. "Good riddance."

"Isn't she coming back?"

"Of course she is. There's money to be had."

I strolled over to look at a series of framed photos propped up on a plate rail that ran along the far wall. Each photo pictured a different luxury vehicle, with a date printed across the bottom, one for each year.

"What are these?" I asked.

"Yvonne's cars. She insisted on a new trade-in every year and always took a photo on the day she brought it home. This was her trophy wall."

I ran my hand along the rail, counting off the pictures until I came to a blank spot. "What happened to this one?"

Imogen walked up behind me to take a look. "No idea. Someone must have taken it, though I can't imagine why."

"When did the tradition start?"

"After her husband died. Heart attack. He was older than her by about twenty years, I think."

"He must have had money."

"That he did. I never met him, but he spoiled her from what I've been told. Bought her anything she wanted. Nothing was too good for Yvonne."

She picked up the closest photo and peered at it through her thick lenses, then plunked it back on the railing. Her look was blacker than the one on Kate Skalding's face when she'd slammed the front door minutes earlier. I had a revelation.

"You hated Yvonne," I said.

Imogen snorted, still staring at the photos. "I didn't like her, but nobody did. She was a mean, spiteful woman who hurt people." She looked at me, and her expression softened.

"I don't suppose you like her much, either, now that everyone blames you for her death."

I drew in a sharp breath. "Do they?"

"I wouldn't worry about it. Leafy Hollow runs on gossip. This time next month, they'll be bad-mouthing somebody else." She walked to the door. "But I won't be around to hear it. I'll be gone. Do you need anything else? I can get you a cold drink from the house."

Imogen stood at the entrance, her smile reminding me of someone. She moved into the sunlight, and the impression faded.

"No, thanks. I really am just leaving."

I followed her out and climbed into my truck to drive back onto Peppermint Lane. Half a dozen houses along, I pulled over under an overhanging tree and switched off the engine. Imogen didn't know where the missing photo went, but I did. It was in the folder I found in Bobbi Côté's apartment and gave to Jeff. But how did Bobbi get it?

I slipped out of the truck and walked along the road in the growing darkness, backtracking to the Skaldings' home, then ducked between the lilac shrubs that provided a privacy hedge between Yvonne's property and the road. I wasn't sure what I expected to see, but I was convinced that something was going on in that house. At the sound of a car on the road behind me, I jerked my head around, half expecting Jeff Katsuro to slip up behind me and slap the cuffs on. Although... I giggled. *Concentrate, Verity.*

Mourning doves hooted in the thicket around me as I settled in, swatting the odd mosquito.

It didn't take long. The swish of tires on gravel alerted me to a cyclist traveling up the Skalding driveway. I peered out to identify the rider in the deepening gloom. It was a man, I could tell that much, but his face was turned away from me. He left the bike by the garage, walked up to the front door, and rang the bell.

Zander Skalding opened the door and ushered the visitor in. From my vantage in the lilacs, I could see the front of the house but nothing inside. I couldn't hear anything, either. After watching for twenty minutes, I weighed the possibility of creeping closer against the odds of being arrested. Should I chance it?

I didn't have to make a decision, because at that moment, the Volvo crunched back up the driveway and the electric garage door whirred up. Kate parked the car, closed the garage door, and walked to the house. She inserted her key in the lock and entered.

I parted the bushes, trying for a better vantage point.

At the sound of a bloodcurdling scream, I tore from the thicket, pulling my cell phone from my pocket to dial nine-one-one. By the time I reached the front door, the screams had turned to shouts. The door opened and the cyclist toppled out, propelled by Kate Skalding's foot. I gasped as he hurtled past me and landed on the lawn. He scrambled to his feet. In the light coming from the open doorway, I recognized Terence Oliver.

He was wearing boxer shorts. And nothing else.

Kate stalked from the house, swinging her handbag over her shoulder, and marched to the garage. "You'll be hearing from my lawyer," she hollered over her shoulder.

She disappeared into the garage, and a moment later, the Volvo tore down the driveway.

"Kate, no," a voice shouted from behind me. "Come back, please."

Zander Skalding stumbled through the doorway on one foot while pulling on his Y-fronts. "Kate, come back," he yelled after the departing Volvo. As the car raced off down Peppermint Lane, he staggered to a halt.

The three of us stood there—Terence in his boxers, Zander in his disheveled briefs, and me slapping mosquito bites—and looked at each other.

Sirens wailed in the distance.

"I'm sorry," I said. "I'm afraid I called the police."

Zander contemplated the empty driveway, and then turned to me. "May I offer you a drink, Miss Hawkes?"

"That would be lovely, thanks."

CHAPTER 31

I STUCK my spade into my aunt's garden and leaned on the handle to plan my next move. Dead and dying plants were piled on the compost heap against the back wall, and the deep, rich soil was ready for the replacement perennials I'd lined up on the flagstone.

My arms and shoulders ached from the unaccustomed movements. I must be out of shape after days of eating baked goods and watching *Star Trek* episodes. Not to mention last night's party, which had left me with a pounding headache this morning.

We drank quite a lot after the police had left. Zander and Terry were celebrating the fact that Kate was gone for good. I was celebrating my survival of Jeff Katsuro's furious reprimand.

I pulled the spade from the ground and started in on another bed. I sensed that Jeff had hidden depths, but I didn't think it possible for him to get that mad. He had pulled me outside by the wrist and turned to face me on the Skaldings' patio. Then he ran his fingers through his hair, puffing. He was so angry that it took several seconds before he could speak.

"You promised me," he said, pointing his finger at me, "that you wouldn't do any more investigating."

"I wasn't, I swear—"

"Yes, you were. You've been skulking around, looking in windows, fabricating conspiracies, and misusing police resources. And that's for starters."

"I don't think I did all that."

"Don't smirk at me."

"I'm not smirking. I'm not."

"You won't be smirking if I charge you with police interference and obstruction of justice."

"No, I certainly wouldn't—"

"Not to mention breaking and entering, which I should have charged you with at the outset." He glared at me, and tears pricked the back of my eyes. If he'd taken the time to listen to my theories in the first place, none of this would have been necessary. Probably. I swallowed my pride, which was getting to be a habit.

"You're right. I've been an idiot and a miscreant and I'm sorry. I'm very sorry." I clapped my wrists together and held my arms out, ready for the handcuffs. "I know you have to arrest me. I'll go quietly." I looked down at the ground, sniffling a bit.

I glanced up and saw him regarding me with one eyebrow slightly raised. "Miscreant?"

"Well, yeah, you know, a—"

"I know what it means."

I shut up and resumed my study of the patio stones.

"You can put your arms down."

When I looked up again, he was shaking his head at me. "I may have to charge you this time, Verity."

"I did not misuse police resources. I heard screaming and called nine-one-one. Anybody would have."

"You shouldn't have been here in the first place. I told you Terence Oliver was not a suspect. Although why I did, I have no idea. The less you know, the better."

"I won't ask you anything else, I swear."

He walked across the lawn to the cruiser.

"Jeff, wait."

He halted and looked back over his shoulder.

"Did you know about Terence and Zander?"

With an exasperated sigh, he walked away.

Once Katsuro and his pals had disappeared, Zander—now fully dressed—leaned out the patio door and waggled a drink at me, hip-hop music booming in the background.

"Verity, get in here. We're having a party."

So, I began the night by narrowly escaping arrest, and ended it with two new friends. Even more surprising, events that would have me hiding under the bed back in Vancouver didn't trigger even the teensiest of anxiety attacks. Not only that, but I now had more friends in Leafy Hollow than I did back home.

That realization sparked my outbreak of gardening. First thing in the morning—after two cups of coffee and a handful of painkillers—I drove to the nursery to buy a few flowers to brighten up the front yard. Before long, I was knee-deep in colorful perennials with the nursery owner enthusiastically pointing out "a few of Adeline's favorites." He put them on Coming Up Roses's business account, and I signed the bill.

In the garden behind Rose Cottage, I placed the pots where I thought they should go, stepped back to appraise their positions, and then rearranged them. As I tapped the bottom of a pot of English lavender and slid out its roots for planting, I realized I was looking forward to seeing it bloom next summer. But for that, I'd have to hang around.

Meeooww. Tom rubbed up against my leg.

I crouched on the paving stones to scratch his back, my fingers combing his sun-warmed fur. "It's time you had a proper name, Tom. What would you say to..." I mulled over a mental list of notable one-eyed characters until I hit on Christopher Plummer's affable *Star Trek* villain. "General Chang?"

General Chang arched his back, purring like a Tribble.

I surveyed the garden. There was plenty of work to be done, but first—I tossed my new gardening gloves to one side —a glass of real lemonade and a few more chapters of *Anna Karenina*.

Anna had finally met Count Vronsky when my phone rang.

"Verity? It's Wilf. I have the information you asked for on that numbered corporation."

Shoving the book to one side, I sat up straight with the phone to my ear. "And?"

"It's an offshore entity incorporated in the Caymans. No local principals."

"Then who looks after their interests here?"

"No idea. There were letters in the file about a proposed transaction in Pine Hill Valley though. They were sent to Yvonne Skalding and cc'd to a local builder."

"And his name was?"

"It probably means nothing, Verity."

"His name?"

"Henry Upton."

I tilted my head back, staring at the ceiling. While it was gratifying to have my suspicions confirmed, it was also alarming. Upton would make a formidable enemy. Hopefully, it wouldn't come to that.

"Does this corporation have a name?" I asked.

My stomach dropped even further at Wilf's reply.

"It's referred to as the Syndicate throughout. Cap S."

My chest grew tight and my arm holding the phone sagged. General Chang rolled over on the sofa and batted at it. With a weak smile at the cat, I pulled the phone back up to my ear. "Thanks, Wilf. I guess that's all for now."

"Verity, hold on." After a muffled, "Harriet? The door, please," he came back on the line. "That's not the only reason I called." He took a deep breath and puffed it out. "I made a mistake."

"Oh?"

"I should not have tried to represent you and Henry at the same time. It was," he cleared his throat, "that is to say, it could have been a conflict of interest. It wasn't, naturally, but—"

"I think I get the picture, Wilf."

"He wasn't straight with me, you know."

"I'm sure—"

"I'm the only lawyer in town, and I sometimes try too hard."

I could picture his pained wince even over the phone. "Are you saying you'd never heard of the Syndicate before this?"

"Verity, I had no idea why Henry wanted Rose Cottage, I swear. I thought it was another one of his monster home schemes."

"I see."

"Also, I'm not charging you for the information."

Wow. He really did feel guilty.

"Thanks, Wilf." I hung up the phone with mixed feelings. Wilf didn't know it, but Upton wasn't the only person who saw those letters. Bobbi Côté also had copies.

A quiver of fear ran up my spine. Is that why she was killed? Who was behind the Syndicate, then?

Realizing I had no way to answer either of those questions, I picked up *Anna Karenina* with a sigh. Surely the police would figure it out. After reading the same paragraph four times, I closed the book again. Could I depend on the police to clear my name? No one had been arrested for Bobbi's murder yet. And as far as Leafy Hollow residents were concerned, the main suspect was right here in Rose Cottage. Besides, what harm was there in a chat between neighbors? Jeff couldn't criticize me for calling Henry Upton because I had the perfect excuse.

Henry answered after two rings.

"Mr. Upton? I've changed my mind. I'd like to discuss the

possible sale of Rose Cottage." I paused. "Great. I'll be there in ten minutes."

I leaned against Upton's granite kitchen island with an empty wineglass in my hand. After my nifty finger snap, I felt confident he wouldn't make any more advances. Still, as he twisted open the wine bottle with his left hand to save the taped fingers on his right, I worried that he might be holding a grudge.

Upton poured Chardonnay into my glass and set the bottle down on the granite with a clink that echoed in the empty room. "So. Rose Cottage. Are you ready to accept my offer?"

After a sip of Chardonnay, I settled onto a wooden stool at the island. "Not quite."

I could tell he was trying not to scowl. "You want more money."

"No, I want information."

"I don't have any information that could interest you."

"I think you do. But first, you should know that I've decided to leave Leafy Hollow and go back to Vancouver. That's why I want to sell my aunt's cottage."

He pressed his lips into a thin line, so I kept talking.

"But the police suspect me in Yvonne Skalding's murder. They're making it difficult for me to pack up and move on. And if I can't leave"—I shrugged—"I can't sell the cottage."

"I don't see what I can do about that."

I put my wineglass down on the island so he wouldn't see

my hand tremble. I could fight back, sure, but he was a big guy, and I'd never seen him mad.

"If I could tell the police who killed Yvonne, I'd be off the hook and free to dispose of my aunt's estate."

Upton gripped the counter with his uninjured hand and leaned over it, his belly pressed against the edge. "You don't think I—"

"No, of course not. No." I picked up my glass and took a big swig of wine. It did nothing to calm my nervous stomach. I put the glass down. "But you might know who did."

He was scowling in earnest now. "I don't know anything about it."

"It could be something you don't realize you know. Something about Yvonne."

He pushed back from the island and paced through the empty room. "And if I told you, you'd sell me Rose Cottage?"

"I'd be more inclined—"

"Yes or no?" he thundered.

"Yes." I hoped he couldn't see the fingers crossed behind my back. "Yes, I'll sell you Rose Cottage."

Henry returned to the island, poured himself another glass of Chardonnay, and tossed it back. "Five years ago," he said, setting down the glass, "there was a bad accident up the road here, at that four-way stop at Concession Nine and Wellington Road. Two women died."

"I heard about it. Hit and run, wasn't it?"

He nodded. "The women were in one of those stupid little subcompacts. The police figured a big SUV knocked it off the road, probably after running the stop sign."

I gasped. "Like a Hummer?"

"Judas Priest!" he bellowed. "It wasn't me."

I held up my hands. "I'm sorry."

He twirled the bottle on the counter and gave a snort of disgust. "Yeah, well, the police thought the same. They came up here the next day to grill me, but, of course, the Hummer was clean. Then they asked about Skalding. She'd been driving a Lexus that autumn, but she intended to trade it in for a black SUV."

"She got a new car every year, didn't she?"

"Yeah. Anyway, Skalding always went south in the winter. I told the cops she left the day before the accident. I told them I saw her leave that afternoon after putting her suitcases into the Lexus." He gestured toward the front of the house. "I can see her driveway from up here."

Yes, you can. If you use *binoculars*.

"So it couldn't have been Yvonne who caused the crash," I said.

Upton picked at the wine bottle's label with his thumb. "Yeah, except, it wasn't true. I did see her leave, but she was driving that new SUV, and it was the middle of the night. The same night as the hit and run that killed those women."

I stared at him, trying to take this in. "Why did you lie to the police?"

He grimaced. "My wife was bugging me about building this house, but Skalding was holding it up. Her damn nonsense was costing me a fortune. I emailed Skalding to tell her what I'd told the cops. I told her if she didn't want me to remember the truth, she better drop her objections."

"And she did."

He waved a hand around the room. "Obviously."

"But... if I tell the police, they can charge you."

He snorted. "Charge me with what? I had nothing to do with the accident. I wasn't involved in it and I didn't witness it. What I told you is pure speculation."

"You withheld evidence."

"Says who?"

A shiver ran down my spine at the look on his face. "Okay," I said, slowly, "but Henry, two women died in that crash."

"So? Knowing who did it wouldn't bring them back."

He poured the remaining wine into his glass and took it over to the windows where he stood looking out across his immaculate lawn. "I'll tell Wilf to get the papers ready," he said, without turning around.

"Papers?"

He twisted his head to glare at me. "For the sale of Rose Cottage."

"Right. Well..." I backed out of the room. "Lorne is waiting for me," I lied. "I better go."

When I let myself out, he was still staring out the window.

CHAPTER 32

THE SKY HAD BLACKENED while I was in Upton's kitchen. Gusts of wind buffeted the truck as I made my way down the winding driveway, puzzling over his admission. I wasn't worried about selling Rose Cottage—a girl can always change her mind, right? I flinched, remembering the look in his face as he stared out at that killer lawn.

Never mind. I'd deal with that later.

Upton had revealed some pretty damning evidence. Yvonne caused an accident that killed two women. Was it possible her death had nothing to do with the land deal? That she was killed because of the fatal hit and run?

But nobody knew she was responsible for that crash except for Upton, and he used that information to his advantage. He had no reason to kill her over it.

I remembered seeing Yvonne on the day that I pruned her wisteria. She came out onto the front porch with a glass in her hand, and she was swaying—drunk, now that I thought about it. Had she been drunk on the night of the crash, five years ago?

But if her death was a revenge killing, why wait until now? What was different? The police had no more evidence today than they did back then.

My fingers tightened on the steering wheel.

Bobbi had evidence though. How did she get it?

I envisioned the sequence of events.

On the day of the crash, Yvonne took a photo of her brand-new SUV to display in her garage, the way she always did with her new vehicles. After the accident that night, she either threw the picture away or took it with her. But in her haste to leave, she must have left a copy behind on her computer, or even in her desk. Bobbi could have found it while recording one of Yvonne's many bylaw complaints.

But Bobbi didn't do anything with the photo, other than squirrel it away in her secret files. If she had been black-mailing Yvonne, she'd be the last person to want her dead.

What if Bobbi didn't realize the significance of the SUV photo? Like everyone else in Leafy Hollow, she believed Yvonne had an alibi for the hit-and-run accident. Only Henry Upton knew the truth, and he didn't care.

Or did he? Upton was so determined to buy Rose Cottage that he offered me twice its market value. Had he been equally intent on purchasing Yvonne's property? The property she refused to sell?

I swerved the truck onto the shoulder and slowed to a stop, my hands trembling. Had I spent twenty minutes alone with a murderer?

I turned the engine off and took deep breaths to calm

down, trying to be rational. Of course Upton wasn't Yvonne's killer. He didn't have to kill Yvonne to get her out of the way. He only had to tell the police about the hit and run, and she would have been arrested.

Could Bobbi have shown the photo to someone else, then? Someone who didn't want money, but wanted to punish Yvonne for what she'd done? The photo alone wouldn't convict her of the fatal crash. The police would need her damaged SUV to prove anything, but it was long gone. I doubted even Upton knew what Yvonne had done with it. She even could have run it off a hill and into the river.

My stomach lurched at the thought of my aunt's ruined Ford Escort. Could that be the Syndicate's go-to method for getting rid of inconvenient evidence—dump it in the river?

A sudden rush of wind slapped an overhanging branch against the windshield. I jumped, clasping a hand over my chest. I was as jittery as a bat. Aunt Adeline would have scoffed at my terror. And then bought me ice cream as a distraction.

Thoughts of my aunt led to another theory, one I didn't want to think about. In her journal, Aunt Adeline referred to Yvonne as "evil." Could she have faked her own death to return in secret and put an end to that evil?

I had to admit it fit the facts. My aunt had access to Yvonne's ladder during her landscaping visits, and the hacksaw used to weaken its rungs came from my aunt's garage. So, possibly, did the coyote trap. With a shudder, I recalled the collection of rusting chains and vicious iron teeth that hung from the ceiling.

A part of me liked the idea because it hinged on Aunt

Adeline still being alive. But even my dubious detecting skills could spot the holes in this premise. How did she sabotage the china cabinet, for instance? And what about motive? It seemed impossible that my aunt could have hated Yvonne enough to abandon her own life and go into hiding.

But somebody hated Yvonne Skalding enough to set that series of booby traps. The ladder and the coyote snare weren't deadly. They were designed to injure, not kill. The murderer wanted Yvonne to suffer before she died.

My thoughts flashed back to the accident report in Thérèse Dionne's scrapbook. The two hit-and-run victims suffered for hours. The coroner said they might have survived if the other driver had reported the accident.

Still, the only evidence of Yvonne's involvement was that trophy-wall photo of her new SUV. It wouldn't stand up in court.

The truck's cab swayed with each blast of the wind that whipped the branches overhead. I should get home before the rain hit. I reached for the key, but my hand froze at another thought.

The SUV photo might not have persuaded a jury of Yvonne's guilt. But it might have convinced a grieving husband. A chill ran through me. Had Bobbi shown the photo to Jeff Katsuro?

Shaking my head in disgust, I turned the key to start the engine. That was ridiculous. Jeff was a dedicated police officer, sworn to uphold the law. Besides, what about Bobbi? She had nothing to do with the hit and run.

Bobbi kept the photo though. It wouldn't have taken

much for her to connect the dots after Yvonne's death and realize what she had.

And how much money she could make.

I thought back to my confrontations with Leafy Hollow's unhinged bylaw officer. Bobbi had been arrogant enough to blackmail a murderer.

Besides, if Jeff was the killer, she likely figured she was safe. Yvonne's murder could be considered a crime of passion, and Bobbi may have thought Jeff wasn't cold-blooded enough to kill again.

If that had been her reasoning, it was faulty. I didn't know much about murder, but I'd seen enough *Mystery Theater* to know the second crime was easier than the first. I'd also seen how mad Jeff could get.

A few drops of rain hit the windshield as branches tossed in the wind.

I collapsed back against the seat, sickened by the plausibility of my theory. Jeff must have been alone in the Skalding house many times while investigating Yvonne's two earlier mishaps. It would have taken him less than a minute with a screwdriver to remove the wall anchors on her china cabinet. Then he warned me off. *Don't do any investigating*, he said. *Leave this to the police.*

Why didn't I listen?

I remembered sitting in the kitchen at Rose Cottage, pulling documents from Bobbi's file and dropping them on the table in front of Jeff. I even remembered the silly joke I'd made. *You'd tell me if my aunt had gone into a witness protection program, wouldn't you?*

I also remembered that he wasn't listening. He'd been

staring at the photo of Yvonne's SUV. The one that had the date of the fatal hit and run printed in computer type across the bottom.

Oh, my God. I was the only person other than Bobbi who'd seen the photo that pointed to Yvonne Skalding as Wendy Katsuro's killer. Jeff knew that because I told him so myself.

Then I gave him my only copy of the evidence.

I opened the door and stumbled to the ditch where I doubled over with one hand on the truck and the other pressed against my stomach, struggling to control my nausea. Jeff said an anonymous caller told the police to search my truck for Bobbi's body. But what if there hadn't been an anonymous caller? What if Jeff set me up?

Rain tore through the branches overhead, soaking the ground and running in rivulets into the ditch. I climbed back into the truck on shaky legs. After wiping my face with a rag from under the seat, I drove to Rose Cottage, my heart thumping at every snap and sway of a tree branch overhead.

I could call Emy and ask her opinion, but her family was related to Jeff's dead wife. Whose side would she be on?

I could go to the police station, but accusing a cop of murder wasn't a wise course of action. Especially since I had no evidence to back my theory—not anymore. The photo was gone. The police would accuse me of deflecting suspicion from myself.

Before making public accusations, I had to find out if Jeff was alone in Yvonne's living room long enough to tamper with the wall anchors. Imogen West would know, but she might be gone by now.

Was I too late?

I walked through the door of Rose Cottage, pulled my cell phone from my pocket, and dropped into the armchair to call the Skaldings' house. When Imogen answered the phone, I let out a sigh of relief.

"Can I drop by for a few minutes?" I asked. "I have something to give you." A farewell gift seemed a believable excuse.

"If you're quick. I'm leaving within the hour."

"I'll drive over right now," I said.

"Come to the back door, then. Zander's gone out, and I'm packing a few things."

I hurried out the back door to grab a potted geranium from the garden, and then climbed into the truck, wondering if Imogen would tell me the truth. Would she condemn a police officer respected by all, to gain justice for a dead woman nobody liked? This could be a tricky conversation.

—————

Except for the rain pelting down on the driveway, the Skalding home was quiet when I parked in front of the garage. Kate and the Volvo were long gone, and there were no lights on in the front of the house.

I grabbed the geranium from the front seat, tugged my hoodie over my head, and climbed out of the truck. I ran around to the back of the house, my feet splashing through puddles on the walkway. On the patio, I peered through the sliding doors and tapped on the glass.

Imogen was seated at the kitchen island with her

handbag and a raincoat tossed on the counter beside her. At my knock, she looked up and waved me in.

I slid the door open and stepped into the room. I placed the dripping geranium on the island beside her. "This is for you."

She tapped the pot with a slight smile and rose to set it in the sink. "Thank you. I'm not sure I can take it on the plane, though."

I settled into a high-backed stool at the island and pushed the hoodie back off my head. "Are you leaving Leafy Hollow for good?"

"I'm going home to Leeds. I'm not coming back."

"I know Kate fired you, but Zander's bound to change his mind about keeping you on now that she's gone. He won't want to clean the house himself. You've worked here quite a while, haven't you?"

"I've been in Leafy Hollow five years, but I only worked for Yvonne the past three."

"Still, seems a bit unfair."

"I don't want to stay. Too many bad memories." She rummaged through her handbag and extracted a set of door keys, which she plunked on the counter.

I nodded sympathetically. "It's been awful for you."

"You have no idea," she said, rubbing her wrists. She got to her feet with a pinched expression. "Where are my manners? Would you like some tea?"

"That's kind, thanks."

It was too humid for tea, but it would take time to brew a pot and drink it—time I could use to grill my host for information.

Imogen filled the kettle and put it on the burner, then took a teapot down from the cupboard. Rain splattered against the darkened doors.

I tried to sound casual as she measured out the loose tea leaves. "Do the police have any idea who did it? Have they said anything?"

"Not to me."

"Did they question you?"

She gave me a level look, the measuring spoon held over the teapot. "What do you mean?"

"Nothing. I only thought that you were in the house, so—"

"I told you, I don't live in. The police think the coyote trap was hidden in the lawn during the night, and that the same person broke into the house to tamper with the cabinet."

"What about the security system?"

"Zander disabled it because he and Kate kept setting it off. Not to mention the officers coming and going."

"It must have been hard to keep track of everybody."

"I didn't try." She set the teapot on the island and added two china cups and saucers. "Milk and sugar?"

"Please." I'd rehearsed the wording of my next question several times in my head, but in the end, I simply blurted it out. "Was Detective Constable Katsuro ever alone in the living room?"

Imogen picked up the teapot and filled our cups. "No idea. I suppose he could have been." She replaced the pot on its wooden trivet without looking at me. "Why do you ask?"

"No reason."

"There were a lot of people coming and going, but Zander and Kate were here the whole time. I don't think anyone was alone in the house for long."

I stirred milk and sugar into my cup. That wasn't the answer I'd been expecting, but I realized it was the one I wanted to hear. My tensed muscles relaxed a bit.

Imogen put a hand on my arm. "I have a confession to make. I told the police about your argument with Yvonne. I'm sorry. I didn't mean to cause trouble for you."

"You told them the truth. What else could you do?"

Imogen picked up her cup with a wan smile and took a sip.

"Besides," I added, "there's a new lead in the case. Remember when I asked why one of those car photos was missing from the garage?"

Imogen fixed her eyes on me. "What about it?"

"It turned up in Bobbi Côté's apartment. And here's the interesting bit." I leaned in. "Yvonne was the hit-and-run driver who killed those two women."

Imogen craned her neck, running a finger under her collar. "What hit and run?"

"Five years ago, at that four-way stop at Concession Nine and Wellington Road."

"How do they know it was Yvonne?"

"They don't, not yet, but Henry Upton admitted to me that he saw Yvonne leave town after the accident. He never told anybody because he wanted to use it as leverage in their legal battle."

"You haven't told anyone else?"

"Not yet." I swung my stool around to face the doors and

windows that looked over the lawn and up to Upton's huge house on the hill. The storm had reduced visibility to a few yards, and Upton's place was invisible in the gloom. "I was afraid that... somebody else might be implicated, and I didn't know what to do about it." I sipped my tea, relieved I'd been wrong about Jeff. "It doesn't matter now."

I swiveled the stool back, but not before noticing Imogen's carry-on case sitting open on the dining table. I got up to take a look. "Need any help with that?"

"No," she said sharply, "but thank you. Tell me about this evidence. Was there anything other than the SUV picture?"

"Now that you mention it, there was. A photo of a girl, eleven or twelve, holding a baby. Weird, eh?" A china foot was poking out of the carry-on case. I pounced on it and pulled out a Royal Doulton figurine of a young girl lifting a puppy in the air.

"Good choice," I said, grinning.

"Yvonne always said she'd give it to me," Imogen said stiffly.

"Frankly, if I were you, I'd take more than one."

When I replaced the figurine in her case, I jostled an envelope with my arm. Several photos spilled out. I pulled out the envelope. "Sorry. I'll straighten those up."

"Don't do that." Imogen darted over to snatch the photos from my hand, but too late. I'd already seen the first one.

It was the original photo of the two girls in Bobbi's folder. This one was bigger than the copy, and in color. When I flipped it over, I saw handwriting on the back.

Imogen West and Lily Reynolds.

Leeds, West Yorkshire.

I had only enough time to remember that Lily Reynolds was the name of the second victim in the hit and run—and realize how much trouble I was in—before everything went black.

CHAPTER 33

WHEN I CAME TO, I was crumpled on my stool with a splitting headache and my hands pinned behind my back. Imogen walked out from behind me and stood a few feet away. Even though my vision was blurry, I could make out a chef's knife in her hand—and a broken teapot on the floor. Liquid dripped from my hair onto my face. I licked some off my upper lip. Earl Grey.

"Imogen," I croaked. "What are you doing?"

"Why did you have to interfere, Verity? Why didn't you mind your own business?"

Believe me, I was asking myself the same question.

Imogen walked around the island to face me from the other side, brandishing the knife. "I can't let you go to the police."

"I won't, I promise." I twisted my arms. They were tied with tea towels, judging from the bulk. "Imogen, please untie me, and we can talk about this. Did you know Lily Reynolds?"

"Not much."

"Then why—"

"She was my half sister, but we never met again after that photo was taken. Her father took her to Canada as an infant. Until five years ago, I didn't even know if she was alive."

I let out an involuntary groan as I struggled to straighten up. My vision was clearing, but I was still groggy.

"My mum was ill most of her life, and I had to look after her. Twenty years I spent in that shoddy council flat." Imogen's eyes flashed behind her thick lenses. "When Mum died, I was alone, with debts I couldn't pay. I had no friends, no family to help me."

"One day, I got an email from Canada. Lily had hired a private investigator to find me. She wanted me to come to Leafy Hollow and join her. We were going to start one of those British shops. You know, the ones that sell imported treacle, Cadbury bars, and Robbie Williams albums? With a big Union Jack in the window?"

"What a good idea. I love treacle."

I had never heard of it, to be honest, but if I could keep her talking, I might have a chance to escape. I wiggled my arms, trying to loosen the towels, my heart fluttering like a trapped bird.

Imogen's voice sounded bitter. "I sold everything I owned, and bought a plane ticket. I thought I could start a new life. I should have known better. I've never been lucky. Never."

"I gave notice on the flat, and I was about to leave when a second email arrived. Lily had been killed in a car crash. The person who sent the email didn't even know who I was. They simply went through her address book and notified everyone who was in it. I couldn't get a refund on my plane ticket, so here I am."

"Didn't you tell anyone you were Lily's half sister?"

"Why would I? I didn't know her friends. I didn't know much about her at all, beyond the emails she sent me. Besides, I had no immigration papers, so I didn't want to attract attention."

"Why did you stay in Leafy Hollow, then?"

"I had nowhere else to go. I took cash-only jobs, like housecleaning, and I rented a cheap flat over the jewelry store." She shrugged. "Then one day, I saved Yvonne from choking to death."

Imogen tapped the knife tip on the island's butcher-block surface, her expression black. "I should have let her die."

I wrenched my gaze from the knife to look her in the face. Now that I knew of the relationship, I could see beyond her thick glasses and spot the resemblance to the young girl in the photo. I'd been an idiot.

"After that," Imogen continued, "Yvonne hired me full time—well, four days a week, she called it, but the hours were so long it was more like five."

"When did you realize she was the other driver in the accident?"

"She let it slip one day. I was cleaning up to go home, and she'd had too much to drink, as usual. But I had no evidence, and she had an alibi. I didn't know Henry Upton had provided it until you told me."

"Then Bobbi Côté moved into the building next to mine, over the hardware store. One night, she invited me in for a drink. Before long, she was bragging about all the dirty little secrets she knew. I had no idea what she was talking about until she showed me her copy of the SUV photo. I realized right away what it meant, but Bobbi had no idea. She simply collected things—business papers, photographs, diaries—that might prove useful. I didn't realize until much later that she copied that photo of Lily and me."

"Meanwhile, I took bus trips out of town every weekend, looking for that SUV. It took me all this time to locate it, but I did, last month. It's in a body shop two hundred miles from here."

Imogen wrapped both hands around the knife and plunged it into the butcher block. I gasped, but she didn't seem to hear me.

"It was up on blocks, no wheels. The front bumper and the hood were damaged, but there were no plates and the VIN number was gone. It was all a waste of time. There was nothing to take to the police."

She twisted the knife in the counter, shaving off bits of wood. "Yvonne Skalding ruined my life, but I made her suffer for it."

Which left only one question. "Did Bobbi..."

"Try to blackmail me? Yes. She shouldn't have done that."

"Imogen, I don't blame you. If you let me go, I won't tell anyone."

"We both know it's too late for that." She put the knife down while she pulled on the raincoat, and then picked up the knife and walked behind me.

I gasped at the sound of fabric ripping.

"Stand up."

My arms were still tied together, but no longer attached to the chair. I staggered to my feet and leaned against the counter as the room spun around me. Then I straightened, trying not to stumble.

Imogen jabbed the tip of the knife into my back. I jumped.

"Move. To the garage."

With my hands tied behind my back, I couldn't pull the hoodie over my head, and the rain scrolled across my face. I shook my head to clear my eyes as we crossed the lawn. I looked up at the Upton house, hoping Henry was outside with his binoculars. The yellow Hummer was gone.

Imogen opened the garage's side door and pushed me through with the tip of the knife. Then she locked the door behind us and poked me again. "Back there." She gestured with the knife at the metal clothesline at the back of the garage.

I staggered over with Imogen behind me, holding the knife to my back.

"Sit down." She pointed at a wooden crate.

I felt a sharp stab of pain. Blood trickled down my back as I dropped onto the wooden box. Imogen reached for the line and pulled it toward me. My breath caught in my throat when I saw the noose.

"Imogen, please, there's no need for this." I twisted my wrists until I had one hand nearly free. "You can tie me up and leave. It will be hours, even days, before anyone finds me. You'll be long gone by then."

She slipped the noose over my head with one hand, the

knife still digging into my back. The metal rope lay heavy on my chest. My breath quickened along with the thrum in my veins.

I twisted my head to look behind me. The rope was looped over the rafter and tethered to the heavy-duty electric winch on the wall.

Imogen's chuckle was raw and evil as she stepped in front of me. She opened her mouth to speak, but there was no point in letting her talk any more. I had to do something. Anything.

I lashed out with my foot, smacking her knee as hard as I could.

Her leg crumpled, and she dropped to the ground with a shriek. The knife flew from her grasp, landing in front of me. As she scrabbled on the floor for it, I kicked it across the concrete.

Behind my back, my hands finally slipped out of the tea towels. But before I could strike, Imogen grabbed my ankle and yanked me off the crate. I hit the concrete floor with a painful thud. The noose tightened around my neck. I clawed at the rope, struggling to breathe.

Imogen scooped up the knife, raced to the electric winch on the wall, and pressed the starter.

The rope grew taut, jerking my neck back. Black spots formed in front of my eyes. I heaved myself onto my hands and knees and staggered to my feet. Standing up loosened the rope enough that I could scrape the metal noose over my chin and off my head.

Imogen frantically jabbed at the starter.

With the noose in one hand, I dove for her.

She took her hand off the starter and stabbed at the air with her knife, ready to sink it into my stomach.

At the last second, I dropped and rolled, grabbing her ankle and scraping past her like a runner sliding into first. As Imogen crashed to the floor, I tugged the noose over her foot and yanked it tight.

Then I dashed to the winch and turned it on.

Imogen screamed as the rope retracted into the drum, dragging her across the floor and up into the air.

When I stepped away from the starter, she was hanging by one foot from the rafter, her arms flailing. Her eyeglasses lay shattered on the concrete floor.

I walked over and stopped just outside her reach. Then I bent over until I was level with her reddened face. "You're going to miss your plane," I said.

Her face contorted, and her body flopped in the air as she reached for me. "Sod off," she screamed.

"I'm afraid I can't do that until the police arrive. Can I get you something while we wait?" I raised my eyebrows. "Treacle?"

CHAPTER 34

I WAS SLICING lemons for an immense pitcher of home-made lemonade when a double rap sounded on Rose Cottage's front door. In the two days since the police had taken Imogen West away in handcuffs, I'd had a steady stream of visitors. Not only reporters, but also Leafy Hollow residents anxious to sign on with Coming Up Roses Land-scaping. If this pace kept up, I'd have to hire a media rep.

Wiping the juice from my hands with a kitchen towel, I walked through the house and opened the front door. Jeff Katsuro stood in front of me, his police cap tucked under his arm.

I pulled the door wide open and gestured at the interior. "Come on in."

He followed me into the kitchen but declined my offer of lemonade.

"I'm on duty," he said with a smile, waving the glass away. "I came by to update you on Henry Upton."

I took a sip of the lemonade before setting it down. "I heard he's been arrested. Aiding and abetting or something?"

"I don't know why I bother." Jeff shook his head, but his smile was friendly.

"I'd love to hear the details, though," I said. "What did he do?"

"He put Bobbi Côté's body in your truck."

My jaw dropped. "Why?"

"Upton was supposed to meet Bobbi at his place that night. She was blackmailing him over the land deal. But when he arrived, he found Imogen in his garage with Bobbi's body. He says she threatened to tell the police that he killed Bobbi if he didn't help her."

"What happens to Upton now?"

"Accessory after the fact to murder is a serious charge. If he's found guilty, he'll go to prison."

"What about concealing Yvonne's hit and run?"

Jeff's expression darkened. "The prosecutors are discussing that, but there's not much they can do." He pressed his lips together.

"I'm sorry that this stirred that up again."

He gave me a dazed look. "Sorry? Don't be. For five years, I've tried to find out who was responsible. You have nothing to be sorry about."

I bit my lip and stared at my feet. I did have something to be sorry about—I'd suspected him of murder. Was there any need to mention that, though, when we were getting on so well? Nah.

"In fact"—he held up a hand in grudging acknowledgement—"you were a big help."

I beamed at him, happy that we were friends again. "Thank you." I swept a hand to my stomach and bowed modestly. "Glad to be of service."

"By the way, forensics is finished with your aunt's truck. They'll drop it off tomorrow."

"Thanks again."

"Don't thank me until you hear this next part." He took a deep breath and exhaled heavily. "The brass refuses to reopen the investigation of your aunt's accident. The force won't look at it again unless there's new evidence. I'm sorry, Verity. I tried."

I was momentarily crushed, but then I brightened. *New evidence.* That was the key. And who better to find it than Verity Hawkes, with her superb investigative skills? This wasn't over.

"Thanks for trying, Jeff." I walked him to the front door. We paused on the porch as he settled his cap on his head. When he looked at me with those dark eyes, goosebumps rose on my arms. Probably just the temperature dropping before the expected afternoon rain.

"Verity, I was wondering—"

"Yes?" I winced at my enthusiastic response. I could have at least let him finish his sentence.

"My bowling team is short a member. I thought you..."

"Bowling?" I stared at him.

"We get together every couple of weeks at the—"

"I don't know anything about bowling."

"No, of course not. Forget I mentioned it. I don't know what I—"

He stopped talking when I put a hand on his arm and

leaned in. "I could learn." At the look on his face, I drew my hand back. Too much? "But you probably don't want a beginner on your team."

Fleetingly, I realized that bowling would mean meeting new people and socializing and... having fun. Wow. Not even a tremor of anxiety. I smiled up at him.

He gave me a thoughtful look. "I could arrange private lessons."

My stomach slid somewhere south.

Jeff set off down the steps with a wave of his arm and a grin. "I'll call you."

I watched him walk to his cruiser. Nice... uniform.

Standing in the open doorway, I reflected on my day so far. Ryker had dropped by earlier to renew his suggestion of dinner. I told him I'd think about it. Two offers in one day was unprecedented. These weren't dates though. I wasn't ready for that. But at least I wouldn't sit home alone every night, not anymore.

At the creak of a ladder, I turned my head.

Carson climbed down from the roof. He spit a couple of nails into his hand before speaking. "That's the west side done."

A flutter of excitement went through me. "Does that mean I can take the pail out of the living room?"

"Yep." He tossed the nails into a pocket of his carpenter's apron and slid his flask from his back pocket.

"Why don't you take a break, Carson? Have lemonade on the porch."

He paused, looking dubious, the flask halfway to his mouth. "Lemonade?" He took a swig, and then climbed up the porch steps to settle into one of the aging rockers. "I could use a break, I guess."

General Chang rubbed up against Carson's legs. Then the tomcat sashayed to the edge of the porch to watch Reuben, who was pecking his way across the front lawn. The General's tail switched in frustration as he narrowed his one eye at the rooster.

By the time I returned from the kitchen with two frosty glasses, Emy's yellow Fiat had pulled into the driveway. She waved out the open front window and climbed out, carrying a cardboard box wrapped in string. Lorne got out of the passenger side.

I handed the glasses of lemonade to Carson and waved back.

Emy climbed up the rickety steps and handed me the box. "Cupcakes." She turned to Lorne. "And?"

He palmed his forehead. "Sorry. I'll get them." Lorne jogged back to the Fiat, extracted a paper-wrapped spray of flowers, and jogged back. With a shy smile, he presented me with a bouquet of pink Gerber daisies.

"Thanks, Lorne. These are beautiful. Why don't you join Carson while I put them in water?"

Emy followed me into the house, but we both spun around at a "Hallo," from the open doorway.

Gideon stood there. He must have been hiding in the bushes because I hadn't seen him a minute ago.

He held out a Tim's box. "Thought you might like some donuts."

I took the box and slid it over top of the cupcakes, so I

could balance both on my outstretched arms. "Thank you. Can I get you a lemonade?"

"No, you're busy with your friends. Do you need help with the, um, hybrid tea roses tomorrow afternoon?"

"I certainly do. Thanks for the offer."

We weren't pruning roses, of course. That was code for our secret project—cracking into my aunt's password-protected files. Gideon had objected to the tea rose part as "too girly," but I insisted. "Make up your own damn secret code next time," I said.

"Don't leave," I told him now. "Stay for a glass of lemonade, at least."

With a shrug, he settled into the other rocker, beside Carson.

We sat under the shade of the elm, watching dark clouds gather and waiting for the rain. Lorne and I leaned against the banisters with our legs on the steps, and Emy sat in a lawn chair. Carson poured a shot from his flask into his lemonade, and then tipped the flask over Gideon's glass with a raised eyebrow. When Gideon nodded, Carson poured in a healthy measure. I averted my eyes.

"Verity, did you ever find out what that syndicate thingy was?" Emy asked. "The one on the survey you found in Bobbi's apartment?"

I caught Gideon's eye before he looked away, raising his glass of adulterated lemonade to his lips.

"Wilf Mullins called about it yesterday," I said. "That syndicate in the Caymans doesn't exist anymore. It's disappeared. At least, according to the records he's been able to find."

Gideon put his glass down on the porch floor. "They'll be back."

Emy turned her gaze to him. "Do you think Adeline knew who they were?"

Her question hung in the air. Both Carson and Lorne twisted their heads to look at Gideon.

A distant crack of thunder sounded. Raindrops spattered on the leaves above us.

Gideon shrugged. "It's possible." He picked up his glass and rose from the rocker. "Let's go inside. It'll pour any minute."

Emy and Lorne followed him in while Carson retrieved Reuben and tucked him into the Ford Escort. Before I could follow the others inside, a crunch of bicycle tires on the gravel driveway made me turn.

Zander and Terence waved from the driveway, and then pulled their matching mountain bikes onto the porch. Two bottles of wine were strapped to Zander's bike rack, and Terence's held a plastic bag of cheese and crackers.

"Great news, guys," Zander said breathlessly as we crowded into the living room. "You're looking at"—he pointed to Terence and then at himself with a huge grin —"the brand-new, all-improved, so-stupendous Leafy Hollow Historical Society. Terry's even making an app for it. We've set up shop in Mom's house."

After a general round of applause, I brought glasses from the kitchen. We poured wine to toast their new venture.

"Salut," we cried in unison.

Behind my back, Emy tapped my arm. She was studying

the mantel and had picked up one of the pictures for a closer look.

"Is this—"

I looked over her shoulder. "Matthew, yes." I smiled at the photo that I'd taken on our hiking trip to the Yukon.

"I'm glad you put his picture here," Emy said, replacing it on the mantel. "It makes it more like home."

"I still have my apartment in Vancouver, Emy. I'm not staying in Leafy Hollow."

"I know. You miss your friends."

Something twisted in my chest as I looked around the room. These were my friends, gathered around me in this ramshackle little cottage.

General Chang wound himself around my legs, purring. He looked up at me. *"Mrack?"*

I bent to pick him up, and hugged him to my chest with both hands, biting my lip to stem the tear threatening to slide down my cheek.

Fortunately, a splatter of rain on the windows diverted my attention. Soon, it was pelting down. Lorne closed the front door. With the din of the storm shut out, I heard a different sound. Dripping.

With my wineglass in my hand, I walked into my bedroom. My *east* bedroom.

"Lorne," I yelled. "Better bring that pail in here."

And then, I tossed back my wine and rejoined my friends.

EPILOGUE

THE PARTY WAS in full swing when we ran out of beer.

"There's more in the basement," I said, remembering the case of twenty-four on my aunt's storage shelves. "Back in a jiff."

I hurried out to the kitchen, heaved open the sticky basement door, and trotted down the steps. At the bottom, I flicked on the light switch and turned to the storage units.

Footsteps thumped down the basement stairs behind me. "Verity, wait," Gideon yelled, limping on his bad knee. "I haven't told you—"

"It's okay," I called over my shoulder. "I can get it." I reached for the beer, but I couldn't quite grab onto it. I reached again.

My hands dissolved.

I stared, transfixed. Just how much alcohol did I drink?

Gideon hobbled up behind me. "Verity—"

"Oh, good grief," I whispered. "It's a hologram. Look, Gideon." I pushed my fingers through the shelf.

This time, the storage unit dissolved, leaving my hands resting on a waist-high pillar topped with a numeric keypad.

I jerked my hands back.

A metallic voice boomed from somewhere over our heads.

"You have fifteen seconds to input the correct code, or this facility will self-destruct."

I stared at the pad with my mouth hanging open.

"Oh, crud," Gideon said. "Control doesn't know your aunt is gone."

"Fourteen..." the voice intoned.

"What does this mean? Gideon?" I twisted my head to look at him. His gaze was riveted on the keypad.

"Thirteen..."

"What should we do?" I wailed, thumping him on the arm.

"Don't panic." Gideon pushed me to one side and touched the pad. It gave off sparks and a bang that pitched him back and onto the floor.

"Twelve..."

Gideon, his glasses askew, rose up onto his elbows. "Blasted thing doesn't know me," he said through gritted teeth.

"Eleven..."

"What do you mean, it doesn't know you?" My voice sounded shrill in the enclosed space. I tried to ignore the hammering in my chest. "Gideon? What is this?"

"Ten..."

"Control," he answered.

"Control? How can this be Control? What are you talking about? Tell me."

"Nine..."

"There's no time. Input the code."

"I don't know anything about a code."

"Think. You must know it."

"Eight..."

I stepped up to the pad, rubbing my hands together. My aunt wouldn't want Rose Cottage to self-destruct. So she must have told me the code. But what was it?

"Seven..."

My breathing quickened as I studied the numbers and letters on the electronic pad. What was it? *Think.*

"Six..."

"Should we leave?" came a voice from behind me.

I turned to see Lorne, with Emy clutching at his arm. Their eyes were wide.

"Five..."

"Yes," Gideon said, scrambling to his feet. "Go," he shouted at Lorne and Emy. All three started up the stairs.

I turned back to the keypad.

"Verity," Gideon hollered. "Get up here. Now."

"Four..."

I forced my trembling body to stay put. That code must be in my brain somewhere. With a shaky hand, I tapped C-I-C-E-R-O on the keypad. I stepped back, clapping both hands over my mouth to keep my heart from leaping out of my throat.

"Three..."

Oh, sheep. It hadn't worked, and I was fresh out of codes.

"Run," I screamed, tripping over my feet as I hurtled for the door.

The metallic voice thundered overhead. "Ha-ha. Just kidding. Welcome, Adeline."

Just kidding? I skid to a halt, gasping, and pivoted to face the keypad, screaming at the top of my lungs, "You son of a—"

The rest of the holographic wall wavered and disappeared, accompanied by grinding and the sounds of locks thudding open.

Gideon, Lorne, and Emy—realizing we hadn't blown up —crept back down the stairs.

We gathered around, all of us gaping at the same thing.

"Whoa," Lorne muttered.

I nodded, unable to speak.

"It's a bad one, Adeline," the voice continued. "The fate of our nation may depend upon it."

We stared. Conga music swirled down the steps from the party. The air conditioning unit rumbled on for a minute or two before chugging to a halt. Still, we stared.

I cleared my throat. "We'll need better flashlights."

"And new balaclavas," Emy added.

"Hold on," Lorne said. We all turned to look at him. "Does this mean there's no more beer?"

ALSO BY RICKIE BLAIR

ABOUT THE AUTHOR

After three decades as a financial journalist, I returned to my real passion—writing fiction. When not hunched over my computer conversing with people who exist only in my head, I spend my time trying to tame an unruly half-acre garden and a mischievous Jack Chi. I also share my southern Ontario home with two rescue cats and an overactive Netflix account.

For information on new releases and special offers, please sign up for my newsletter at www.rickieblair.com.

Made in the USA
Monee, IL
20 February 2020